Black Moss

By

David Nolan

Fahrenheit Press

For the dark, Satanic hills of Manchester.

BLACK MOSS

This edition first published 2018 by Fahrenheit Press.

ISBN: 978-1-912526-33-8

10 9 8 7 6 5 4 3 2 1

www.Fahrenheit-Press.com

F 4 E

PART I

ONE

7.05 am Friday 6 April 1990

The location instructions that Danny Johnston had been given by the news desk were odd, even by the standards that he'd come to expect over the last six months: *Take the A62 out of Oldham. Pass through Diggle. Stop at Brun Clough Reservoir car park. Pennine Way sign on your right. Walk PW path until you reach another reservoir (Redbrook). Next one is Black Moss Reservoir, with Little Black Moss next to it. Look for a beach and police activity.*

Look for a beach... *Seriously?* It was bad enough being sent this far out of his patch. The radio station Danny worked for as a reporter was supposed to cover Greater Manchester and no more; Danny was almost certain that this far up the moorland A62 road he could practically smell Yorkshire. There was certainly a glow of amber light over the next heather-covered brow and he had a strong suspicion it was coming from Huddersfield. *This isn't our patch – this is wild goose chase bollocks. That's bad enough in itself. But look for a beach? Come on. That's taking the piss.*

Spotting the wooden Pennine Way marker that the instructions had mentioned, Danny parked up the radio car with its distinctive rooftop mast and yellow-and-blue Manchester Radio logos. He turned off the cassette that he'd been playing as he drove – Technique by New Order.

Pulling a can of Coke from his pocket, he popped the ring pull and drank half of it. His head throbbed, and his throat was parched. The shock of sugar and caffeine didn't cure it, but experience told him it would see him through the next twenty minutes or so.

As he got out of the car he pulled a tie out of his pocket – it was already looped into a tight knot – and pulled it over his head and around his neck, tucking it roughly under his collar. *Proper reporters wear ties,* he'd been told on his first day at Manchester Radio. *In some of the places you'll be going, people treat you like God if you're wearing a tie.*

Danny put the strap of a black, Marantz cassette recorder over his shoulder, shoved the microphone attached to it into his trouser pocket and locked the car. You could always tell reporters from independent radio stations from their BBC counterparts by the tape machines they used. The BBC favoured hefty, reel-to-reel German Uher machines. The indie reporters were issued with the much lighter Japanese Marantz units. *The BBC are slow and safe, like their tape machines* – another piece of wisdom he'd been issued with – *we are light on our feet and fast. In and out. No messing.*

Lighting up a cigarette and swearily muttering about the boggy conditions and his inappropriate footwear, Danny set off down the windy Pennine Way path. The gravel soon gave way to paving slabs, which rocked and squelched under his feet – the ground below was soaked through with water. Pockets of icy snow still lined either side of the path, the result of a slightly freakish series of spring-time snow showers earlier in the week.

The path forked right at the first reservoir and then headed upwards, following the soft, rolling flow of the moorland. The slabs that formed the path were drier here, the slope of the route allowing the moisture to drain off the watershed. Danny looked right; down through the valleys he could see the lights of Manchester.

He looked left. More lights, telecommunications towers and buildings, *that's definitely Huddersfield,* he thought. *There's no story out here and even if there is one, it probably doesn't belong to us.*

Danny had never been out here before. He'd heard the

moors were bleak, but he wasn't prepared for the sheer unrelenting *nothingness* of the area. It was like the world had been horizontally cut in two — sky at the top, moor at the bottom, with nothing to provide any form of relief from the two themes. *Not even a tree. Not one. In any direction. Bleak.*

As he crested the hill he could see a second reservoir; there were figures there. Activity. There was clearly *something* going on — whether it was happening within the Manchester Radio broadcast area was quite another matter.

The thin blue jacket and off-white shirt that Danny wore gave precious little protection from the wind as it nipped and pinched at his upper body. The situation wasn't helped by the fact that halfway down the front of his shirt, one of the buttons was missing. Every push of wind seemed to find the gap. Danny pulled his jacket together, held it shut around his slight frame with both arms and continued.

The wind pushed his dark brown hair back from his face. Danny's hair had been fashioned into the floppy, fringey haircut adopted by the majority of Manchester males in their mid-twenties over the last eighteen months. The hairdo was so omnipresent it was probably no longer fashionable, but Danny hadn't had the time or the inclination to do anything about it.

He got closer to the second, grey sheet of reservoir he'd been told to head for. The wind pushed tiny, quick waves across the top of the water. The Pennine Way's paving slabs gave way to grit and small stones and then to sand. Danny saw two police officers close to a patch of land between the path and the water's edge of Black Moss. One policeman was waving his arms at the other, shouting at him. Danny looked past the officers and his eyes were drawn to a dark, yellowy strip that separated the mossy moorland from the reservoir. Next to the reservoir — there was no other word for it — was a beach.

The police close to the water spotted Danny approaching and held up a shiny, white sheet to mask something in the sand. The sheet made a plasticky, crackling sound, like something used on a building site to wrap up bricks. 'Morning,' Danny said. 'I'm from Manchester Radio. Is the senior officer about, please?'

'Fuck off mate,' one of the PCs shouted, struggling in the wind with the white sheet. 'We're not supposed to talk to you... But fuck off anyway.' The officer was a similar age to Danny. His face was as pale as the sheet he was grappling with and he appeared to have vomit down the front of his uniform. His helmet was lying on the floor close to his feet. It was speckled with wet sand.

Danny was about to go into his spiel – the one he had been told to trot out in circumstances like these – about how that this was a public right of way and he wasn't causing any obstruction. The usual stuff. As he was about to start speaking the harsh moorland wind whipped hard against the sheet and pulled it from the hand of one of the policemen. One side of the plastic flipped left to right and flew into the face of the other PC, exposing the area of beach they'd been trying to hide. Danny looked down and saw the body of a small child lying face down in the sand. His tiny legs just touched the path. It was a boy. At least, it looked like a boy. A bloated, puffy, white thing, but a boy nonetheless. Nine, maybe ten years old. He was wearing socks, sandals and grey school shorts. His hands were bunched into fists and looked unnaturally dark, like they'd been dipped in black paint. His arms and neck were bare, but his torso was covered with a shiny black strapping that had been wrapped around and around his back and chest. His face was almost entirely buried in the sand, but Danny could just make out the corner of his mouth. It was curled up. Like he was smiling. Danny had never seen a dead body before. Ever. 'Christ Almighty,' said Danny. 'Poor kid. *Christ.*'

'No pictures, you fuckin' vulture,' said a third officer, who ran towards the group as his colleagues struggled to put the sheet back in place. 'Get back to the road. I mean it. Fuck off out of it. Right now.'

Danny half-heartedly waved his microphone in the

policeman's direction and stepped back. 'I'm from the radio,' he said quietly. 'We don't do pictures. We do sound. Christ. *Poor kid.*'

Danny began to walk back up the path. Then he glanced back at the scene and again caught a glimpse of the body, this time over the top of the sheet. The officers were still struggling with it against the wind and they were arguing between themselves again. The strapping across the child's back seemed to shine in the early morning light. Then the wind eased, and the sheet began to behave, doing the job it had been commandeered for in the first place: that of stopping people from seeing the body of a little boy, half buried in sand next to a grim, moorland reservoir in the middle of nowhere.

Halfway back to the radio car, Danny saw a middle-man in a dirty, fawn-coloured rain mac and crumpled suit walk towards. *Here's the boss,* Danny thought. *He must be in charge – he has a moustache and he looks pissed off.* Danny recognised him: *Detective Inspector... Smithdown? Yes.* DI John Smithdown from Greater Manchester Police. *Good bloke. Old school cop. Meat and potatoes... as straightforward as his name. Snap out of it and do your job. Talk to him.*

'Mr Smithdown? Danny Johnston from Manchester Radio. Remember me? I interviewed you about a thousand times over the Oldham prostitute murder a few months back. Good result for your team that was.' *Shameless flattery, but it might work.*

'Yes Danny. Morning. Nice bit of flattery there. Well done. It won't work, you know.' The detective stopped and glanced at Danny's tape recorder. 'Bit far away from the bright lights and wine bars of Manchester for you this, isn't it? How are you coping alright with the altitude?'

'I got a mild nosebleed as I drove through Diggle, but it soon passed,' Danny replied. The slightest of smiles appeared briefly across DI Smithdown's face. *Good sign,* Danny thought. The golden rule of Manchester Radio was: *Never Come Back to the Station*

Without an Interview. Ever. So, he continued trying to engage the DI in chat. 'This is bloody miles away from anywhere though,' added Danny. 'Where's the border with Yorkshire?'

'You're standing on it, young man,' said the policeman. The two looked at the stone-flagged Pennine Way path beneath their feet. The DI stamped his feet. 'This is the border right here.'

'Terrible business down there at the... well, beach I suppose,' Danny continued. The two men looked at each other. The officer was in his late forties. His face was grey, so was his moustache. And his eyes. Danny suddenly felt very young and inexperienced. Long pause. DI Smithdown said nothing.

'Your lads let the sheet slip for a second,' Danny said, pointing down the path with his microphone. 'Easily done in this wind. Not their fault, I'm sure.'

Danny looked directly at DI Smithdown and made a point of holding eye contact with him. 'I saw the kid's body. Just awful. Couldn't have been more than nine or so, would you say?' Again – the pause. Danny instinctively wound the flex of his microphone in a loop around his hand. This stopped the lead from touching the ground, in case anyone was to step on it and disconnect the mic. *Habit.* 'Could I get a few words, Mr Smithdown? For our next bulletin?' Very long pause. 'I've come a long way. As you yourself pointed out.'

DI Smithdown looked away from Danny and up the path towards the road. There were headlights approaching. Forensics, more officers, scenes of crime personnel – they'd make a better job of shielding the boy's body than two PCs with a sheet. He looked back at Danny and pulled a crumpled, black pack of John Player Special cigarettes from his coat pocket. There was one left. He lit it and again looked directly at Danny – so much so, it made the reporter feel slightly uncomfortable. 'How come you were here so quickly?' the detective asked. 'You journos normally hunt in packs. There's always a huddle of you. You're streets ahead of everyone this morning. How come?'

'We got a tip off,' Danny said. 'An anonymous call about an hour and a half ago. I suppose I was the next person due on shift, so they got me out of bed and sent me straight here. Everyone else has been too busy covering the riot. Just my bad luck, really. And yours.'

The riot that had started at Strangeways Jail on Sunday of that week had electrified the Manchester Radio newsroom. Ever since prisoners had broken through the upper ceiling of the jail and taken up residence on the roof, coverage had been wall to wall and the story led every bulletin. Nothing else seemed to matter other than the latest news on the rooftop protests at the prison. There'd been talk that dead bodies were piled high inside the jail and that the SAS were preparing to go in. One remand prisoner, who'd been attacked by other inmates on day one of the disturbances, had already died in hospital from his injuries. Danny had gleaned most of this by listening to the radio and reading the *Manchester Evening News*, because he hadn't been near the jail since the riot had started.

'All the proper reporters are covering the riot, I reckon,' said DI Smithdown. *You probably have a point there*, Danny thought. 'Right,' sighed the detective. 'Get your microphone out. But, let's be clear...' The DI took a pull on his cigarette and took a step closer to Danny. He was head and shoulders taller and smelled of alcohol and mints. 'You didn't see the body, did you?' he said, softly but very, very firmly. '*No, I did not, Mr Smithdown*,' the DI said, providing his own answer before Danny could reply. 'Because my lads never dropped that sheet, did they? *No, they did not, Mr Smithdown*. So, you can't ask me anything specific about the body, can you? *No, I cannot, Mr Smithdown*. Clear?'

'Crystal clear, Mr Smithdown,' said Danny. He pressed play and record on the Marantz recorder and held the microphone about six inches from the DI's mouth. 'Could you identify yourself for the tape please?'

'DI John Smithdown, Oldham CID, Greater Manchester Police... tired, hungry, pissed off and eager to get this over with very quickly indeed.'

Okay. Best keep this straightforward, Danny thought. 'DI Smithdown, what can you tell us about the discovery officers have made out here this morning?'

DI Smithdown switched immediately into copperspeak, the bland, verbal autopilot that the police tended to use when they wanted to give as little away as possible: 'At approximately 5.30 am this morning the body of a juvenile male was discovered by a man out walking his dog. The area is currently being sealed off and a fingertip search of the scene will commence shortly. The age and identity of the juvenile male are not yet known, and I have no further details to give at this present moment in time.'

The officer gave Danny a small nod, a semi-polite half smile and walked off towards Black Moss. More vehicles and officers had arrived. *Not the greatest interview ever*, thought Danny, *but it will have to do*. He looked at his watch: 7.45 am. If he could get a decent signal going from the radio car, he'd be able to make the 8 am bulletin. He rewound his tape, turned up the volume on the built-in speaker and pressed play to check that the interview – such as it was – had recorded. He heard Smithdown's words about a 'juvenile male' – all was well. 'Thank you, Mr Smithdown,' he half shouted at the officer as he walked behind him up the path. Then he thought of something. 'Mr Smithdown?' The policeman half turned. 'Who's in charge then, Greater Manchester or Yorkshire?'

'We are,' the DI shouted back. 'The body's lying right across the border but the bloke who found it called it in from Diggle. That makes it GMP.' He carried on walking.

There were more police vehicles gathering now. It looked to Danny like they were setting up an incident room. Soon the scene and the story would be locked down. The police press office would take over and there would be no more opportunities to talk to officers at the scene like this. 'Mr Smithdown? One more thing. The recorder's off by the way – what was that stuff wrapped around the kid's chest?'

DI Smithdown carried on walking but half raised both hands in a universal gesture that anyone would recognise for *how the hell should I know?* He carried on down the path towards the reservoir.

Danny ran the opposite way up the Pennine Way and arrived back at the radio car; he unlocked it and sat in the driver's seat. He had things to do and they needed doing quickly – the eight o'clock news was now less than ten minutes away. He pulled a small pad from his inside jacket pocket, took a green, Pentel pen from the breast pocket and pulled off the cap with his teeth. At the same time, he pushed a large red button on a control panel behind the handbrake. It operated the mechanism that raised the huge, sectioned mast that sat in the middle of the car. The motorised mast groaned, scraped and moved upwards, its sections separating one by one, pushing the mast from the roof of the car and into the bright, moorland sky. Danny had to keep one hand on the button at all times to keep it moving. There was a reason for this: if he had forgotten to check for overhead power lines and was electrocuted, the mast would stop moving upwards, thus reducing any further damage to the expensive radio car.

With his other hand, Danny started to write a rough script for his piece. It came in two sections: first a cue – a few sentences for the newsreader to say to introduce the piece – then Danny's report, with a gap in the middle for DI Smithdown's 'interview'. The words came quickly: murder squad detectives... *that was always a good way of suggesting it's a murder without actually saying it.* Grim discovery... *Dramatic. The station bosses loved that kind of stuff.* He decided to put the name of the reservoir in his SOC – the 'standard out cue' that signified the end of his piece. Black Moss Reservoir: *that sounds spooky.*

When the mast was fully upright it stopped. Danny picked up the chunky mobile phone that was embedded into the dashboard. He uncoiled the spiral lead and dialled the number that was taped to the dashboard of the car and marked 'Master Control Room'.

'MCR, Gary speaking,' said the voice on the end of the line.

'Gary, it's Danny.'

'Danny boy!' yelled Gary Keenan, the radio station's chief engineer.

'The very same. Right, I need to get a signal up to feed a piece for the eight and I'm on the outskirts of fucking nowhere. Or just past Diggle, as it's also known.'

'Telling you now – shit signal from there mate,' Gary responded, in a slightly offended tone, as if Danny had gone there on purpose just to annoy him.

'I don't care, as long as it's audible.'

'Absolute philistine. Right, no guarantees, but let's give it a whirl. Powered up?'

'Yes.'

'Waving your wand in my direction?'

Same chat every time. To get a signal, the head of the fifteen-foot mast had to be literally pointing at the radio station – nothing more technical than that. Once the engineer had located the position, the mast was then twisted and fine-tuned until the best possible feed could be established. Danny put his hand around the mast ready for the engineer's instructions.

'Absolute shit,' Gary said, looking at the signal display in the control room. 'Let's see what we can do. Okay, turn right. Right. Right again.' Danny edged the mast in the direction he was told.

'Stop there,' Gary ordered. 'Stop. *Stop, you twat!* Back a bit. Bit more. Done. Shall I transfer you to the news desk?'

'Yep.' Danny heard a short blast of the station's output – 'Dub Be Good to Me' by Beats International – and the transferred call was answered. One of the curses of working at a radio station was that Danny knew every record in the chart, whether he liked the song or not.

'News desk,' came the answer.

'It's Danny, who's that?'

'It's Beth and it's five to eight,' the voice replied.

'Fully aware,' Danny mumbled. He really didn't like Beth Hall. She was Manchester Radio's morning news presenter. She was ex-network news and everything she said – and the way she said it – was designed to remind you of the fact.

'Cue,' she said. It wasn't a question.

'Right,' Danny spoke slowly, giving Beth time to type the introduction to his piece. He heard the clatter of an electric typewriter as he read out the words. 'A child's body has been found close to a reservoir on the outskirts of Oldham. The grim discovery was made in the early hours of this morning. Murder squad detectives have sealed off the area close to the main A62 road at Diggle. From the scene, Danny Johnston has this report.'

'Are there any other journos there?' Beth asked.

'Not yet.'

'This *exclusive* report,' she corrected. Beth swung her chair around, expertly wound some quarter-inch tape into the Studer reel-to-reel machine behind her and jabbed the illuminated button marked 'OB' on the control panel next to it. At his end, Danny knew the drill. He plugged his tape recorder into the mini sound mixer fixed into dashboard and lined up the tape to where DI Smithdown began his brief statement. Danny paused the tape just as the officer took a breath before saying his first words. At the same time, he plugged his mic into the adjoining input. He needed to give a sound level. Without being asked he began speaking: 'Two, two, one two, I can count, and I am giving you a sound level by counting… Two, two,' he said as his voice jarred the sound level needle from its resting place. In the newsroom, Danny's signal should have been wavering around five on the sound meter but was struggling to hit four.

'The signal's crap, give it plenty of oomph,' said Beth. 'And it's four minutes to. If you balls it up you're doing it live. And we both know you're shit at that.'

Thanks for the confidence boost there, Beth, he thought. *What a cow.*

A few weeks earlier, Danny had lost his way during a live piece outside a local town hall. His words had tumbled into each other and the sense of the piece had been completely lost. Beth had cut his item short and continued with the rest of the bulletin.

'Okay,' said Danny. Two minutes to eight now. He prepared to do a count in, so Beth knew when to press record.

Three, two, one... (pause). 'The body of the child, thought to be around eight or nine years old, was found at the edge of Black Moss Reservoir a few miles outside of Diggle. It's believed the body had been discovered on the exact spot that marks the border between Greater Manchester and Yorkshire. Officers are now sealing off the scene. Detective Inspector John Smithdown is in charge of the operation...'

Danny released the pause button and played in the recording of DI Smithdown's brief chat. When the officer finished off by saying, 'present moment in time,' Danny picked up and continued his voiceover: *'Forensic teams are now arriving, and murder squad officers are now overseeing the removal of the child's body before a post-mortem examination can reveal the cause of his death. Danny Johnston, Manchester Radio News, at Black Moss Reservoir.'*

He heard Beth jabbing at buttons and his own voice play back down the telephone line. It had recorded fine at the other end. He expected a word from Beth that all was well, but the line went dead. He didn't mind. It was nearly one minute to the news. Danny turned on the radio and stepped out of the radio car, leaving the door open so he could hear. He lit a cigarette as the DJ spoke over the outro of 'Loaded' by Primal Scream and introduced the news. The jingle stated that Manchester Radio was 'always first with the news that matters.' Then Beth introduced herself: 'Manchester Radio news at eight o'clock, I'm Beth Hall.' The crabby, bad-tempered tone she had used with Danny was gone. In its place was a smooth, soft and low delivery as she read the first item... about the ongoing riot at Strangeways jail. *She hasn't even led on it! Fucking cow!*

Danny leant into the car and switched off the radio. He looked down the A62 road and saw more vehicles approaching. Other journalists were arriving – the BBC's radio car was bringing up the rear. Looking over his shoulder to the crime scene he saw the boy's body was now covered by a portable white tent. *The professionals have arrived*, he thought. He saw DI Smithdown walking back down the path, briefing a scene of crime officers. The whole area was now cordoned off with 'Police Do Not Cross' tape. *No one else will be getting near the reservoir today*, he thought. *Or the kid's body*.

He pulled on the last of his cigarette. *God, it's freezing*. He thought about what he'd seen, about the little boy, the edge of his mouth curled into a deathly smile. That thought – and the cold bite of the Pennine air – made him shiver. He constantly told himself he wasn't going to become one of those clichéd reporters that didn't care and seemed to take pleasure in boasting about the fact. Those hard cases that let everything just wash over them like it didn't matter. Something truly terrible had happened out here at Black Moss and Danny Johnston cared about it. It mattered.

TWO

9.35 pm Friday 20 May 2016

His first thought wasn't... *How badly am I hurt?*

Nor was it... *Have I hurt anyone else?*

No. It was... *I wonder if this is the same tree Marc Bolan crashed into?*

Daniel Johnston leant forward and looked at the tree he'd hit. The shattered windscreen made it difficult to see, but it set his mind at rest on one issue: *Can't be the Bolan tree,* he thought. *It would have flowers and ribbons and messages on it. Definitely.*

Hang on a minute, you daft sod, Johnston thought. *That tree's in Barnes. This is Clapham Common. Thank fuck for that! You're not thinking straight, Daniel... God, you really are pissed.*

He grabbed at his seat belt and tried to find the release catch. Then he realised he wasn't wearing a seat belt. *Good, that'll save some time. Best get out of the car.*

He opened the door of his high-end four-by-four, fell forward, twisted and somehow landed neatly on his back. He looked at the sky. A young couple in their twenties leaned over him and partially blocked Daniel's view of the stars. The woman seemed concerned. The young man with her had an iPhone in his hand and was pointing it down at Daniel. The light from the phone glared white into his eyes. 'Are you okay?' the young woman said, looking down at him.

'He's absolutely wankered is what he is,' the young man

said, shaking his head. 'Wasted.'

The woman prodded her friend with her finger. 'It's him, isn't it? The guy off the telly. The documentary journalist guy.'

'The Mr Totally Wasted Guy, more like,' the young man said. 'All self-righteous on the TV and here he is all pissed up, falling out of his flash car. Absolute joke.'

'Hi,' said Daniel from down on the floor. 'I don't suppose I could ask you not to film me at this rather difficult time?'

'You don't ask permission from those guys you chase down the street on the telly, do you?' the man replied.

'Fair point,' Daniel conceded. He tried to get up, thought better of it and decided to stay put. The ground felt cool on his back. Two police officers joined the small group of people now looking down at him. Blue lights danced across the faces of the staring group. One officer was speaking into his radio: 'Yeah, white male, late forties/early fifties, RTA on Clapham Common Southside – junction with Rookery Road. Male is conscious. Just about. Injuries not yet ascertained. Front-end damage to vehicle. Looks like no other vehicles involved. Request ambulance.' The officer paused. 'Drink apparently taken,' he added.

Copperspeak, Daniel thought. *Never changes.* He rolled over and got to his feet with a speed that surprised the people around him. He made a grab for the young man's camera phone but managed to half punch one of the police officers on the shoulder instead. The chatter of the people around him – about a dozen by now – suddenly stopped.

Silence.

'I'm not taking a breathalyser!' Daniel suddenly shouted. The police officers and the group of bystanders all stared at him. He sat down with a dull thump on the grass verge close to his car. The young man with the iPhone shook his head as he deftly topped and tailed the video of Daniel shouting. He then posted the clip out onto five different social media platforms at once.

I am massively, massively in the shit, thought Daniel Johnston. He lay back down on the ground and closed his eyes.

THREE

9.30am Friday 6 April 1990

Danny drove the radio car up the spiral ramp to the first-floor parking area in the city centre slab of concrete that housed the Manchester Radio studios. The City Tower and Piazza was also home to a hotel, shops and a few cafes, all of which had seen better, busier days. The twenty-year-old facade of the hotel was blackened with car fumes and many of the shop units had 'To Let' signs taped to the windows. Rubbish and leaves swirled in the wind across the half-empty car park in a series of rather depressing mini twisters.

The site was being deliberately withered on the vine of the city's commercial property market. The owners wanted a fresh start, so life for the current occupiers was being made as difficult as possible to gently force them out. Many businesses had taken the hint and moved on, but Manchester Radio still had a few years left on its lease, so Danny and his colleagues were stuck here for the time being, regardless of how unglamorous things became for them.

He parked the radio car in the covered space marked RESERVED FOR MANCHESTER RADIO OB VEHICLE. For a moment, Danny stopped and stared through the windscreen at the concrete wall in front of the car. He leant an elbow on the steering wheel, put his hand across his nose and mouth and began to cry. Just two or three big sobs. Then he took a deep breath and stopped. He paused for about ten seconds, again staring at the concrete wall ahead of him. Then Danny got out of the car and plugged the charger cable that hung from a hook into the side of the vehicle. He'd once forgotten to do it after a job and the station's news editor Mike Sharston had made a big deal of telling Danny what an idiot he was in front of the whole newsroom. That kind of thing happened a lot at Manchester Radio: *why have a quiet word in a new reporter's ear when you can shout at them in front of everyone else in the newsroom?*

Danny trotted down the steps from the car park and walked across the filthy, deserted piazza that stretched under the car park towards the Manchester Radio reception. He saw the yellow-and-blue station logos attached to the windows and felt a nervous grind tug at his stomach as he approached the door. The same feeling he'd had every day since he'd started the job the previous October after three years on a local newspaper. The feeling could be could be summarised along these lines: *I'm shit at this. Everyone knows I'm shit at this. They are currently discussing how shit I am right now, and they'll go suddenly quiet when I walk in. Mike Sharston thinks I'm shit. Gary the engineer thinks I'm shit. Beth Hall KNOWS I'm shit. Why am I putting myself through this? I should pack it in and go back to local papers. Or get a job in PR. Anything but this.*

Then another thought put a stop to his train of thought like a cold, hard slap.

Christ, that kid.

Spotting Danny as he approached the glass door, the middle-aged receptionist smiled and buzzed him through. 'Morning, Danny!' she said. She was wearing a blue blazer with a white, ruffled shirt, her red hair styled into an elaborate bun. 'Terrible business up at Oldham. Just awful.'

'I know, Pauline. Shocking stuff, even for round here.'

The reception was a dazzlingly bright collage of primary colours, lit by rows of spotlights suspended from the ceiling. Framed gold-and-silver albums scrawled with cheery messages from the singers and bands responsible for them lined the walls. Alongside them were photos of the station's main presenters. Most had alliterative names or Christian names for surnames – *Jonathan Jones, Stuart Simon, Mike James.*

Their hair, their clothes, their smiles, everything about them was the antithesis of what was happening outside the radio station. Manchester was now *Madchester*. The city was exploding with music, art and nightlife. Little or nothing of that was reflected in the reception of Manchester Radio. It was 1990 outside, but inside things felt distinctly 1983.

Danny kept walking. A few people looked through a small rack of cassette tapes sitting on the counter of the chest-high reception desk. *Billys*, thought Danny. It was what the station staff secretly called the listeners. Billy Bunters. *Punters*.

Pauline buzzed a second door that connected the rear of the reception to the radio station itself. There was a third door, where guests were able to go straight to the studios, but that wasn't for the likes of Danny. 'That was a really good report, Danny,' Pauline said as he walked by. 'No one else got an interview at the scene. Well done.'

'Thanks Pauline.' Danny pushed the door. 'Didn't think anyone would notice with Strangeways still going strong.'

Pauline gave Danny her best sympathetic face then turned to serve someone who wanted to buy a tape. She'd been here since the station opened nearly twenty years earlier. She saw everything and knew everything. *At least Pauline doesn't think I'm shit,* he thought.

Danny stepped through the second door and the bright, pleasant surroundings of the reception instantly gave way to a wash of dirty grey and beige. The carpet was stained with scores of uneven, brown splodges, where endless cups of tea and coffee had been spilt over the years. Plastic cups – most with cigarette ends in them – were everywhere. The edge of every available surface was dotted with scorch marks where lit cigarettes had been balanced on table edges and window ledges – and forgotten about. The building had recently gone smoke-free, but you'd be hard-pressed to know it. There was a smoking room off to the left of the corridor. Two people were standing in the corridor having an argument. Both had lit cigarettes in their hands; their arms were outstretched so their hands were a few inches inside the smoking room, meaning they were sticking to the letter of health and safety law but studiously avoiding the spirit of it. Danny squeezed past them and headed towards the newsroom.

'Danny boy, you little fucker!' Gary Keenan cried as they passed in the corridor. Heavyset, bearded, ponytailed and sporting large teardrop glasses with a sticking plaster holding one of the arms to the frame, Keenan wore a plain grey sweatshirt and misshapen jeans that were being tugged to one side by a huge bunch of keys attached to his belt loop. He was eating a bacon roll. And smoking. He had a plastic cup of tea on the go too. 'Good piece by your standards that was,' he boomed as he walked in the opposite direction. 'Piss poor by anyone else's, but quite good by yours.'

'Stop flirting with me Gary,' Danny replied. 'I'm straight. I've told you before.'

'You wish, Danny boy. You wish. By the way, Sharston's after you.' Gary disappeared into the reception in a cloud of cigarette smoke. Danny could hear Pauline shouting at him for smoking in her reception area as he headed out onto the piazza.

Danny pushed open the door of the newsroom with his shoulder. The noise of the place would have shocked anyone not used to it. A wall-mounted TV was on with the sound of the *Kilroy* debate show underscoring the still image of the CEEFAX news headlines. STRANGEWAYS' STAND OFF CONTINUES was the lead story. Mixed in with *Kilroy* was the sound of the Manchester Radio station output, plus that of their BBC opposition. Then there were the typewriters: manual and electric. There had been talk of word processors – computers even – but they had yet to arrive at Manchester Radio. Across the top of this wash of noise was the sound of voices – arguing, shouting, laughing, swearing. There were about fifteen people in the open-plan space. Some were on phones, some were talking face-to-face. Some of the voices were on tape, being edited by reporters who should have been wearing headphones but couldn't be bothered. The words and sounds were being pulled back and forward across tape heads on giant Studer editing machines as journalists tried to find the exact point to mark their edit with a chinagraph pencil, before cutting the tape with a one-sided razor. Voices. *Everywhere.*

'Danny! Here. Now.' Danny looked at Mike Sharston though the glass of his office which was separate to the rest of the newsroom. Sharston was a short, wide man in a very tight suit. He was balding with a red face. On several of his fingers were heavy signet rings. No radio reporter in his or her right mind would wear rings like that – they'd bang on the metal microphones as you were recording and ruin the audio. But Mike Shartson never did interviews these days. He never seemed to leave his tiny office. He was there when Danny arrived for an early shift and he was there when Danny finished a late shift. He never seemed to go home. Danny lifted his tape recorder, waggled it in Sharston's direction and pointed at the charging dock where all Marantzs were supposed to go as soon as possible after arriving back at base. That was the rule. It was Mike Sharston's rule.

'Now!' Sharston yelled.

Danny caught Beth Hall's eye. She was typing quickly at the seat reserved for whoever was reading the news that day. Possession of that seat and that typewriter meant she was in charge of the news output too. She looked across the top of her rather unflattering, large-rimmed glasses, poked her lower lip at him and fluttered her eyes, like a child would do when they want to express a sentiment along the lines of, *there, there, don't be a cry baby.* Then she winked at him.

Nice, thought Danny. *What a cow.*

Danny did as he was told but walked slowly towards the news editor's office and casually leant against the door frame. He didn't want to appear as if he was scared of Sharston and was jumping to it. Even though he was. 'Danny. Hi. Right. What was it I wanted to talk to you about?' said Sharston, tugging at the neck of his grubby, off-white shirt.

'A massive pay rise and a shot at reading the morning bulletins?' Danny replied.

'No. It definitely wasn't that,' Sharston replied. He moved some papers around his desk and looked at his notebook. Then he moved the papers again. 'Ah yes. Right. Oldham. The kid's body. That was wasn't too bad this morning. You got on air first too, I'm told. If the post-mortem says it's definitely murder, we may have a story on our hands.'

Oh, it's definitely murder, thought Danny.

'There'll probably be a press conference at Oldham nick first thing Monday morning,' continued Shartson. 'Go along. Stick with this story. Make something of it. Make it your own.'

Danny tapped his fingers on the door frame of Sharston's office. 'I was hoping to get down to Strangeways. Everyone's been covering it except me. It's the biggest story ever. The whole world is there.'

The riot had started on Sunday lunchtime a few days earlier. Trouble had broken out during the lunchtime church service and had spread quickly throughout the jail. After raiding the prison medical centre to get their hands on prescription drugs, the rioters targeted the jail's E wing where sex offenders were housed – in the eyes of inmates, they were the lowest of the low. The chilling, grunting chants of 'Beasts. Beasts. Beasts' could be heard from the road outside the prison as the rioters got nearer and nearer their targets.

The *Manchester Evening News* was busily proclaiming that, according to their sources, Strangeways was filling up with corpses: '20 DEAD' their latest headline proclaimed. There was no actual proof of this yet, so the Manchester Radio reporters had been told to steer clear of such in their reports. It was the UK's biggest independent radio station outside of London and they had a reputation to maintain. They were pushy and fast, but they were also fair and accurate.

After the inmates had taken control of the jail, they'd armed themselves with scaffolding poles and smashed through the ceilings of the upper floors and accessed the roof, where they were currently putting on quite a show for the TV cameras that had taken up residence around the jail. Every aspect of the rooftop protest was being lapped up by the media. As far as Danny Johnston was concerned, the riot was the chance for him to prove himself, prove he was the real thing.

'No Danny,' Mike Sharston said. 'I don't want you at Strangeways. We've got it covered. It'll probably all be over this weekend anyway. There's talk of the SAS going in. Maybe even today. I want you to stick with this dead kid thing. This could be a good opportunity for you. I suggest you take it. Now off you trot.'

'Maybe I could go to the jail after I've finished at Oldham?'

'Got it covered, Danny. On your way.' Sharston went back to the task of moving paper around his desk. Danny returned to the noise of the newsroom, looking for an unoccupied typewriter so he could freshen up his 'dead kid' story.

Beth Hall walked past him, heading towards the small booth next door to the newsroom to read the next news bulletin. She was seven or eight years older than Danny. She was wearing faded jeans and a black polo neck jumper. Her long red hair was a mess, pinned up on top of her head with hair grips and held together with a large elastic band. She was carrying several scripts and a small pile of 'carts' – plastic boxes containing loops of tape that could be played into the news report. 'Haven't you freshened up your piece for this bulletin yet? Shame on you,' she said. And exited in a waft of expensive but intrusive perfume. *She even smells annoying,* thought Danny.

FOUR

10.25 am Thursday 2 May 2016

Leaning into the intercom, Daniel pressed the button next to the speaker and waited for his cue to talk. Nothing. He buzzed again.

'Hello?' the female voice said.

'Hi. It's Daniel Johnston. I've an appointment with Jo McGuire.'

'Push the door and come through,' came the reply. Daniel tried to do as he was told but pushed too soon. The door didn't move. After he'd finished pushing, the door buzzed, and the latch was opened. By the time he realised he'd missed his cue, the door had locked again. He pressed the intercom again. 'Hi. It's Daniel again... I... sorry...'

The door buzzed again and this time he made it through and into a tiny reception area with enough room for two people, three at a push. There were two layers of glass between him and the receptionist. A large sign warned that the physical or verbal abuse of staff would not be tolerated. The receptionist – a woman in her thirties with tattoo-covered arms – glanced at him over the top of her large, black-rimmed glasses. 'Are you here for the needle exchange?' she said.

Daniel returned her look. Then he realised that she was talking to him. *Needle exchange?* 'No,' he said. After a pause, he added: 'I'm with the alkies.' He smiled at the receptionist, quite pleased with his attempt at keeping the situation light. It didn't seem to have worked – her face was unchanged.

'Alcohol support,' said Daniel. 'I'm with the alcohol support programme.'

'Alcohol is to the left. Go through, take seat.' A second door buzzed, and Danny went through into the waiting area. *Things are bad,* he thought, *but they could be worse. I could be turning right.*

Daniel sat down. The furniture was dark beige and blocky. The floor was a chessboard of dull, dark brown and light brown plastic tiles. There were framed pictures on the wall that were abstract and bland. One wall was completely covered in leaflets and flyers: self-help, support groups, psychotherapy, yoga, Pilates, massage – all the kind of things that he would normally have given a very wide berth to. He sat very still. Very still indeed. *Don't look right,* he thought.

After a few minutes of sitting very still and not looking right, Daniel was approached by a woman in her forties. She was wearing black, skinny jeans, Converse trainers and a white t-shirt. Her long blonde hair was parted in the middle and looked slightly wet, as if she'd just arrived after a hasty shower. 'Daniel?' she asked.

'Yes,' he replied, getting out of his seat. 'Yes. That's me.'

'I'm Jo McGuire.' A handshake. 'Do you want to come with me?'

Not especially, Daniel thought. 'Yes. Sure.'

They walked towards a series of brown, wood-effect doors that were, much to Daniel's relief, to the left of where he'd been sitting. Jo motioned for him to go into room six and she slid a sign on the door over to one side. IN SESSION, it now said. PLEASE DON'T DISTURB.

Daniel went into the small room and was asked to sit down. More beige furniture and another nondescript framed print. There was a small wooden table and on it was a box of tissues, with a single tissue sticking out of the box, ready to be plucked out and used. Daniel stared at it.

'Right Daniel, can I get some details from you before we start? Full name?'

'Daniel Johnston.'

'Date of birth?'

'July 12, 1966.'

'Big birthday coming up soon then?' said Jo, without looking up.

'What?'

'Big birthday. Coming up. For you.'

'Right. Yes. Big five oh. Can't wait.'

Daniel looked directly at Jo as she tilted her head up from her clipboard. 'Great,' she said.

'I have your address as Abbeville Road, Clapham. Is that right?'

'Yes. *No*. I'm staying at a hotel at the moment. Trying to keep a low profile.'

'Are you currently taking any medication Daniel?'

'Yes. Tons.'

'And what are the names of these items?'

Daniel fished into the pocket of his fashionable black, collarless jacket and produced a series of cardboard strips. He'd torn the lids off the pill boxes before he came to the treatment centre, knowing full well he'd forget the names of them otherwise. He looked at the ripped packaging: 'Prozac, diazepam and some kind of vitamin E supplements,' he said. 'I'm down to half a diazepam tablet at a time now. After today, it's a quarter. Then nothing.'

'The diazepam is to help with the alcohol withdrawal, yes?'

'Yes, indeed.'

'And how have you been getting on with the diazepam?'

Daniel remembered taking the first one just over a week ago. It had knocked him senseless. 'They're refreshingly strong,' he said.

'They're supposed to be,' said Jo, still looking down at her notes. 'That's why they've told you to drop down to a half and then a quarter to wean you off them slowly. They're highly addictive.'

'No point replacing one addiction with another,' said Daniel.

'No. No point in that,' she agreed. 'The vitamin E is to

27

help repair damage to nerve endings that may have happened because of long-term alcohol abuse. The Prozac is, well, to take the edge off any depressive feelings that might occur during withdrawal. It's quite usual to sort of... start looking inwards in these situations.'

She looked through her notes. 'Are you driving at the moment?'

'No. I had a crash. I refused a breath test at the scene. There's talk of challenging it – some loophole lawyer says he can get me off. Some technicality. I'm not so sure it's a good idea. It'll probably make me look even more of a giant twat than I do already. Sorry. No need for that kind of language, is there?'

Jo looked directly at him for the first time. 'Why are you here, Daniel?'

Pause. 'Is this the bit where I'm supposed to say, "because I'm an alcoholic"?" Daniel overdramatically wobbled his head and waved his hands to make his point.

'No. It's the bit where you tell me why you're here in whatever way you see fit.'

Long pause. 'Because I've been pissed for the best part of the last quarter of a century,' Daniel said. 'Because I massively, massively fucked up my life and my career. Because I crashed my car and somehow, miraculously, didn't kill anyone. Because I need help. That's why I'm here. I suppose.'

Jo and Daniel looked at each other. Daniel was breathing heavily. Jo glanced at the tissues. He shook his head. 'So yeah. That's why I'm here.'

'A perfectly good answer. Thank you.'

'Plus, private rehab clinics leak like sieves – the press pay staff for information and pictures. I thought an NHS place would be more discreet.'

'Sure,' Jo said.

'Can I ask something?' Daniel said, leaning forward in his chair. 'Why am I not in a group? Why am I not sitting with a bunch of people in a circle? I thought that's how this kind of thing worked?'

'We thought having you in a group would be... distracting,' she replied.

'How do you mean?' Daniel asked, despite already knowing what Jo was about to say.

'Because you're well known. You're on the telly. There was a lot of publicity about your crash.'

TV Daniel in Drunk Drive Smash.'

'Exactly.'

'I see.'

'Distracting.'

'Got it.'

Pause. 'So, how can I help?' said Jo, putting her clipboard on the floor and making herself comfortable.

'I don't really know,' Daniel replied. 'I've never done this before.'

Jo put down her paperwork. 'Well, the diazepam will be finished within a matter of days. That basically keeps you pleasantly out of it for a week or so... you're just about high enough that you can't be bothered with drinking, basically. It only takes about 10 or 14 days for your body to be free of alcohol. Amazing really. After what it's been through. Beyond that it's all in here.' Jo tapped the side of her head with her pen. 'If you decide you want to start drinking again, you probably will. If you decide you don't, you probably won't. It's not up to me. It's up to you. You're in control. Drink or don't drink. It's up to you. I've worked with hundreds and hundreds of people over the last fifteen years with drug and alcohol problems. I'm here to talk a bit but mainly listen. That's it. I can't prescribe you more drugs. I am not on call to you. I'm available once a week for an hour at a time. To talk. To help you with this...' For the second time, Jo tapped the side of her head. A pause. The longest one yet. 'Why not tell me about when you started drinking? And why.'

FIVE

10.15 pm Friday 6 April 1990

The carnival was in full swing when Danny arrived at Strangeways. He turned off Bury New Road, finding a parking spot alongside a clothing wholesaler, whose window was full of garishly coloured gear aimed at the current *Madchester* market. *Counterfeit*, thought Danny. *Every last stitch of it. No one seems to care though. Criminality that they turn a blind eye to, right outside a prison.*

Music drifted across the road as Danny locked his car, an aging blue Ford Escort. Then he double checked he'd locked it properly. The song was 'Ghetto Heaven' by Family Stand. There were scores – no, *hundreds* – of people milling about in the side roads and wasteland that surrounded the jail. Many were drinking from tins of beer – there was a man selling them from a makeshift stall made from what looked like a decorators table. An additional boozy waft was provided by the Boddington's brewery next door to the jail. It only added to the party atmosphere – as did a heavy smell of weed in the air.

Danny spotted a kid of about 12, selling t-shirts. He had a swathe of them across one arm and he waved one in the air with his free hand. Danny looked at the design as the boy passed him: it was a silhouette drawing of the jail and the words *Strangeways Breakout 1990* written underneath. *Must get one of those*, thought Danny, as he weaved through the crowd, looking for the Manchester Radio outside broadcast car that had been parked outside the jail since the start of the riot on Sunday.

On top of the main roof area of the prison – to the left of the jail's distinctive red brick central rotunda and tower – figures could be seen scurrying about. The hole they had punched through the roof could be clearly seen to the left. One inmate – wearing what looked like a prison officer's uniform – was waving a hand-made sign that said: 'TOLD WE WILL DIE'. A prisoner next to him was shouting into a makeshift megaphone fashioned from an orange and white traffic cone. What he was saying was a mystery, because every time he tried to shout, 'Mr Blue Sky' by ELO would blare out from within the prison compound. Danny had heard that the prison authorities had been using music to keep the rioters awake and to stop them relaying messages to the outside world. It was clearly true; what's more, it was apparent that the Home Office's taste in music was as suspect as their riot containment techniques.

Lights glimmered in the upper windows of a huge warehouse to the right of the jail. The words PAKASTANI UK TRADE CENTRE were written in huge white letters on the gable end. Danny had heard that several news operations had hired out space in the warehouse, so their cameramen could get better shots of the rioters.

On a side street to the right of the jail, Danny spotted the radio car, parked between an ITN satellite truck and a BBC outside broadcast vehicle. Manchester Radio engineer Gary Keenan was standing at the front of the car – the bonnet was up, and he was fiddling with the engine. And swearing. In the driver's seat was Robert Crane, the radio station's chief reporter. Crane was a foot taller than Danny, five years older and twice as experienced. Despite being a radio journalist, Crane was wearing a black suit and a red tie as if he was all prepared for his big TV break. He had the air of a man who didn't think he'd be staying long at Manchester Radio. Leaning through the radio car window and chatting to Crane - with a tin of beer in one hand and a joint in the other - was

Beth Hall. Danny was about to turn around and walk back to his car when Gary Keenan spotted him: 'Danny boy!' he shouted. *Fuck,* thought Danny. Reluctantly, he carried on walking towards the radio car.

'Come to check out the party for yourself, have you?' Gary asked, still ferreting around under the car's bonnet.

'Yeah. What are you doing?' Danny knew nothing about cars and wasn't remotely interested in what was going on, but would rather talk to Gary about car maintenance than chat to Beth Hall and Robert Crane.

'Swapping the battery. It's knackered. It needs a drive around to re-charge it, but we can't move from the spot otherwise some BBC bastard will pinch it. So - old battery out, new one in. What you doing here? Thought you were on kiddie murder patrol out in the swamplands of Oldham?'

'I was. I am.' Danny looked at Beth through the radio car windscreen. She was still talking to Crane. They were laughing. Beth caught Danny's glance and he looked away. 'Still waiting on the post-mortem result, but it's a bit of a dead end, Gary, to be honest with you. There's isn't a single house near the scene, so no doors to knock on to see if anyone saw anything. No ID yet on the kid. Cops are stumped. So, I thought I'd come down here and see what all the fuss is about.'

'And what do you think of it so far?' Gary asked, tugging at the battery connections to test they were secure.

Danny looked across the scene outside the prison. With the amount of drinking and drug taking going on, it reminded him of a nightclub, but with no walls or roof. He saw a TV reporter give a young man in a shell suit some cash – about £50 by the look of it – to give an interview. He heard the man, who's back was to the camera, so his face couldn't be seen, describing how his friend had just given himself up and that there were 'bodies all over the place' inside the jail.

'It's a circus,' Danny said.

'It's a fucking madhouse, Danny boy,' Gary said, slamming

the car bonnet closed. He tapped on the windshield to get Robert Crane's attention. 'Right, Bobby Boy, fire it up.' Crane started the engine.

'I keep thinking I should be here, Gary. That I'm missing out. Letting Max Headroom there get all the glory.' He motioned towards Crane, who was writing his script and simultaneously checking his hair in the rear- view mirror of the radio car. Again, Danny accidentally caught Beth's eye. She got out and started walking around the car towards them. *Shit.*

Danny started thinking of more things he could talk to Gary about, but didn't manage to think of one by the time that Beth got to them.

'Daniel...' she said. Beth was the only person who called him that. 'Thought you'd been told to stay away from here. The grown-ups have got this covered.'

'I'm on my own time, Beth. I'm not here for work – purely for pleasure.'

Danny looked at her. Her hair – normally piled up on top of her head in a messy bundle – looked freshly washed and styled. Her usual jeans and jumper had been replaced by a leather jacket and short black dress. The glasses that she normally glared at him through at work were gone. *Contact lenses? She's on the pull!*

'How about you - on your way out, Beth?' Danny asked, glancing briefly at Robert Crane as he rehearsed his piece in the radio car.

'Just passing though, Daniel. Very much like yourself.'

'You should take care, Beth. Some right nasty types to be found around Strangeways you know.'

'I can see that,' she replied.

Danny smiled at Beth and she walked away. 'See you on Monday, Gary,' Danny said.

Gary leaned in. He smelled of oil and cigarettes. 'Don't take the bait Danny boy,' he said, quietly. 'That's what she wants. Steer well clear. Do your own thing. You'll be fine. You're good.'

33

'Cheers Gary.' Danny walked towards the perimeter mesh fence of the jail and looked up at the rioters. One of them was swinging a makeshift hangman's noose above his head. Another had taken all his clothes off and was walking tightrope-style across the apex of the main prison building. A fire had started behind him. 'Mr Blue Sky' kicked in again. Danny stood and stared. *Gary's right. It's a madhouse.*

On the way back to his car he bought a four pack of Red Stripe beers from the man with the decorating table. The man asked Danny for ten pounds. 'A tenner?' Danny said, digging into his pockets to find more money. 'They'd barely be a fiver, ordinarily.'

'These are extraordinary times, mate!' said the beer seller, smiling at Danny and exposing missing front teeth. He plucked Danny's ten-pound note with a flourish.

'Not all the robbers are in the jail, are they?' Danny took his beers and got into his car.

The beer-seller shouted after him. 'Extraordinary times, mate!'

Danny opened one of the beers and drank about half of it. He thought about the men inside the jail. He thought about the circus outside. And he thought about the little boy, face down on the beach at Black Moss reservoir. He put the half-empty beer can into the coffee cup holder near the handbrake. *Yes. No question about it… It really IS a fucking madhouse*, he thought as he drove away.

SIX

10.30 am Thursday 9 June 2016

'So, Daniel, before we start. Can I ask – have you consumed any alcohol or taken any drugs since our last meeting?'

'Danny,' he said. Jo looked at him, looked at her notes and looked back. 'Call me Danny. And no – other than the diazepam I was kindly given. I was never really that bothered about drugs. I've tried the lot, been right through the menu, but it never really grabbed me. Not like drinking did.'

'Why do you think that is?' she asked.

'Have we started now?' Danny was aware that his tone was more defensive, more bristly, than he intended. He sat back slightly in his chair and held up both hands in an apologetic gesture. *Try not to be an arse, Danny boy,* he thought.

'Sorry, Jo,' he offered. 'Do you know what? I think it's the people. Drinkers tend to be pretty straight, if you know what I mean. You know where you stand. All the people I've ever met who take drugs have all been quite shocking wankers. They'd pick your pocket to fund a wrap of coke. But a boozer will share his last tenner with you. And buy you a drink with it. And one for himself obviously.'

'Was that important to you, the company of other drinkers?'

Danny thought of his regular coterie of drinking buddies: a few film editors, a director, a photographer, an actor and an accountant. He'd seen them almost every day for years yet couldn't have told you where they lived. 'Yes. We were a like an army unit. A band of brothers. All for one and all that.'

'When was the last time you saw them?'

'The day I crashed the car.'

'Is it worth talking about that?'

'I suppose it must be.'

Again. The bristle.

Danny exhaled, long and hard. 'We'd just finished a show, an expose about dodgy landlords. Hidden camera stuff. Nothing special. We'd finished early, so we went on the medicine – sorry, went for a drink – about 6.30. I'd been in there at lunchtime as well. We tended to drink at an Italian restaurant near the TV studios. It was our place that we'd kind of adopted. We had this idea that no one would find us. Nonsense, obviously. Everyone knew we drank there. Anyway, I put a few hours in there then got off. I'd taken some food with me to eat at home. A bit of seafood pasta. I'd gone back to the studios to get my car. I've got my own parking spot... *had* my own parking spot. Then I headed home. I know that boozers always say this, but my driving was fine. I'm extremely experienced at driving with a few drinks in me. I'm really good at it. I know. We all say that. It's bollocks, isn't it? Anyway. That's what happened. I set off for south of the river and was a few minutes from home...'

A pause.

'Then I saw something.' Danny paused again. 'This is confidential, isn't it? I didn't mention this to the police. Don't know why. I just didn't want to.'

'Of course it is,' said Jo leaning forward ever so slightly.

'Then I saw this little kid. Eight or nine years old. A boy. He ran across the road right in front of me. He was wearing shorts and had no top on – bare-chested like he was on holiday or something.'

Danny Johnston looked at the tissues on the table, as if to check they were still there. They were. There was one sticking out of the oval hole in the top of the box.

'He looked right at me as I was swerving and skidding. *Right at me.* And smiled. The little bastard! Then I hit the tree.

Then everything went to shit. Or not. Maybe hitting that tree was the best thing that has happened to me or a very long time.'

'Was the little boy okay?'

'Yes. I think so. Yes. I didn't see him after the crash but I didn't hit him, I'm sure of it.'

'Why didn't you mention it to the police?'

'Not sure. Maybe I... I don't know. I don't want to just make up an answer for you, Jo. I'd just be saying words for the sake of it. No point. I don't know why I didn't mention it.'

Danny and Jo sat in silence for about thirty seconds.

'You look different,' Jo said.

Danny, never particularly heavyset, had lost more than a stone in weight since he'd stopped drinking. He'd had his hair cropped close, which revealed its true colour; underneath the expensive dye job he'd had for the last ten years his hair was a very light grey. He'd also stopped shaving and the developing beard was virtually white.

'I am different,' Danny said.

SEVEN

8.45 am Monday 9 April 1990

Danny pulled the radio car up to the barrier of Oldham Police station and wound down the window. There were rarely any spare parking places at Oldham nick, especially when a murder press conference was being held. But today, Danny was waved straight through and told to park in the visitors' section. *That's a first.*

The police station – a grey, pebble-dashed piece of sixties brutalism – formed part of a series of equally grey and brutal buildings that greeted you as you came into Oldham town centre and drove the seven unlovely miles from Manchester city centre. Nothing said: 'Welcome to Oldham' less than Oldham Police station.

Danny signed in at reception and was told to wait. There was only one other reporter there – a woman in her early twenties – that Danny had never seen before, was sitting in the waiting area. She had short, jet-black hair and was wearing what appeared to be a chamois leather skirt. An alarmingly short chamois leather skirt. Danny sat opposite her and made a point of keeping his eyeline perfectly horizontal. She had no technical equipment with her. *Must be a print journo*, thought Danny. *They think they're better than us.*

'Hi. You from *The Messenger*?' Danny asked. The death of a child in these circumstances would make the lead story for weeks for a daily teatime paper like the *Oldham Evening Messenger*. It was always a good idea to keep it friendly with the local reporters. *Especially with Ms Power Skirt here,* thought Danny.

'Yes I am.' she replied in a medium-strength local accent.

'Here for the press conference on the kid?' Danny asked, tweaking his slightly grammar-school accent to mirror hers, a habit he'd developed recently. It was another piece of advice he'd picked up: *blend in, adapt, talk to people in the same way they're talking to you.*

'Correct again.' She glanced at Danny's Marantz. Her attitude towards him became a few percent friendlier. 'Are you from Manchester Radio? We monitor it in the office. You were first there weren't you? Jimmy something, isn't it?'

'Danny Something. Danny Johnston.'

'That's right. Hi, Danny Something. I'm Kate.' She leant forward and put out her hand. Danny shook it. *No, I won't tell you anything about what I saw out on the moors,* Danny thought. *That skirt has no power over me.*

'Did you see much out on the moors? What do you know that I don't?' she said, leaning even closer to him as she spoke.

'Not really,' replied Danny, trying to make the story sound as dull as possible. 'Bit of activity. Noncommittal coppershit from the local DI. Usual stuff, really.'

'How did you get there so soon? It's way out in the sticks for you lot. Must be nearly out of your patch.'

'News desk got a tip off. Yeah, it's the very ends of the earth for us. Proper *Deliverance* country.' Danny crossed his eyes and played an imaginary banjo to make his point.

Kate smiled at him. Not the friendliest smile Danny had ever seen. 'I'm from near there,' Kate replied, leaning back into her seat.

'Right.' *Bloody hell,* he thought. 'Some really lovely countryside around there.'

A middle-aged man with a clipboard approached them. His name band identified him as Brian Lake – GMP Press Office. 'Right, you here for the press conference. Only two of you? That's a bit disappointing. Ah well. You'd better come this way.'

Danny and Kate followed the press officer through a series of double doors. 'How's your mum keeping Kate?' the press officer said as they walked down a long corridor.

'Not bad, thanks. Keeping herself very busy – you know what she's like.'

Danny felt even more out of place than usual. *No, I don't know what she's like, actually. Do feel free to fill me in. And how come she knows the press office guy so well?*

The two journalists were led into a large conference room with thirty or more chairs – set out like a school play– facing a long-top table. Danny sat a few seats away from Kate on the front row. He felt it might be a bit odd if he sat next to her. At the table facing them sat DI Smithdown. He looked like he'd made a real effort with his appearance, but still looked rather uncomfortable. Danny tried to catch his eye; he was sure the DI would remember him from the moors. If he did, he made no indication of it – he just looked around the room and the out of the window – anywhere apart from at Danny and Kate. Next to the DI, according to the triangular nameplate that sat in front of him, was Detective Superintendent James Pym. He was a similar age to DI Smithdown but looked altogether more comfortable in his well-pressed suit and bright white shirt. His hair was well-cut and suspiciously dark brown.

The two policemen leant in and spoke quietly to each other. Then DI Smithdown called over the press officer. He looked at the journalists who were currently taking up precisely two of the forty seats and moved his arm in their general direction. His facial expression suggested something along the lines of: *is this it?* Danny couldn't be sure, but he was fairly certain that DS Pym said something back along the lines of 'fucking Strangeways, isn't it?'

Danny left his seat and placed his Marantz recorder on the table in between the two detectives. He gave the DI an awkward smile, like a workman who knew he was slightly in the way. He attached his microphone to a small stand, pressed play and record and went back to his seat. 'So that's you done then?' Kate stage-whispered to Danny. 'Easy job being a radio journo. Just press record.'

'Play *and* record,' Danny corrected. He folded his arms, quite pleased with himself.

Glancing at a few sheets of notes and leaning slightly too far into Danny's microphone, DS Pym began speaking: 'Ladies and gentlemen, thank you for coming this afternoon.' He paused and looked at Danny and Kate. 'Both of you. I'm Detective Superintendent James Pym and this is Detective Inspector John Smithdown. We're here today to issue an appeal on behalf of Oldham Police in relation to the discovery of a young, deceased male. The body was found in the early hours of Friday morning close to Black Moss Reservoir. Those of you who know the vicinity...' the DCI glanced in Kate's direction, slightly annoying Danny... 'will be aware that this is a very remote area, just off the A62 Oldham to Huddersfield Road, beyond Diggle. The body was removed from the scene later that same day. It appears to be that of a male child, approximately nine to ten years of age. The body was discovered partially-clothed. A post-mortem took place over the weekend. The exact cause of death hasn't been one hundred percent ascertained but the boy had suffered multiple catastrophic injuries. I don't want to go too deeply into the nature of those injuries at this stage, but any one of them could have caused his death. Suffice to say, this discovery is being treated as murder. With that in mind, we have an appeal to make to the public today.'

DS Pym put his notes to one side and looked directly at Danny and Kate. *Are we about to disengage from copperspeaky?* thought Danny. 'We urgently need to identify this child,' the DS said. 'We don't know who he is. We don't know how he came to be up there at Black Moss. The one thing we do know is that something has gone horribly, horribly wrong for a young boy to be found in this place in this way. Horribly wrong.'

That's my clip for the next news bulletin, thought Danny.

The DS continued: 'We would appeal for anyone who saw anything suspicious in the Black Moss area over the last seven days to come forward. Although the reservoir is very remote, the nearby road is busy. It has particularly heavy traffic in terms of lorries and HGVs driving to and from Manchester and Huddersfield. I'd also ask if anyone has information about any missing children in the Oldham or surrounding areas to come forward. They can contact us on 856 2220 – ask for the Oldham incident room. Alternatively, they can call Crimestoppers anonymously on 0800 555 111. That ends this appeal. I will answer any questions you have as best I can, but I'm limited in what I can say at this present moment in time.'

Danny hated asking questions in front of other journalists. Fortunately, Kate half raised her hand and asked: 'DS Pym. Has anyone reported a child missing in the area?'

'No, they haven't, Kate.'

'Isn't that unusual? For a child's body to be found without a child being reported missing?'

'Yes, it is unusual.'

'How unusual?' she pressed.

'Very.'

'Are you following any particular lines of inquiry?' In the same way as coppers spoke copperspeak, journalists spoke *journalese*. This was a coded question, meaning: *do you know what happened here and can't actually tell us at the moment?*

'Not at the moment, no,' the DS replied. 'We're keeping an open mind. One matter of interest to us is that the body was found exactly on the border with Yorkshire, so we'll be liaising with our colleagues on the West Yorkshire force who are taking a great interest in this case.'

Kate continued to gently pepper the officer with questions, deftly writing extremely neat shorthand notes into a spiral-bound notepad as she spoke. 'Should we read something into the fact that the body is in that spot?' she asked.

'Again, we're keeping an open mind, but it would be astonishing coincidence that it just happened to have been placed exactly on the county border.'

'Can you tell us the nature of the boy's injuries?'

'I'm not going to release that information at this present moment in time as I feel it might prejudice our inquiries.'

That's copperspeak for 'only the police and the killer know the nature of his injuries and I want to keep it that way' thought Danny. He looked at DI Smithdown, trying to get a sense of whether he'd told his boss about Danny seeing the boy's body. *He hasn't told him,* thought Danny. *That's interesting.*

DS Pym looked across to DI Smithdown, who had sat in silence with his head down and his arms folded throughout his colleague's statement and answers. 'Anything to add, Mr Smithdown?'

'No. I think you've got it covered, Mr Pym,' he said. His arms remained folded.

DS Pym began to get up out of his chair. 'Thanks very much for your time,' he said. 'We've a lot to do as you can imagine and if you don't mind, we need to crack on.'

Kate put away her notebook and took out her purse, foraging for change. 'See you again, Danny Something,' she said as she half ran from the room. She was obviously planning to phone some copy through for the late edition and needed a payphone. She smiled at the press officer and left in a chamois leather blur.

'See you,' said Danny, largely to himself.

Danny was in no such rush. He was way too late for the nine o'clock news so he had another half an hour, at least, to file his report. Not that anyone would notice. *Strangeways, Strangeways, Strangeways. That's anyone seemed to care about.* He sauntered over to the top table. DS Pym was in a huddle with the press officer a few yards away. DI Smithdown hadn't moved. Danny reached over for his Marantz. 'Mr Smithdown,' he said, quietly. The officer, arms still folded, was looking out of the window. 'Why no mention of the tape on the kid's body?'

DI Smithdown turned away from the window. He looked at Danny. Then he looked at the tape machine – its twin wheels were still turning, and its red recording light was still lit. He looked back at Danny. *He's not daft, this guy,* thought Danny. He pressed the stop button on the Marantz. The wheels stopped turning, the red light faded away to nothing. DI Smithdown looked at Danny and stood up, pushing his chair back.

'Tape? Pure speculation, young man.' DI Smithdown rummaged thought his pockets and pulled out a packet of cigarettes. 'There's a time and a place for speculation.' He leant in slightly. 'And this definitely isn't the time or the place.' DI Smithdown gave Danny a flat smile and walked away.

EIGHT

11.35 am Thursday 9 June 2016

'What do you mean... a *kill payment*? What the fuck is that? I've never heard of it.'

Standing outside the drug and alcohol unit after his appointment, Daniel Johnston was shouting at his agent, George Pritchard, via his mobile phone. The ache for a drink had sucked all the moisture from Danny's mouth and the bottom edges of his rib cage throbbed. He wanted to retch but managed to hold it back. Rather stupidly, after all these years, Danny had started smoking again. He pulled a Silk Cut Ultra Light from its white packet of ten and lit it. *I'm only buying them in tens,* he thought. *It's not like I've really started again. Not full-on.*

Then, he continued with the business of shouting.

'But I've already started work on it. It's my big book. My proper book. My fucking take-me-to-another-level serious book. They can't just change their minds and cancel it.'

'They can, and they have,' said George Pritchard on the other end of the line. Pritchard had been Daniel's agent for fifteen years. He'd steered Daniel from jobbing local TV journalist to full-on celebrity righter-of-wrongs. When you thought of campaigning TV journalism, you thought of Daniel Johnston. But since his car crash, work for Danny had been haemorrhaging out of George Pritchard's Soho office.

'But I signed a contract!' Danny shouted, even louder this time. He threw his cigarette into a flower bed outside the unit and lit up another.

'Yes, Daniel,' George said patiently. 'But the publishers didn't. The contract needs both signatures for it to be valid. They hadn't signed – now they don't want any part of the book since your... *accident.*' This was George's preferred word for what had happened: *accident.* A less diplomatic person might call it *driving your car into a tree while pissed out of your mind then taking a swing at a policeman*, but George preferred *accident.*

'Unbelievable,' said Daniel.

'They've offered you the kill payment to not write it basically. It's quite good of them really. They could have just walked away.'

'So, I'm being paid not to work.'

'Correct.'

'To go quietly like a good little boy?'

'In a sense, yes.'

'They can stuff their kill payment.'

'No, they can't, actually,' sighed the agent. 'It'll be received with considerable gratitude, thank you very much. It's the only money you've got on the horizon.'

Danny took a few paces left, then right, the sat down on the steps of the drug and alcohol unit.

'How much is it?' he asked.

'Five grand.'

'Okay. Could be worse. What else have I got coming in? Surely, I've got money owed from *2016*? I've done three episodes for them already this year.' The TV show *2016* – the name cunningly went up a digit every year – had been Daniel's main employer for nearly ten years. ITV's flagship popular current affairs show had made his name. He'd interviewed dictators, exposed con men and changed laws as the programme's best-known reporter. He'd even saved a young girl's life after bullying a regional health authority into changing its mind over her cancer treatment. *Won a bloody BAFTA for that,* Daniel reminded himself. *What was the kid's name? Briony or Bonnie or something.*

'*2015* have been looking at their contracts too,' sighed Pritchard. 'You should have told them you'd been arrested at the scene of the accident. It's in the fine print. You have to tell them if you get in trouble with the police. It affects their brand. There'll be no work forthcoming from them for the foreseeable. They're within their rights to withhold payments too, because you've brought the company into disrepute. You've tarnished their image.'

Oh, come on. Even I can't tarnish ITV's image, Danny thought. For once, he kept the thought to himself.

'But you're technically still an employee, albeit a freelance one,' George continued. 'So, they have a duty of care towards you. They've asked about your treatment. How's it going?'

'Swimmingly.'

'You're not helping your cause you know, Daniel.'

A long pause. 'I won't lose sleep over *2016*. I should have moved on from there years ago. But the book was a big deal.' Danny had made a well-received episode of *2016* about celebrity historical child abuse. It had touched on the connections with the establishment and politicians. Cover-up or conspiracy fantasy? Not hugely in-depth but that was TV half hours for you. But he'd been offered the book deal on the strength of the programme and he'd recently started to work on it. He'd started to structure it, play with it, shape it, finesse the idea. It really had the makings of something very special indeed. He hadn't actually written anything yet, but that wasn't the point.

'I know the book was – is – really important to you,' soothed George. 'Look. Lie low. Maybe go back to Manchester for a while. Let things blow over for a few months, then we can get the PR guys on the case. Do some redemption-type pieces – rehab your image. How the accident was the best thing that ever happened to you... Pulled you from the brink, that kind of thing. Then we can get you some reality TV gigs. Daring-do stuff. Channel Four has a ski-jumping show you know?'

'I'm not standing next to Davina Mc-fucking-Call in a lycra onesie George,' Danny stated. 'Not for anything.'

'Have a think. Look, I've got to go. Got a call on the other line. I'll be in touch. Bye, Daniel.'

'Okay, George. Look – thanks. I mean it. And sorry for being an arse. Thanks for being there for me.'

'That's what I'm here for mate,' said George. 'Take care.'

Danny ended the call. He headed off towards the main road adjacent to the unit and looked for a taxi to take him home. He found one quickly and gave the driver the address. The driver pulled away from the kerb and looked at Danny in the rearview mirror. His face lit up in recognition of his passenger.

'You're that telly bloke, aren't ya? The car crash telly bloke? That's it. Off the telly.'

Danny slid down into his seat. 'The very same,' he confirmed. *This is going to be a very long cab ride,* he thought.

Thankfully, his phone pinged, notifying him of an email. It was from George. The email said that George was terminating their existing terms and agreements as client and agent forthwith, citing an irreconcilable breakdown in their professional relationship.

He'd already drafted it, thought Danny. *Bastard.*

NINE

5.45 pm Monday 9 April 1990

Danny stood at the bar of the Three Tunnes pub in Oldham town centre, smoked his third cigarette and started on his second pint. He looked around the pub. It was the kind of pub with horse brasses above the bar and a very regular clientele. Nearly everyone there was male, middle-aged and smoking. *This is the copper-iest pub I've ever been in,* he thought. *DI Smithdown is bound to drink in here.*

Danny may have been a stranger in Oldham, but some things were true wherever you went. Journalists drank in the nearest pub to their newsroom, no matter how rundown, expensive or unpleasant that pub happened to be. The closer the pub, the more time you got to spend drinking. By the same logic, police officers always drank in the nearest pub to their police station. Walk straight out of Oldham Police station and just past the magistrate's courts and you came to the black and white frontage of the Three Tunnes.

Danny had long since filed his piece after the police press conference but had decided to return to Oldham after his shift was done. There was nothing to particularly drag him back to his flat in Didsbury, south Manchester. He didn't have a girlfriend. He had a ragtag gang of drinking mates at a pub near his flat, but he didn't really *know* anyone in Didsbury. He didn't know anyone in Oldham either; in fact, he didn't know anyone who *knew* anyone in Oldham. But still, here he was.

As he continued to search the faces of the early evening

drinkers, Danny spotted someone he recognised: Kate from *The Messenger.* She was standing on the other side of the pub with a female friend. They were the only women in the pub, yet strangely they seemed to fit right in. She nodded to Danny, who took that as a signal that he should go over and say hello.

'Hi Kate,' he said. He smiled at her friend. 'This your pub?'

'Kind of. What are you doing here Danny Something?'

'Just having a drink, soaking up the atmosphere,' Danny said in the most casual manner he could muster.

'Rubbish. You're looking for DI Smithdown, aren't you?

'Why, does he come in here?' Danny asked.

'No. He drinks in the Indian restaurant over the road,' Kate said.

'Alright, no need for sarcasm.'

'We don't do sarcasm in Oldham, there's no market for it. I'm deadly serious. It's weird, but that's where you'll find him.'

Kate looked at him and narrowed her eyes. 'This story has got under your skin a bit, hasn't it, Danny Something? You broadcast guys never hang around. Straight in, straight out. Yet, you're still here. Why's that then? What did you see out on the moors?'

'A dead kid,' he said, sipping his pint. Danny looked at Kate's friend. She was the same age, but she didn't look like a journalist. Probably an old school friend. She showed no interest in their conversation whatsoever. 'Just a dead kid.'

'It's terrible, just terrible.' sighed Kate, taking a glug of her lager. She was drinking a pint, Danny noticed. 'It really is. But no one seems interested – it's Strangeways or nothing at the moment. I filed a piece about the kid for tonight's paper, but now I've been told to track down rioters who come from the local area and get their families to talk.' A pause. Danny looked at her. Her eyes were so dark they were nearly black. Very striking. *Bit scary.*

'I'm sure they'll soon ID him,' she continued. 'I've not heard anything weird about the body or how it was found, have you?'

Danny thought about mentioning the tape, then decided not to and shook his head. He finished his drink. 'I'm going to get off home. It's been a long day. See you again.'

Danny smiled at Kate's friend – got nothing in return – and headed for the door.

'Say hello to DI Smithdown for me, Danny Something,' said Kate as he walked away. Her friend said something quietly in her ear and the two young women laughed. Fortunately, they couldn't see his face flush red as Danny walked out of the pub.

Outside the Three Tunnes, Danny looked around the precinct. He quickly saw what he was looking for and headed up the sloped street to The Raj restaurant. As he went in, a customer came out with a takeaway; there was a small bar with two high stools at the far end of the restaurant. There was only one person sitting at the bar: DI John Smithdown. What little colour there'd been in his face earlier in the day had all but disappeared. He looked exhausted. He wasn't drunk, but he was several pints ahead of Danny. He made his way through the tables – all of which were empty – towards the bar. Danny pointed at DI Smithdown's near-empty pint of bitter 'Another one?' he asked.

'Well done for finding me,' the detective said. 'We'll make a journalist of you yet. A large half, please.'

'Why do you drink in here?' Danny asked, ordering himself a pint of strong lager and another pint of bitter for the DI. The waiter seemed to know that Danny wasn't here for food and didn't bother offering him a menu.

'I come in here because all the coppers go in the Three Tunnes, that's why,' the DI said. 'Sometimes you need a break from them. All they talk about is crime.'

'Can I talk to you about a crime, Mr Smithdown?'

'Depends which one.'

'You know *exactly* which one.'

DI John Smithdown shifted his weight on his bar stool. He started peeling apart a beer mat, then spun it away across the top of the bar. 'Didn't think anyone was interested in that kid,' DI Smithdown said. He was looking at the bar top, not at Danny.

'*I'm* interested Mr Smithdown. Otherwise I wouldn't be here.'

'Why Danny? Your radio station covers the whole of Greater Manchester. There's a murder every five days in the GMP patch. Take your pick. Why this one?'

That, thought Danny, was a perfectly reasonable question. 'Maybe it's because I *saw* him. Mr Smithdown,' Danny said, taking the stool next to the detective. 'When there's a murder, we cover the press conferences, interview the officers, do the "emotional appeals for help"… It's the way it works. It's the same every time, a ritual. You do your bit, I do mine. But this is different. I *saw* him. No kid deserves to end up like that.'

DI Smithdown grabbed a handful of Bombay mix that was in a bowl on the bar. 'Ordinarily I wouldn't be seen dead talking to the likes of you Danny,' he said, washing the mix down with a big gulp of his pint. 'No offence – cheers, by the way – but I wouldn't. Truth is, I'm fucked with this case. It's barely started, but I'm fucked. I need the oxygen of publicity, but every bit of it is being sucked out of Oldham nick, across Greater Manchester and straight into Strangeways fucking jail. We have a dead child and the only people we can convince to cover it are you and Kate from *The Messenger*. Pathetic. No offence. I've got no resources, no staff. Most of our cells are full of rioters who've either given themselves up or been dragged backwards out of Strangeways. People are too busy staring at the roof of that prison to realise what's going on around them.'

'What *is* going on Mr Smithdown?' said Danny.

The policeman rubbed a hand across his unshaven face. It was speckled with grey stubble. His eyes were red with tiredness. 'Something terrible happened to that kid. Yet my boss won't release it. Says we should wait. Keep our powder dry, he says.'

'The placing of the body is very telling, isn't it?' said Danny. 'Right on the border...'

'Bollocks. You've been watching too much telly. So has the DS.'

'How do you mean?'

'They panicked,' Smithdown said, staring at himself in the mirror behind the bar. 'Whoever did this was *shitting* themselves. They left that kid there because they got scared and ran off. Must have been pretty weird, carrying a kid across the moors in the dead of night. Fuck me, he might even have been still alive. But I don't think there was any intention to leave him on the border. That's bollocks.'

'How do you know?' Danny asked his question quietly, leaning in,

DI Smithdown took a hefty swallow of his pint and turned to look at the reporter. 'Because of the tape, Danny. The tape that you saw. That tape you weren't *supposed* to have seen.'

'Sorry, I don't get it, Mr Smithdown.'

'Because that little lad had weights attached to his body. Strapped to him with tape. They had no intention of leaving him in the sand on the county border. They probably didn't even know the border was there. They were going to sink him in Black Moss. Maybe they panicked. Maybe they thought they saw someone coming. Who knows? But the idea that he was left on the border as some symbolic act is pure DS Pym bollocks.'

'How did he die, Mr Smithdown?' Danny had no idea why DI Smithdown was telling him all this. At that moment, he didn't care.

'Asphyxiation. He was probably half dead already. After what had been done to him.' DI Smithdown reached across the bar and took back one of the split beer mats. He took out a pen.

'What had been done to him?' Danny asked.

DI Smithdown made light work of the rest of his pint. He

nodded to the waiter. 'Everything, Danny. The full fucking works. We won't identify that kid anytime soon unless we accidentally get a DNA match with someone we arrest for something else, or we trace a relative, or someone walks into Oldham nick and tells us who he is.'

The detective was writing as he spoke: 'He had no teeth – they'd been knocked out or pulled out, probably a bit of both. His hands had been burnt – probably with a blow torch or over a fire. So, no fingerprints. For a kid of that age, they were really hedging their bets with that one, belt-and-braces stuff. Christ, I hope he *was* dead by the time they'd got him to Black Moss. Poor little shit.' He took another hefty gulp, finished his pint and leant close to Danny. 'Which is why we can't let this be buried because of Strangeways and my stupid twat of a DS. No way.'

DS Smithdown handed Danny the split beer mat. A number was on it. 'Call me tomorrow. Early doors.'

The waiter handed DI Smithdown a takeaway bag. He took it with a nod and left. Danny watched him leave then turned his attention back to his pint. He was feeling stunned by what had just happened. And very nervous. He was also strangely elated.

TEN

2.20 am Friday 10 June 2016

That, thought Danny Johnston, *was a fucking horrible dream. Jesus Christ Almighty.*

Since he'd stopped drinking, the ferocity and realism of Danny's dreams had increased massively. He was feverish and hot, yet the sweat all over his body was already starting to chill him. Maybe it was down to the pills he'd been taking. Or the fact they had run out. Maybe it was because he was actually sleeping now rather than simply passing out after a night's drinking. Blackout boozing doesn't tend to encourage dream-filled sleep. Either way, he was starting to dread going to sleep.

He looked around his hotel room. He swung his legs around and sat upright on the edge of his bed.

He'd dreamt he was back on the common. But this time he was searching for something. He staggered and stumbled as he looked – dream Danny clearly knew what he was looking for; asleep Danny didn't.

He turned around and saw his car was on fire. He didn't care – the search was more important. After what seemed like hours, Danny came across a quieter, more still area of the common. He could hear the sound of rippling water but couldn't see where it was coming from. Pushing apart some branches from a large bush, he saw a small boy lying asleep on a single bed. The boy was tied to it; the bed was filthy – the boy even filthier. He was close enough for Danny to reach out and touch, yet when he tried, the boy seemed to be a hundred feet away.

Behind him, Danny heard the sound of an explosion. He turned and saw a fireball where his car had been. Again, he didn't seem to care.

He turned back to look at the bed.

The boy's face was inches from his. His breath stank of rotting vegetables. He spat wet earth into Danny's mouth then screamed at him.

That's when he woke up.

What kind of a person has a dream like that?

ELEVEN

Noon Wednesday 11 April 1990

Danny had agreed to meet with DI Smithdown at a tiny, side-street cafe close to Oldham Police station. Despite not feeling his best, Danny was bang on time. The cafe was busy with people visiting the nearby market. DI Smithdown put up a hand and waved Danny over to his table when he spotted him.

Smithdown was drinking coffee and screwing a cigarette out into the ashtray. He seemed to be ageing in dog's years – he looked ten years older than when they'd first met out near the reservoir less than a week ago. There was a woman sitting with him. She was dressed in some white shirt and black trousers – not a uniform, but she was clearly a copper. Her dyed blond hair was scraped back from her head and tied back tightly. She was tall and strong-looking, like a PE teacher She also looked rather annoyed at being there. No words were spoken between her and DI Smithdown.

Danny nodded in the DI's direction and ordered a slice of toast and a can of Coke at the counter. The Coke was for caffeine and sugar, to try and wake himself up. The toast was because he felt he ought to eat something. He hadn't eaten properly for days. After finishing his last shift, he'd gone drinking at his local pub; on returning, he'd found half a bottle of malt whisky tucked towards the back of his kitchen cupboard and demolished that too. Then he'd fallen asleep. Or passed out. *Depends how you look at it.* Today was supposed to be his day off.

He took his Coke and toast over to the table where Smithdown and the female officer were sitting. Still no words between them. *Funny old dynamic going on here,* Danny thought.

'Alright Danny,' the DI said. He gestured at an elderly couple at the next table to see if a chair was free and pulled it over for Danny when they indicated that it was. 'Danny, this is Detective Constable Jan Cave.'

'Hi,' said Danny and put out his hand. She shook his hand – the thinnest of smiles appeared.

'DC Cave is the closest thing we have to a child safety expert round these parts,' said DI Smithdown. 'She's been on a course.'

'Oh right. Great,' said Danny and bit into his toast. It made him feel a bit sick. He had no idea why he was here but thought it best to say as little as possible and see where it went. He put the toast down and drank the Coke instead.

'I thought it would be a good idea for you to meet DC Cave and get an idea what we're up against when it comes to unidentified and missing kids. I'd like to tell you that the system is under strain, but the truth is, there isn't really a system.'

'Do you think the kid might have been a runaway? From a kids' home or something?' Danny asked him. The question was more for DC Cave.

'Possibly,' she said. She looked at DI Smithdown. Then back at Danny. 'Not sure.'

'Okay,' said Danny trying a different tack. 'Well, what happens when a kid goes missing? What procedures kick in?'

Again, the female officer looked to DI Smithdown. He nodded, as if to say, *Go on, tell him.* 'You're not recording this are you?' she asked. She had a strong North Manchester accent.

'No, I'm not,' Danny said, smiling in what he thought was a reassuring way. 'I'd have a microphone out and it would be near your face if I was. We're just talking, aren't we, DI Smithdown?'

'Just talking,' he confirmed.

'Sorry,' said DC Cave. 'I've only ever had dealings with the press once before and it wasn't a very nice experience. *The Messenger* printed my picture a few years back. I was on duty outside a house where there'd been a domestic murder. Dad killed two kids with a claw hammer. Absolute horror story. My neighbours on the estate where I lived didn't know I was with the police. After the paper appeared, I got all sorts of hassle. The dad who hammered his kids got flowers outside his house – I got dog shit through my letterbox. I had to move. Not right, is it?'

'No. It isn't,' agreed Danny. 'Are you a child safety specialist, DC Cave?'

For the first time, the female officer smiled. There was almost a laugh. She pushed her cup of tea away and leant on the table. 'Let me tell you how it works,' she said, and the smile fell quickly from her face. 'Missing kids, kids in danger, vulnerable kids – these jobs always fall to female officers. Most of the blokes at the station have kids – I don't, I've never changed a nappy in my life, but I'm supposed to know more about kids because I'm female.'

She looked at DI Smithdown as if to check she wasn't speaking out of turn. 'If a kid goes missing – a kid that's actually *cared* for, in a good community surrounded by good people – there'll be search parties out within the hour combing the streets and parks looking for that child. Children that are cared for – that are *loved* – very rarely go missing. On the odd occasion that they do, they're normally found before the police even arrive at the scene. Because the people that love them will move heaven and earth to find them.'

'So what kind of kid was the lad up at Black Moss, in your opinion?' asked Danny.

'Well, he was almost certainly a kid that *wasn't* cared for – and kids that aren't cared for tend to end up in care.'

'In a care home?' Danny asked. 'Looked after by social workers?'

'No,' said DC Cave firmly. 'The homes are staffed by *residential* staff, they aren't qualified social workers. They're there to do a head count. If the head count doesn't add up, they fill in a missing from home report and hand it to the police. Some of the kids go missing so often, the homes have the forms already filled out to save time. The forms are handed from shift to shift at the police station and that's it. It's just a bit of paper and that can go missing as easily as a kid who wants to hitch a lift into Manchester and see the sights. How much effort goes into looking for a kid that's already gone missing ten times so far this month? Not a lot. You guys from the press aren't interested because they're, well, they're kids in care.'

'Not sure that's true,' said Danny.

'These kids go missing *all the time*,' stated DI Smithdown, jabbing the table with his finger. 'I can show you case after case of kids who've just disappeared into the mist and I can count the column inches we've had about them on one hand. Without using my thumb. These kids aren't a story to you guys. That's not a criticism – it's a fact. Actually, it's a criticism *and* a fact.'

'So, what's different about this case?' asked Danny.

'We've had scores of kids go AWOL in this division over the years, but we've never had a dead one before. Not a dead one we've known about anyway. And not one that had been subjected to serious sexual assaults like this lad was. Attacks that were... *sustained*. It probably went on for several days before he ended up at Black Moss.'

Danny looked straight at DC Smithdown. He'd felt hangover sick when he arrived at the cafe. Now he felt an altogether different kind of sickness.

'Mr Smithdown thinks this boy was snatched – stolen to order,' said DC Cave. 'I'm keeping an open mind, but one thing's for sure: the best way of stealing something, Danny, is to take something that no one will miss. That way, less people will come looking for it.'

'Okay,' said Danny. 'I get it. But what do you want from

me, Mr Smithdown?'

'Interest,' said the DI. 'Time. Publicity. I need you to keep chipping away at your bosses to keep running this story. Keep it in the public eye as best you can. I know that all that anyone's interested in is Strangeways at the moment, but we need you to keep it in the news. But I also need to trust you not to release what we know until I say so. Especially about the way the kid's body was found. Hardly anyone knows about that – if it gets out, I'll know it was you that blabbed it. Stick with it and, when the time is right, I'll give you everything. The big exclusive. Young guy like you, it could make your career.'

'I'll need new audio,' Danny said. He saw the slightly puzzled look on the officers' faces. 'A new interview, to freshen things up. Maybe you'd like to do it DC Cave? My recorder's in my car.'

'No chance,' she said. Danny could see there was no point in trying to cajole her.'

'I'll do it,' said DI Smithdown. 'I'll come with you to the car – we can do it there.'

Danny and DI Smithdown both got up. 'You settle up, DC Cave, while I escort this young man to his vehicle. Make sure you get a receipt.'

'Just one thing,' said Danny. 'Can I ask – why me, Mr Smithdown? There's better journalists than me about.'

DI Smithdown looked at DC Cave and back to Danny: 'Because you saw him. You're involved. Tell me you haven't thought about that kid since the other morning out on the moors?'

'I haven't thought about much else,' Danny said.

'Then that's your answer. That's why.'

'What about Kate from *The Messenger*? Can't she help?'

DI Smithdown leant in, so he was close to Danny's face. 'Two things. One: *The Messenger* doesn't have the same reach as you guys. I need to spread my net good and wide. Second – and this is very important – the shit who did this is off the scale. Fucking evil. And I don't want my daughter anywhere near him.'

TWELVE

10.30 am Thursday 15 June 2016

'So, how have you been, Danny?' said Jo McGuire.

'Okay. Not bad,' he replied. 'Lying low. I've moved back into my house. And no, I haven't had any drugs or alcohol.'

'Fine. Good. Thanks for the update.'

Danny pulled some extra strong mints from his pocket and popped one in his mouth. Since he'd stopped drinking he'd had a constant, foul, metallic taste in his mouth. Plus, he was aware of his smoker's breath. He offered a mint to Jo, but she shook her head. 'Actually,' he said, 'there is one thing. I'm having problems sleeping.'

'Insomnia is a very common side effect of alcohol withdrawal,' the counsellor offered.

'I can get to sleep fine, but the dreams – they're waking me up every night. Never had anything like it.'

'What kind of dreams?' she asked, popping out the point of her pen.

'Just the usual sort of thing – car crashes, screaming children, that kind of thing.'

Danny crunched on the mint in his mouth and it made a harsh, cracking noise that sounded much louder because of the quietness of the small meeting room. 'I'm alright, though. A bit of disturbed sleep. A few bad dreams. There's plenty of people worse off than me.'

'Did you check with the police about that boy you saw? It might set your mind at rest. You must know a lot of police officers in your line of work.'

'Not really, no. I used to – I used to be a proper journalist. In those days, my God. The kind of things the police would tell you over a drink or two in a smoky pub. Unbelievable. But I've had people to do that kind of thing for me for years. That sounds crap but it's true. To be honest, I'm just a front man. A presenter. I read things out that other people have written, ask questions that have already been prepared… I'm not a proper journalist. Not like the old days. Anyway, you can just Google it these days, can't you? So, I Googled it. No reports of any kids hurt that night.'

Danny was going to offer Jo a mint – then remembered he'd already done so. He played with the wrapper. 'You've never mentioned your family or relationships,' she said. 'Do you have anyone, Danny? Anyone to help you with all of this?'

Danny paused to think. He knew the answer but was slightly embarrassed to say it out loud. 'Not really. I've been in London for years now, but all I've ever done is work and drink. Very often at the same time. So, no wife, no kids. All my friends are really just drinking friends and I've broken the code of honour by packing it in. I've deserted them, basically. So, I can't see any of them coming round and having a heart to heart about my sleeping habits, to be honest.'

'You're from Manchester originally though, aren't you?'

'Yes, I am. But I haven't been back there for years.'

'Any family? Brothers and sisters?'

'No. No brothers and sisters. My parents died about ten years ago. I wasn't that close to them, to be honest.'

'Do you want to talk about that?'

'Not really. It's not a big deal. Sorry, that sounds a bit harsh, but it isn't. It wasn't then, and it isn't now.'

'This might sound a bit clichéd,' Jo said, 'but were you unhappy when you were young? Is that part of all this?'

Danny shifted in his seat. 'I'm very wary of going down the whole *woe is me* route. It's too easy, isn't it? *I hated being a kid and it made me get pissed for thirty years.* No. You won't get that from me. Maybe I just really liked the taste of alcohol. That's as good an explanation as anything, isn't it?'

Silence for a while. 'Sorry,' Danny said. 'It sounds like I'm getting angry at you, but I'm not. You're just... well, you happen to be in the same room as me, don't you?'

'Is there anyone back in Manchester that you could talk to? Maybe they can help you?'

'Maybe,' said Danny. 'Yeah. I've been thinking about that.'

THIRTEEN

2.30 pm Wednesday 11 April 1990

After interviewing DI Smithdown in his car – a couple of copperspeak soundbites, nothing too earth-shattering – Danny decided to take a trip back up to Black Moss. It had only been a few days since he'd first been here, but so much had happened since then, it seemed like months ago.

After saying his goodbyes to the DI, Danny had a swift couple of pints in the Three Tunnes then headed out of town up towards the moors. The sun was shining. The sky was blue, crisp and clear. *There were worse places to be on a Saturday afternoon.* Danny parked up and headed down the Pennine Way path, moving quickly past the first reservoir and heading up the slope towards Black Moss. He was more appropriately dressed this time around, with boots and a fleece, but the cold still bit at him as he crested the hill.

There was a single policeman standing at the spot where the body had been found. A woman was talking to him. Danny looked to see if there was a route on the other side of Black Moss so that he could bypass the two figures. There wasn't. Plus, it was too late; the woman had spotted him and was running up the path in his direction. *Fucking hell*, thought Danny.

'Danny Something! Hang on!' shouted Kate.

'Ah. Kate from *The Messenger*,' said Danny as she approached. 'Kate *Smithdown* from *The Messenger*, daughter of DI Smithdown, who chose not to tell me that her dad was running the investigation while pumping me for information in a chamois leather mini skirt. *That* Kate Smithdown.'

'He isn't running the investigation, that's half the problem,' she said, slightly out of breath after running up the path. 'Don't be so paranoid.' Danny noticed he'd made her blush. Only a little, but it showed quite strongly across her pale complexion. He was quite pleased with himself.

Kate continued: 'The bad guys are the people who know how that kid ended up dead out here, not me.' Her Oldham accent began to push through as she raised her voice... *owt 'ere.*

'It's bad enough being a copper's daughter round here as it is, let alone when you're a journalist and everyone thinks you're biased towards the police. I wasn't singling you out. I don't tell *anyone* who my dad is.'

'What the hell are you doing out here, anyway?' Danny asked. 'Shouldn't you be harassing the families of Strangeways rioters?'

'I live near here. Remember?' Kate crossed her eyes, reminding Danny of the look he'd given her at the police station. She pulled a packet of Benson & Hedges from her shoulder bag. There were only two left in the pack; she put one in her mouth and offered the other to Danny. He took it. She lit hers then his. 'Look, Dad's really worried. There's something very, very grim going on here. You should be flattered that he is trusting you with this. He likes you. He *trusts* you.' She looked down the path towards the reservoir. 'He obviously sees something in you that I don't.'

'I have no idea what you're talking about,' Danny said. He motioned for Kate to continue down the path towards the water. Despite the sunny sky above it, Black Moss looked greyer than ever, as if deflecting any attempt the beautiful day might make to brighten it up.

'Does your dad know you're here?' Danny asked as they walked.

'I'm not thirteen you know!'

'I know, but he seems keen for you to keep well clear of the case.'

'Is that what he told you?' Kate asked.

'Sort of.'

They walked past the officer on duty at the spot where the boy's body was found. Danny wasn't sure, but he thought that he might have been one of the men on duty the other morning. The policeman wouldn't make eye contact with him but nodded at Kate. They carried on down the straight path alongside the edge of the reservoir. There was a small, derelict jetty halfway long. They stopped. 'Have you been down to Strangeways yet?' Kate asked. 'The inmates are coming out in droves now. Oldham nick is full of them. They say it's a matter of hours until it's all over.'

'They've been saying that since April the first when it all kicked off,' Danny said. 'No one knows what the fuck is going on. It's a riot. The people in charge aren't in charge anymore. The guys on the roof are and they're just making it up as they go along. Anyone who claims to know what's about to happen next is kidding themselves.'

He picked up a stone and was about to skim it across the water. He changed his mind and dropped it in the sand instead. It didn't seem right, somehow. 'The riot will play itself out soon enough, I reckon,' Danny continued. 'I don't care anymore, to be honest. I kept thinking I was missing out being by not being there. Maybe I'm not.'

There was silence for a moment, apart from the wind, the birds and the distant burr of cars from the main road. 'What did you see the other morning, Danny?'

He thought for a good twenty seconds before answering. 'Well, the kid was in a bad way, that's for certain,' said Danny. He wasn't sure if he was being too cautious. *But what if this was a test?* What if DI Smithdown was checking to see if Danny really was discreet, could really keep his mouth shut when told to? He might have sent Kate to test his resolve. He couldn't chance it. 'All I saw was a poor little lad face down in the sand. That's enough, isn't it?'

Kate looked back at the lone policeman next to the reservoir. 'Dad said you've been speaking to DC Cave?'

'Uh huh,' confirmed Danny. 'She's not a million chuckles, but she does seem to be trying to help. She thinks the kid was from a home – it could explain why no one has reported him missing. The system's a shambles – just a bit of paper passed from one shift to the next to keep tabs on kids that no one cares about anyway. If someone loses that paper, it's like the kid never existed. It stinks.'

'So, what happens next?' Kate asked. She hugged herself to keep out the cold.

'Your dad wants me to keep the story on the go – keep broadcasting appeals for information. It's not going to be easy.'

'Well, that's the Strangeways effect for you,' said Kate.

'It's more than that. You know the deal with murders – the police run them to a system. After the initial release of information, the cops put a grieving relative up at a press conference; they make an emotional appeal. We always describe them as an "emotional appeal" don't we? Hopefully, they'll cry a bit and that's the bit we'll use. It keeps the story going. But with this – there's nothing. There are no grieving relatives. There's no one to make an emotional appeal. There's *nothing*. No cares about that kid. Just your dad.'

'You seem to care, Danny Something.'

The two journalists stood silently next to the water. It still refused to take on any hint of colour other than grey. 'Why did you come back up here today?' Kate asked. 'I know you were seeing Dad, but it's not exactly on your route back, is it? I imagine you live in Didsbury or somewhere like that.'

Danny smiled. The south Manchester suburb was well known to be populated by radio and TV types. It would be a terrible cliché for Danny to live there. 'Yes. I do live in Didsbury actually,' he admitted. 'I'm a walking, talking stereotype, aren't I?'

'I don't know what you are, Danny Something. But Dad seems to like you. So that's in your favour, I suppose. Anyway, back to my question. Why are you here?'

'Don't know, really. Just thinking about the kid, I suppose.

This seems the best place to do it. Anyway, I'm heading off,' Danny said. 'Back to my fantabulous Didsbury *pied-à-terre*.' He began to walk up the path. 'We all talk like that in Didsbury, you know, it means – '

'I know what it means,' interrupted Kate. 'It's French for dickhead's flat.'

Danny carried on walking. He nodded at the policeman as he approached him. *I'm sure that's the cop who was sick the other morning.*

Kate spoke again, louder this time. 'Why d'you come back up here, Danny Something?' she shouted. Like Kate's father had done the other morning, Danny gave a gesture universally accepted to mean... *how the hell should I know?*

Danny reached his car, a small Renault he'd had for two years and never washed once. If the outside was bad, then the inside was a disgrace. The back seat was covered in newspapers, takeaway cartons, empty Coke cans, notepads and chocolate bar wrappers. *I should probably clean this out,* he thought. *Or get rid of the worst of it, at least.*

Danny leant in and found a screwed-up plastic bag. He filled it with the most unpleasant looking rubbish – not all of it, by any means – and walked across the car park to a concrete bin by the side of the road. He put the bag of litter into the bin. He had to push it down as it was already full. As he did so, a white, Manchester Radio van drove past. It was going very fast in the direction of Huddersfield, but he had time to see the person behind the wheel – Danny recognised him. And he was pretty sure that the station's engineer, Gary Keenan, had recognised him too.

FOURTEEN

10.30 pm Thursday 15 June 2016

In the previous two hours, Danny had managed to walk around the various tree-lined sections of Clapham Common three times. Head down, hands in pockets, he was walking fast as if he had a purpose. Which, in fact, he didn't. An old joke kept circling around his head: *My dad had a problem with his legs... they wouldn't walk past pubs.*

Danny couldn't get the joke out of his head. *Maybe that's what I'm doing – seeing how well my legs will walk past pubs.*

He'd walked past a lot of pubs in the last two hours. And off-licences. And mini markets. And restaurants. *Some people drink in restaurants*, he thought. *People who want to avoid other people – people with a lot on their minds – they drink in restaurants. It's not that unusual.*

Tucked away in the far corner of the common – Clapham Old Town, they called it – was Danny's favourite pub, The Mitre. In the various loops, routes and permutations he'd taken around the common, he'd so far managed to avoid The Mitre. Now, he was very clearly walking down a slim road called The Polygon and could see the pub dead ahead of him. *Fuck. There's a pub my legs haven't walked past very often. Fuck.*

Danny stopped across the road from The Mitre. He sat on a bench and watched. He listened to the thrum of sound that wafted across the road. The *rat-a-tat-tat* of glasses and chatter; the punctuation point created by a loud peel of laugher; the muffly bass of the music. The way the sound changed

71

and wavered as people came in and out of the pub door.

Danny stared at the front door of The Mitre, his favourite pub. *Where everyone knows your name.*

At 11.30 pm, after the last of the drinkers had left, he went home.

Until he'd stopped drinking, Danny had never really noticed how bland his house was. It was a desirable Clapham terrace – the value just kept going up and up – but it was un-lived in and cold. There were no photos, mementos or individual touches. There was furniture and basic practicalities but no imprint of ownership. It was like a house that had been bleached of all personality in order to sell it. Danny had lived there for nearly a decade. It had been like that since the day he moved in.

It took an hour or so for him to get to sleep. It seemed like only minutes for the dreams to come. This time, it was Danny who was on the bed, his hands tied behind his back. The bed was sinking into water – water so dark it looked like black gloss paint. There was relief for Danny as the bed slipped away and left him struggling yet afloat on the surface. Then fear – real, chest-punching fear – as he realised he was chained to the bed and it was dragging him down.

FIFTEEN

7.30 am Friday 13 April 1990

Seeing Gary Keenan out on the Huddersfield Road had bothered Danny for two days. He couldn't shake the thought of it. *What was he doing out there, driving past that very spot? That's just so weird. Maybe it's just me being paranoid. I don't know who the fuck to trust anymore. But I'm sure he saw me, and knew I was up there the other morning when the body was found. But he said nothing. Why?*

He needed to settle his mind, and to do that, Danny needed an excuse to talk to Gary. He'd come up with an idea and he was quite pleased with it. He'd arrived at Manchester Radio half an hour early for his day shift. Just before leaving home he'd uncoupled the microphone of his Marantz recorder from the main unit. Exposing the five pins that made the connection, he'd rammed a kitchen knife into it and deliberately bent the pins out of shape. When he tried to re-connect the microphone, it wouldn't fit. *Rather than just marching up to him and asking outright, I can go and see him about my busted Marantz and see if he mentions seeing me. If he doesn't mention it, I will.*

It was too early for Pauline to be on the reception, so Danny punched in the security numbers on the door and let himself in. Station output was piped into the building twenty-four hours a day and 'Real Real Real' by Jesus Jones was ending; then Beth Hall read the 7.30 news headlines.

Because it was Friday the 13th, many journalists seemed to

have decided that today would be a convenient time for the Strangeways' riot to end. It would, at least, suit their headlines: 'Prison authorities at Strangeways' prison in Manchester are hoping that Friday the 13th will prove unlucky for the remaining rioters still holding out inside the jail,' he heard Beth say via the corridor speakers.

'Absolute bollocks,' Danny muttered to himself. 'Clutching-at-straws shite. She should be ashamed of herself.'

If he was quick he could sneak past the news booth without having to talk to Beth. Danny saw her through the small square window embedded into the door. *Cow*. All doors into rooms with microphones on the other side had windows in them, so you didn't walk in on someone who was recording or live on air. Danny could see the back of Beth's head as she read the news. Each story was in a separate piece of paper. As she read each story, she threw it away with a flourish.

Despite the heavy door that separated him from Beth, Danny walked quietly. He passed the news booth and headed around the building towards the engineering section where Gary Keenan's office was. There was a sign above Gary's door. It said: THE ANSWER'S FUCK OFF – NOW, WHAT'S THE QUESTION? Danny went in anyway.

There was a fizzy, metallic smell in the room. Gary was using a soldering iron with his back to the door. 'Enter, Danny boy,' he shouted over the sound of complex, progressive rock that Danny thought might be early Genesis. The room was one of the few spaces in the Manchester Radio that wasn't filled with station output. Gary had disconnected it. Instead, the music came from a filthy, double-cassette player perched on a shelf above the wooden work station that dominated the room. There was barely a square inch of the workspace that wasn't covered in tools, tape, wire, screws and the internal workings of tape machines, record decks, CD players and speakers. Danny didn't wonder why Gary had known it was him, despite having his back to him. The engineer had a wing mirror mounted on his desk, so he could see who was approaching. 'Morning, Gary. Sorry to bug you. Got a problem with my Marantz. The mic won't plug in and I don't want to knacker it any more than it already is. Have you got a minute to take a look?'

Gary pushed aside an armful of debris from his desk and cleared a Marantz-sized space. He jabbed at the space with his finger, indicating that Danny should place the offending item right there. 'Bet you a tenner you've fucked up the pins,' Gary said. For a moment, Danny thought he'd been rumbled; then he realised the engineer was talking generally. Reporters were forever breaking the connection pins. Gary looked at the recorder's microphone input: 'Guess what?' he said. 'The pins are fucked.'

'Right,' said Danny. 'Is it up for a swift repair or should I grab another Marantz? I need to get up to Oldham for the kiddie murder.'

Danny waited to see if Gary would chip in about seeing him out on the moors. The engineer swung around in his leather swivel chair and looked directly at him. 'I've just refurbed one,' he said. 'You can have it while I give your one a bit of resuscitation.' He grabbed another Marantz and gave it to Danny. He placed Danny's machine into a heavy-duty plastic box marked with a handwritten sign. It read: 'Fucked'.

'Cheers,' said the reporter. 'I think I might have dropped it out on the moors.' Again, he left a space. It was something radio reporters are taught to do – if you want someone to speak, then say as little as possible. Leave them room to do the talking.

'Serves you right for going out into the arse end of nowhere,' was all that Gary offered.

'Do you know it round there?' Danny asked, trying a different tack.

'No. But I imagine it's a horrendous shithole.'

'It isn't exactly Chelsea, but the countryside around the

ervoirs is amazing. Especially near Black Moss.'

Gary looked at him blankly. 'I'll take your word for it, cocker,' he said. 'Now toddle off and leave me to it.' Gary turned back to his work bench and carried on soldering. Danny looked around the room. It was chaos. 'Gary, how the fuck do you find anything in here?'

'It's all for show this,' said Gary. 'People expect it don't they? But it's all smoke and mirrors mate. You only need two things in this game. Because there's only ever usually two problems that need dealing with. Either something isn't moving, or something is moving too much. And you know what they say, don't you, Danny boy? If it won't move and it should do, squirt it with WD40. If it moves when it shouldn't do, you need to bang a load of gaffer tape on it.'

Danny waited. Nothing. 'Now fuck off and let me pretend to work,' Gary said.

Danny turned around, left Gary's office and pushed open the door of the newsroom. No wall of noise this time. It was still early, and the other daytime reporters hadn't arrived yet. The late reporters were probably still at Strangeways. On the wall was a piece of A3 paper with the words '24- HOUR CLUB' scrawled across it in marker pen. Several Manchester Radio reporters' names were on it – it signified those who had worked around the clock covering the riot, which was by now heading towards the end of its second week. At the top of the list was the name of Manchester Radio's chief reporter Robert Crane – his name appeared several more times too. Danny's name was nowhere to be seen.

The appetite for the story hadn't reduced in the slightest, although those initial claims of '20 DEAD' made by the *Manchester Evening News* were now being played down. The inmates had even fashioned a makeshift banner with the words 'NO DEAD' on it and displayed it from the rooftop. After a prison officer had died from a heart attack he suffered while helping inmates to evacuate the jail, the rioters made another banner, this time expressing their sympathy for the officer's family. Not that he had anything to compare it to, but Danny doubted that prison riots usually panned out this way. It was showy and theatrical. It was articulate yet surreal. Danny thought about the party he'd seen outside the jail. The music, the drugs, the t-shirts. *It's a very Manchester sort of riot,* he concluded.

Danny looked at the CEEFAX headlines on the dusty, wall-mounted TV in the corner of the newsroom. NO END IN SIGHT FOR STRANGEWAYS' RIOT was the headline. The newsroom was even more of a mess than it usually was. Pink and white sheets of paper seemed to cover every surface – and a reasonable portion of the floor. Pink sheets were used by newsreaders to read a scripted cue that would be followed by a piece of audio. White sheets were for straight reads, short stories not worthy of a fuller report, like less-serious crime stories, the weather or 'and finally' light stories. Since the riot started, 'and finallys' had largely been abandoned.

Beth Hall came though the door at the other end of the newsroom. She glanced at Danny but said nothing, instead dropping her spare scripts to the floor and adding to the mess in the news room. She lit a cigarette; smoking rules were largely ignored before 8 am. She began clattering on her typewriter and the cigarette wobbled between her lips as she typed. After about fifteen seconds, she spoke: 'Yes, Danny boy? Something on your mind? You're early. You're never early.'

'I got a fresh interview on the Oldham case.'

'What Oldham case?' said Beth over the *pak pak pak* of the typewriter.

'The dead kid at the reservoir,' Danny said, not quite shouting in frustration but getting pretty close. *That stuff you read out on the news… does any of it go in, or does it just pass straight through you?*

'Oh, that. Sharston isn't convinced it's our patch. And he is the head of news, after all.'

'It *is* our patch. It's Oldham Police's case. Oldham is in Greater Manchester. We cover Greater Manchester.

Therefore, it's our patch.'

'Wasn't it found over the border?' Beth wasn't looking at him as she spoke. The *pak pak pak* continued.

'On the border. HE was found ON the border. *He* was a boy, not an *it*.'

Pak pak pak.

'You alright, Danny?' said Beth. 'You're being weird even by your standards.'

Danny cleared some pink sheets from a seat close to Beth's and sat down. He was in serious danger of having a proper conversation with her and it felt a little odd. 'It's a little bit frustrating, to be honest,' he said, quietly. 'Actually, it's a *lot* frustrating. It's very, very fucking frustrating, in fact. Every reporter who can hold a microphone and speak at the same time is down at Strangeways soaking up the glory. I can't even get near the place. Instead, I'm sent off to the back of beyond to cover a story that actually turns out to be really important. But, no one cares about it. I feel like I'm really close to something big and serious and fucking awful, yet I'm struggling to get it on air.'

The *pak pak pak* stopped. The silence made Danny drop the volume of his voice by fifty percent. 'Very... frustrating,' he added, one more time. Danny looked at Beth, expecting to get a mouthful. She offered him a cigarette. He took it and lit it up.

Beth looked at him with a slightly offended expression on her face, as if she'd caught a whiff of an unpleasant smell. 'Are we about to have an actual proper conversation?'

'Don't know. Are we?'

Beth dropped her cigarette into a plastic cup of coffee. It hissed as it extinguished. 'Look, Danny. I get it. I understand. But you've got to understand that for a station like us, Strangeways is a once-in-a-lifetime story. Our listening figures have, well, they've gone through the roof, if you'll forgive the expression. We aren't Radio Four, you know? Half of our demographic knows someone inside that jail. That's the kind of station we are – and those people are looking to us to keep them updated. It works both ways too – we're getting scoop after scoop because families are coming to us first with news of what they know. The BBC aren't getting a look in and as long as those scrotes are up on that roof, we are not going to let the opposition off the hook. It's Strangeways all the way.'

Danny rolled up a pink script sheet and put it to his eye like a telescope. 'Yeah, I get it,' he said. 'But there must be space for other news too?'

'Course there is – or there will be. This riot will be over any time now. Maybe even today. Then we'll lead with your kid story every bulletin. Look, do me a copy read for the 8 am and I'll try to squeeze it in.'

'I've got some fresh audio too,' Danny added. 'Of the main cop. Appealing for witnesses, that kind of thing.'

'Like he did last week?'

Danny put down his paper telescope. 'Kind of, yeah.'

'I'll take a copy read for now and maybe some audio for later.' A pause. 'Listen, Danny. Stick at it. Sharston must really rate you to give you this story all to yourself. Maybe the glory isn't out at Strangeways at all – maybe it's out in the wilds of Oldham.'

'Maybe.'

'Do me the calls and that copy read, okay?'

'Okay.'

Beth stuck out her lower lip. 'Now fuck off and stop being such a soft arse.'

Danny found the least messy desk in the newsroom and sat down. He inserted a sheet of white paper into the typewriter. Instinctively he typed the time and date of the bulletin onto the top left corner of the paper and a tagline for the story on the top right – a word or two to describe what it was about to save someone having to read the whole thing. Danny wrote 'Oldham Kid' then quickly banged out two paragraphs about the case: *police still baffled, appealing for witnesses, care home theory…* Not great, but something. Danny pulled the sheet from the typewriter and placed it into a wooden tray marked 'New Copy'. Beth was busy shouting at someone on the phone, so Danny left it at that and returned to his desk.

He turned his attention to the calls. Attached to the newsroom wall were two black display boards covered in white lettering. The pegged letters were stuck on by pressing them into hundreds of holes that peppered the boards. They were the kind you'd normally see in takeaways or pubs to show what the establishment served and how much it cost. Instead of prices, the letters spelt out the names and numbers of police, fire brigade and ambulance contacts across Greater Manchester and the adjoining counties. Reporters had to call them every hour to see if there were any ongoing incidents that might be newsworthy.

Danny never quite understood why a Manchester radio station felt the need to ring ambulance stations in North Wales, but those were the rules. He started with Greater Manchester Police, asking for the duty sergeant. Then he moved on to the fire and ambulance stations. It took him nearly twenty minutes to get through the list; by the time he'd finished, Beth had gathered up her scripts and walked through to the news booth to read the 8 am news. Danny stood up and noticed his 'Oldham Kid' story was still in the tray. He sat down and waited for Beth to start reading the news on the internal feed. Then he rang the *Oldham Evening Messenger* and left a message for Kate Smithdown.

SIXTEEN

10.35 am Tuesday 14 June 2016

'Just to cut to the chase,' Danny said to Jo McGuire as he settled into his seat at the drug and alcohol unit. 'No, I haven't consumed any alcohol since I last saw you. Yes, I'm taking my medicine, though the heavy-duty diazepam ones have all gone. I miss them, they were great. What else? Yes, I'm still dreaming like a bastard. No, I'm not working at the moment. Yes, I think it's a good idea to stay away from my old friends. No, I haven't consumed any alcohol. Yes, I think about it all the time, but no, I haven't consumed any alcohol.'

'Good,' said the therapist, looking at her notes. 'How often do you think about it Danny?' she asked. Her voice was very soft, so was her accent. Danny had never noticed before. *Derbyshire, maybe,* he thought. *Edging towards the east Midlands. But not too 'eh up me duck'… good voice for radio, actually. Late night though, not morning or daytime.*

'About what?' he asked momentarily distracted by the accent issue.

'Drinking. Drinking alcohol. How often do you think about it?'

'Well, during the week after I stopped, about five hundred times a day. Now I'm down to about a hundred.'

'Seriously?'

'Seriously.'

'If you were to rate the level of temptation that you feel out of ten, would would you rate it at?'

81

'Twenty to twenty-five, I'd say. Even talking about it now sets off a taste in my mouth. Horrible, metal taste like I've been sucking on tin foil. Vile. But it doesn't matter though, does it? Very binary this not drinking game, isn't it? It's on or off – either you have or you haven't. There's no middle ground. And I haven't. So that's good, isn't it?'

'Okay.' She made a note of what Danny had said. A pause. 'You mentioned work. Do you have plans? You were very successful.'

'Being on the telly and being successful are two separate things,' Danny said, slumping in his chair and folding his arms. 'If you put a packet of biscuits on TV people will recognise it – doesn't make it any good. People just assume they're good biscuits – because why would anyone put rubbish biscuits on the telly?'

'Don't you think you were good? You seemed good to me.'

Danny breathed out long on hard. He rubbed his beard – it was more accurate to call it white now, rather than grey. He sunk even lower into his chair. 'I'm not sure I deserved it. I was just a front man, a talking head, a turn, an act. I didn't find the bad guys – I was just plonked in front of them after a team of researchers found them. It's not proper journalism. It's showbiz. Showbiz bollocks. Big, daft showbiz bollocks. The fact that I could literally do it when I was pissed sort of proves that, doesn't it?'

'How are you for money?' Jo asked.

'I'm cash poor. I've got no money coming in. No one with any sense will touch me at the moment. I had a book on the go but that's been strangled at birth. I've been given a few quid to not write it but that won't last long. Do you know what that's called in publishing circles? A "kill payment". Charming. I've got the house in Clapham and a pension pot but that's about it. So, cash poor – asset... okay.'

'So, what's your plan?'

'I'm not sure yet. My agent suggested I go back to Manchester for a bit. Before he stopped being my agent that is. I don't know. I'm thinking about it.'

'You mentioned your parents last time,' said Jo. 'That you weren't that close. Is that right?'

'Yeah. We weren't, really.' Danny pulled at one of the ever-present tissues from box in front of him. It was a different box from last time. He tugged it slightly so it began to rise up. Then he stopped.

'Thing is, they weren't actually my parents. I was adopted when I was pretty young. My real parents couldn't look after me – didn't have the skills I suppose someone in your line of work might say. The folks who adopted me were perfectly decent people, but when I left Manchester for London in the nineties I just sort of drifted away from them. I came back less and less. Just Christmas for a while, then not even that. They died a few years back. Shame, really. Decent people.'

'So, who would you go and see if you went back to Manchester?'

Danny looked at the therapist. And thought. He tugged the tissue out of the box and put it in his back pocket.

SEVENTEEN

5.30pm Friday 13 April 1990

Danny walked through the front door of the Three Tunnes and spotted Kate ordering a pint at the bar amongst a grim-looking gaggle of teatime drinkers. She caught his eye and pointed to her drink with a questioning look. Danny raised a thumb and a pint of lager arrived at the bar at the same time as he did. He took a sip – it was what Danny referred to as 'cooking lager', the weak kind, Carling or Skol. Danny preferred stronger stuff like Red Stripe or Stella Artois. *It's the thought that counts, I suppose.*

'Not to your taste, Danny Something?' Kate said, pulling up a high stool and sitting down.

'It's a perfectly acceptable aperitif,' he said.

'You like a drink, don't you Mr Something?'

'I'm not the only one,' he replied, gesturing towards Kate's pint.

'Comes with the territory,' she said. 'They give you a pint on your first day of work in journalism, don't they?'

'Yes, they do. And a packet of fags if you're lucky.' Danny lit a cigarette, largely for effect.

'What are you after Danny Something? You're in Oldham more than me at the moment.'

'I'm looking for something else, another angle on the reservoir kid. Your dad gave me a fresh interview, but it was all a bit…'

'Copperspeak?'

'Yeah. Copperspeak.'

A brief clip of DS Smithdown talking about the case – how they were working on the theory that the boy could have gone missing from a care home – had run on the afternoon bulletins. Once.

'He still got a right telling off for doing it by his DS,' said Kate. 'He's treading a bit of a fine line at the moment between keeping the story going and getting bollocked by his boss. You'd think they didn't want to catch the killer or something.'

'Not exactly top of their priority list at the moment is it?' said Danny, drinking a quarter of his pint in his first few gulps. 'No one's going to get a promotion by helping a dead kid that no one cared about in the first place. Keeping the Strangeways lot banged up nice and neat for the Home Office until the riot is over... that's where the silverware is.'

Kate went digging into her handbag and pulled out a bulging red Filofax. It was rammed with so many additional bits of paper, Kate had put a large elastic band around it to stop the catch from popping open. She removed it and flicked through the A to Z section. 'What about Peter Jeffries? Bet he could give you a different angle.'

Danny took the next quarter of his pint and let out a long, disappointed sigh. 'Paedo Pete? Really?'

Oldham MP Peter Jeffries was the kind of politician who boasted that he didn't count his votes come election time, he weighed them. Despite representing an overwhelmingly working-class area,

Jeffries was an old school hang 'em and flog 'em Tory. He could be relied upon to provide a rent-a-quote response to any journalist with access to a pen and a bit of paper, particularly on his pet subject: paedophiles. He'd become so overexposed on the subject that Manchester Radio had an unwritten policy to avoid him after some of his more outlandish claims about local satanic abuse cults had proved to be completely without foundation. 'We tend to steer well clear of Jeffries wherever possible. He's round the twist.'

'Yes, I'll give you that,' conceded Kate. 'He is a bit round the twist. But he knows more about child-related crime than anyone I've ever met. He's actually trying to get the system changed to force the police to set up specialist child protection units in each area. He knows his stuff.'

'Apart from the whole Satanic business.'

'Look, I'm trying my best to help you here,' Kate said. 'I've got his contact details if you want them.'

'Everybody's got his contact details,' Danny said. 'He's in the papers more often than a page three girl.'

'I mean his home address. It's only a few miles away. I thought we could both go.'

'I'm not sure your dad would approve,' Danny said.

'Dad totally approves,' Kate said, reassuringly.

'You haven't mentioned it to him, have you?'

'Not as such, no,' Kate said. 'Danny, you've got nowt else, to be frank. What have you got to lose?'

Danny finished his lager and looked at Kate. He didn't quite understand her and was still concerned he was being taken for a ride with this story. On the other hand, if he still wasn't being allowed anywhere near Strangeways, then where was the harm?

'Okay. Can we have another drink first?' he said.

'It's your shout, Danny Something.'

Peter Jeffries' home was a good fifteen-minute drive out of Oldham, Kate had said, through a village-come-housing estate called Alt. 'Welcome to the real Oldham,' Kate said as they passed through several sets of grey, pebble-dashed terraced houses.

'Jeffries lives here?' Danny said, as he dropped gears to counter the uphill climb.

'No,' replied Kate. 'He lives up there.' She pointed to a detached farmhouse that overlooked the estate. As they pulled off the road onto a snaking dirt track, several hefty brown dogs appeared and proceeded to give them a noisy escort all the way to the front door. There were several classic cars parked outside – *hardly farm vehicles*, thought Danny. A sky-blue Jaguar in particular caught Danny's eye.

'What the hell is an MP doing in his constituency on a Monday teatime?' asked Danny as they came to a stop. 'Shouldn't he be in London at the House of Commons?'

'Jeffries comes and goes as he pleases,' Kate said. 'He's never going to get a cabinet post, so he doesn't feel the need to suck up to the Prime Minister – although apparently she's a big fan of his.'

The front door opened and a large man in his late fifties stepped briskly out to meet them. He was wearing a slightly-too-tight three-piece suit and a vivid blue tie that matched the Jag parked in the driveway. His hair was cut brutally short and his neck bulged slightly around his collar. He looked more like a sergeant major turned bouncer than a Tory MP, but that, for many, was part of his appeal. 'Miss Smithdown, with a plus one. What an unexpected treat. You'll come in for a cheeky one, won't you?' His accent was vaguely local but with slightly forced hint – like someone who was putting on a more upmarket voice for effect. Or had decided they didn't like the way they spoke and had chosen to alter it. Jeffries put out his hand towards Danny and proceeded to crush Danny's fingers in a ludicrously firm grip.

'This is Danny from Manchester Radio,' said Kate.

'Ah. The same Manchester Radio to whom I appear to be currently *persona non grata?*' Jeffries asked, with a strange mix of bullishness and theatricality. 'Well step inside young Daniel and let's see if I can't persuade you that I'm not all bad.'

Danny and Kate went inside the house, passing a packed suitcase by the door. 'Go through to the lounge,' Jeffries shouted, heading towards the kitchen. 'I'm on my way to Westminster, but who's in a rush to get to that place?'

'Why are we here?' Danny whispered to Kate as they walked into the lounge. The walls were covered with photos of Jeffries standing next to an array of sportsmen, middle-of-the-road musicians and TV personalities. Some of the pictures went back to the 1970s; many were signed. Danny pointed to one photo of the MP with a famous DJ. 'This is why we don't use Jeffries,' he said quietly. 'He's a fame-chaser, not a proper politician.'

Jeffries came in with a bottle of red wine and three large glasses. He motioned for Danny and Kate to sit down as he sluiced the whole bottle into the glasses and handed them out. 'So,' he said, tugging up his trousers slightly as he sat down. 'Is this about the lad up at Black Moss? Absolutely monstrous business.'

Kate motioned for Danny to take the lead and talk to the MP. 'Yes. Yes it is,' he began. 'The case is getting ignored because of Strangeways. The police have got nothing. I was wondering – we were wondering – if any information had come your way. Given your sort of, interest in this area. As it were.'

'I've been thinking about this a great deal actually,' Jeffries said, taking a healthy glug of his wine. 'Would you like to hear my theory?'

Not really, thought Danny. 'Absolutely,' said Danny.

Jeffries pulled a coaster from a dispenser sitting on the coffee table in front of him. He placed it onto the table and carefully set his wine glass down on top of it. 'I've heard a lot of talk about the placing of this boy's body – that there is some great significance about it being placed on the border. I think that's nonsense. That's what people want us to think. It's not where it was found that matters, but *when.*'

'It was in the middle of the night,' offered Danny.

'No, I don't mean the time, I mean *when.* Right in the middle of the biggest news story we've seen round here for years and years. I think someone did that little lad in, using Strangeways as a cover. They realised that all eyes would be on the jail, especially the eyes of the media, and figured out it would be the ideal opportunity to do something truly terrible, truly heinous and avoid all the usual attention.'

Danny sipped his wine and looked at Jeffries. He was annoyed. Not at the MP, but at himself. There was no bullishness now. He was talking quietly and convincingly.

The theatricality had all but gone too.

Jeffries looked directly at Danny. 'I know you lot think I'm just here to get my picture taken with the likes of Jimmy Savile,' he said, waving at his celebrity photo gallery. 'But I've been investigating the way children without worth are treated by society for decades. You've been at it a few days.'

'Would you be willing to go on the record with this, Mr Jeffries?' Danny asked.

'Of course! But will you run it? That's the question. There's a sickness in society and you lot are more interested in the easy stuff – the murders, the robberies, the riots. Are you willing to get your hands really dirty, young Danny Johnston?'

Danny looked at Kate. She returned his glance. 'They're quite filthy as it is Mr Jeffries,' he replied.

'Excellent! Then get your tape out and let's get at it then.'

'It's in the car. Give me two minutes.'

'Not a problem. Kate and I can catch up in the meantime.'

Danny walked towards the door. 'Do you want to know what else I think, young Danny?' Jeffries said. 'I think it was a try out. A test. Whoever did it was dipping a toe into the water up there at Black Moss, if you'll forgive the expression.'

The MP's tone became even firmer. Quieter. He wasn't showing off now. He was deadly serious 'There's more to come. Mark my words. The police are chasing their tails over Strangeways and so are all you media types. It's the perfect time to do something utterly terrible. It was hardly flawless – definitely room for improvement – so it would be silly not to try it again, wouldn't it?'

Jeffries leant back into his leather chair and smiled at Kate, then at Danny. 'Just a theory, of course.'

After swapping numbers and leaving Peter Jeffries' house at around 6.30 pm – they'd managed to split another bottle of red three ways after the interview was done – Danny dropped Kate off in Oldham centre before heading home.

He then left his car off near his flat. Danny lived on a road called The Beeches where most of the media types lived in West Didsbury, south Manchester. Then he walked over to the nearby Roebuck pub. He didn't particularly like The Roebuck; it just happened to be the nearest pub to his flat. As Danny walked in he noticed that an actor from *Coronation Street* was holding court; he was drunk and loudly telling the people gathered around him about the drug habits and sex life of one of his female co-stars. Danny went to the other end of the bar, bought a pint but found he had no taste for it. He still finished it, though. Then he left and went to the nearby deli, bought four cans of super-strength foreign lager and took them home.

The flat was part of a 1970s block situated at the end of a Victorian cul-de-sac. Danny didn't know any of his neighbours other than to offer the occasional swift nod as he came and went. He let himself in, popped open a can of lager and checked his mail.

A dim red light flashed from the front room. It took Danny a moment to realise what it was: an answer machine message. He didn't get that many. *Probably work,* he thought. There were two messages. He pressed play; before the first voice spoke, he heard a quick snatch of Indian restaurant music: 'Danny, it's DI Smithdown.' He sounded like he'd had a drink or two. 'Listen, can you please not be dragging my daughter around Oldham on this case? I'd appreciate it. The whole point of involving you is to keep her away from it, you dickhead. I know you've spoken to Jeffries by the way – he's not as daft as he looks, you know. He's nearly as daft as he looks but still, you could do worse than listen to what he has to say.'

A pause. *He really sounds quite pissed,* Danny thought.

'Look. I know this is all a bit weird but stick with it. It's not right what happened to that lad. *Obviously,* it's not right but… yes *obviously.* But it's *more* than that.'

Again, a pause – more Indian music.

'I thought really, really hard before involving you in this,

Danny. Really, very hard. I wanted you to know that I didn't do it lightly. I'm worried that… it might be a bit much for you. Bit much for anyone, frankly, but *especially* you. Perhaps it might help you in a funny way. I don't know. No. Forget that. It's bollocks. It's enough for *anyone* – leave it at that. So, anyway. Thanks for sticking with it. Yeah, right. Anyway. Ring me tomorrow. We'll see what's what. Okay? Good. Ignore my bollocks. You're doing great. Okay… Bye.'

Beep. Message two. 'Young Danny, it's Peter Jeffries here. I'm en route to London on one of these dreadful mobile phone things. You will not believe what I've found out. Give me a few days and I reckon we can go public. You won't believe who's in on this. What an absolute shower of shits. Speak later in the week. Over and out.'

EIGHTEEN

3.30 am Wednesday 15 June 2016

Danny lay on his bed. *No point in getting in it,* he thought. *I can't sleep. I don't want to sleep.*

He looked around his bedroom. And thought. Since the crash – since he'd stopped drinking – he had started to think about things. *Really* think about things.

He never had much of a tendency towards introspection; that had changed, drastically. He'd started to think about things he'd never space to before. He had always been aware that his tastes were a little sparse compared to most people, but now he noticed how bare and soulless his bedroom was: no photos, no keepsakes no nothing. A bed. A wardrobe. A rug. That's it.

The house was the same - four walls that contained some clothes and practical things, but no more. *It could be beautiful... a real showstopper. It was worth a fortune compared to the price I paid for it.* But Danny had done nothing to it since he'd moved in. It even had the same curtains and decoration that had been here when he'd first bought it. He'd put his everyday essentials inside the house, but nothing more. He'd bought a new oven but wasn't sure he'd ever used it. The awards he'd won were in a box under the stairs – they certainly weren't on display. There were no paintings or posters on the walls.

He'd never invited anyone round. Ever.

It was a shell. A box that contained a bed and his clothes. Nothing more.

Danny got up and opened his laptop. He booked a train ticket for the first available train to Manchester – it was leaving from Euston at sixteen minutes past six later that morning.

Danny checked his watch. He rang Jo McGuire and told her he was taking a break from their sessions for the time being. Then he began to pack.

PART II

NINETEEN

10.30 am Monday 20 June 2016

In the old days, it was a reasonable morning's work to track down someone if you didn't know where to find them; you might have to plough through the phone book, apologetically ringing all the numbers that had the same initials and surnames as the person you were seeking. If all you had was a road – or even just a rough idea of an area – then you'd go 'on the knocker', calling in person and asking whoever answered the door if they knew the subject of your search.

Things were very different now. By the time Danny left Euston Station he had traced Kate Smithdown via her Twitter account and messaged her. She'd replied at 8.30 am as Danny passed through Wilmslow station and they arranged to meet later that morning at her office in Salford Quays. He spent the rest of the journey digging through the internet and matching names to various profile pictures on Facebook accounts and company websites. *My God,* he thought as he looked at some of those faces, *we're so fucking old now, aren't we?*

Danny had booked a hotel as he travelled too – it caught his eye because it was on the same site as the old Manchester Radio building near Piccadilly Gardens. When he arrived at Piccadilly train station, instead of getting on the Metrolink tram or ordering a cab, he walked down Piccadilly Approach and arrived at the hotel on foot. Danny hadn't been back to Manchester since his adopted parents' funeral. Things had changed. No local politicians would say it out loud, but the city had benefited greatly from being continually targeted by the IRA in the late 1980s and early 90s, before the detonation of the largest ever bomb on mainland Britain in 1996. The bomb – and the subsequent rush to rebuild – had cut through years of red tape and the centre of Manchester now looked very different to the city Danny remembered. Where there had been a few greasy spoon cafes and chip shops, there were mid-range chain restaurants, fashionable retro stores and street food outlets.

But Danny didn't remember the brutal, seemingly pointless thick strips of concrete that now curved around Piccadilly Gardens. Nor did he remember the sheer volume of homeless people that seemed to dot every corner as he walked from the station to his hotel.

Danny checked into the hotel and went to his room. He dumped his small suitcase onto the bed. He paced the room then checked out the toiletries in the bathroom – Danny was a big believer in judging a hotel by its toiletries. They were okay. He opened his case and decided he couldn't be bothered to unpack. Instead he changed into a clean white t-shirt to complement his black Harrington jacket and expensive-looking jeans. He looked at himself in the mirror. He pushed a hand through his hair. He looked again, then went back to the bathroom and brushed his teeth. Then looked at himself again. He took a complimentary pen and a notepad from the small desk in the corner of his room and tucked them into the inside pocket of his jacket.

Then Danny looked out of the window and cast a glance across the skyline – there were cranes dotted across the west side of the city towards Salford. Lots of them.

He put the hotel key card into his wallet and headed out into the adjoining city of Salford. Kate Smithdown's office – her *building* – was a fifteen-minute tram ride away in Media City, the shiny temple to the area's newfound status as a magnet for all things TV, radio and internet. Danny remembered the former Salford dockland area as previously being home to nothing. The docks had long gone by the time he was born and the area had been a blank canvas for years, with only a taste of the impressive deco-style dock company buildings left standing. Kate's building, tucked between the BBC and an achingly hip supermarket, was called KSM House.

A very young, very fashionable young man with an impressive collection of piercings, facial hair and tattoos was manning the reception and said hello to Danny by name. 'Kate's expecting you, Mr Johnston,' the young man said. 'Great to have you here. Big admirer. Take a seat.'

Danny gave the receptionist a smile and sat down on a geometric set of brightly-coloured foam blocks that seemed to be the seating area. Retro ashtrays on stands stood next to the blocks. They had sweets in them. Retro sweets. *I hate all this shit,* thought Danny. *Hipster bollocks. She's just showing off. Couldn't we just have met at a cafe?*

As Danny cast a disapproving eye over the lollies and chews in the ashtrays, a well-dressed, very striking looking woman in a slim-fitting black trouser suit and white t-shirt walked towards him. She had jet-black hair with a white streak rising from her hairline at the front and she wore expensive-looking black-rimmed glasses. Apart from that, Kate Smithdown had changed very little in the intervening decades. 'Danny Something,' she said, smiling.

Danny wasn't quite sure what to do – they hadn't seen each other for more than twenty-five years. As he hesitated, Kate pressed her cheek against his. Her hands gripped the top of his arms and she held him there for a few seconds. Then she pulled back and looked him in the eye. She smiled. 'Now,' Kate said. 'Where *were* we…?'

TWENTY

4 pm Monday 16 April 1990

After several missed calls were exchanged between DI Smithdown and Danny, the detective left a message for him at Manchester Radio, telling him they should meet that afternoon at an address near to Alt, the area he and Kate had passed through on their way to Peter Jeffries' house. He pulled up outside a grey, pebble-dashed semi on the edges of a sprawling council estate. Kids were running through the streets – some with fearsome-looking dogs – and every other house seemed to have a household item in its front garden: a fridge, a sofa, an armchair.

Throughout the day, Danny had been to-ing and fro-ing the question of whether he should mention the answerphone message the DI had left him. At first, he thought: *maybe he was just pissed – just rambling. He didn't mean anything by it.* Then he thought: *he may have been pissed but he's nobody's fool. What did he mean by it?*

Danny's internal debate was immediately silenced when he saw that DI Smithdown was accompanied by DC Jan Cave. As before, she didn't seem too pleased to be there. *No way am I asking him when DC Chuckle Pants is around,* he thought. *It can wait.*

Danny approached the officers and nodded a greeting. DC Cave looked directly at Danny and held eye contact. When DI Smithdown began to speak, Danny felt like she was still staring at him. 'Danny, lad. Glad you could make it.' Unlike his female colleague, DI Smithdown seemed to be having difficulty looking Danny in the eye. He shifted a cigarette end on the pavement with his foot and stared at it as he spoke. 'Right, so. This is one of two dozen care homes in the area – this is the biggest. It's a pair of semi-detached houses that have been knocked into one big house. The staff here... they're good people... they want to help.'

'Have they ID'd the kid?' Danny asked, adjusting the strap of the Marantz recorder that tugged at his shoulder.

'No. No they haven't.'

Danny felt a tinge of disappointment. 'But they know of a kid who fits the description of the lad. They want to help. One of the staff is willing to talk to you.' The DI finally looked at Danny – he made a twirling motion with his finger. 'With your tape rolling.'

Danny nodded, glanced at DC Cave, noticed she was still staring at him and followed DI Smithdown to the front door. The DI pushed the door and shouted a hello, identifying himself, DC Cave and Danny. A female voice shouted: 'Kitchen!' and they walked through the narrow hallway, following the direction of the voice. The kitchen was large, as if a wall had been knocked down to accommodate it. It was cluttered to the point of being chaotic; a dozen different brands of cereal were lined up across the main kitchen surface next to the sink, which was full to the brim and beyond with dirty dishes. Every horizontal surface was covered in schoolbooks, comics, clothes empty biscuit and sweet wrappers, bottles of juice and fizzy drinks. Danny noticed DC Cave's face was set to slightly-more-disapproving than usual.

A woman in her forties wearing an oversized, colourful jumper and black leggings beckoned them over to the large wooden table that stood in the middle of the kitchen. She was cradling a mug of coffee with both hands. 'Sit down, sit down,' she said. Her voice was soft and warm; there was a hint of Irish in her accent – not unusual in Manchester.

'Brenda this is Danny Johnston, the journalist I was telling you about. Danny, this is Brenda Graham, she runs this place.'

'Ha!' Brenda exclaimed, offering her hand to Danny. 'I wouldn't kid myself. No one runs this place. Anarchy rules here.'

She put down her mug and started work on a roll-up cigarette. Danny could sense a dozen pairs of young eyes, watching him. There were kids everywhere, though none were actually in the kitchen. They hovered and floated at the edges, in doorways or by the stairs. Watching. Listening. Danny caught the eye of a small boy of about ten with hair cut back as short as possible; the boy turned towards the stairs.

'Mr Smithdown thought you might be able to shed some light on this case up at Black Moss?' Danny said. 'The police think it might have been a care home kid. I've also spoken to Peter Jeffries…'

The voice of a teenage boy interrupted them from somewhere beyond the kitchen. 'Pete the Perv? He gives me the creeps. Fuckin' weirdo.'

'Shut it, Brian, you don't know what you're talking about,' Brenda admonished with a smile. 'He's done a lot for us has Mr Jeffries. Won't have a word said against him.'

'Have you got a missing kid at the moment, Brenda?' Danny asked.

'Every kid here is what we call a "persistent missing", Danny,' she replied. 'That's why they're here. They do more runners than Sebastian Coe. They go missing so often the police can't be arsed looking for them.' She nodded at DI Smithdown. 'Present company excepted, of course.'

DC Cave strummed her fingers on the back of the kitchen chair she was standing behind but said nothing.

'We did have a lad of ten go missing around the time the kid's body was found up at the Moss,' Brenda continued. 'But he turned up safe and well about an hour ago.' Brenda turned to look at a boy sitting on the stairs, looking at them through the wooden spindles. 'Didn't you Little Paul? Ya wee shit.'

The boy with the brutally short haircut, that Danny had

noticed as he came in, flicked a v-sign in their general direction and then ran up the stairs.

Brenda returned the boy's v-sign with one of her own. She turned to DI Smithdown. 'Sorry John, I should have let you know. You know what it's like here. In and out like nobody's business. I can't chain them to their beds you know?'

'Have you any other children missing Brenda?' Danny asked.

'Here's the thing,' she said, licking the edge of her roll-up to seal it and then lighting it. 'Every single kid who is supposed to be here... is actually here. Normally, we'd expect about a third of them to be out and about, on their toes and missing in action, only to turn up a few days later. Not at the moment. Don't you see – they're *all* present and correct. All accounted for. All where they should be. All *here*.'

'And why do you think that is?' asked Danny. In the background, he was vaguely aware of a heavy-handed knock at the door. Footsteps immediately followed it – no waiting for an invite with this visitor.

A smartly-dressed figure appeared in the kitchen. He looked out of place in the kids' home. 'A word *please* DI Smithdown,' said Detective Superintendent James Pym. 'Now.'

The two policemen walked out of the kitchen. Brenda looked at Danny. 'Who's pissed in his chips?' she whispered loudly to Danny.

'You can't go behind a senior officer's back and expect there to be no repercussions,' said DC Cave, quietly. It was the first time she'd spoken since they'd arrived.

From his chair at the kitchen table, Danny had a clear view through the hallway and out into the street through the open front door. DS Pym had his back to him, but Danny could see DI Smithdown's face. He was just as angry as his boss, but his eyes were on the floor. He spoke intermittently, as if he was being continually cut off by the senior officer. After less than a minute, DC Pym left. The DI stood for a moment then came back into the house. 'We'd best be off

Brenda. Now we know the lad's safe. We'll leave you and Danny to chat. DC Cave? Keep me posted, Danny.'

The two police officers left. They didn't speak. Danny watched them through the window. They didn't speak as they walked to their car either.

Several of the children who had been waiting and listening around the periphery of the kitchen, now came in and helped themselves to snacks and drinks. Chatter started. Whispers. Laughter.

'As we say in Oldham,' began Brenda, 'what the fuck was all that about?'

'Absolutely no idea,' said Danny. 'No idea at all.'

'I think he's a good man that John Smithdown,' Brenda said, smiling as a young girl of about thirteen leant across her and took an apple from a bowl on the kitchen table. 'But his boss doesn't seem to agree with me.'

'I sense that too.'

'He's done a lot for kids round here, has John. More than anyone will ever know.'

'What about these kids, Brenda,' Danny asked. His hand gestured towards the youngsters in the kitchen. There was now about ten of them, aged between about nine and sixteen. 'You were telling me that they're all present and correct at the moment. Why?'

Brenda finished the last of her tea and put out her roll-up. 'I think it's because they're shit scared of being *out there,*' she tilted her head in the direction of the window. 'They might hate it here, but right now they're more afraid of whoever or whatever is outside of these four walls.'

'Have they said anything specific?'

'No, but these kids know when something isn't right – *really* not right – and they stay well away from it. That's why we have a full house right now. Nothing scares these kids, they've seen it all. But for the first time I can remember, these kids are *afraid.*'

TWENTY-ONE

10.10 am Monday 20 June 2016

Kate's office was on the top floor of KSM House – in fact, it *was* the top floor. The walls were bare bricks with some original and expensive-looking modern art attached to them. They were softly lit with industrial-style lamps attached to the exposed beams of the ceiling. The few items of furniture that were present were pure white and looked very uncomfortable. She motioned for Danny to take a seat at a u-shaped sofa at one end of the room. At the other end was her desk. She tapped a few words into her laptop – virtually the only thing on the desk apart from a photo in a frame – and went over to join Danny. The sofa was huge, but she sat close to him.

'So how are you then?' Kate said, taking off her glasses and putting them on top of her head. 'I heard about your accident. Maybe we should take you on as a client. We do a bit of image management work.'

'I think my image is beyond redemption,' Danny replied. 'Is that what you do here?'

Another fashionable young man brought in a tray filled with a variety of fruity and exotic teas and some tiny bottles of water. Danny opted for a water.

'Digital marketing, social content, viral campaign, that sort of thing. We're doing pretty well. You didn't think I'd still be on the *Messenger*, did you?'

'No not at all – thought you might have gone into radio or telly. You'd have been a natural.'

'I did.'

'Really?'

'Yes – and I've got you to thank, in a funny way.'

'How do you mean?'

'I got your old job at Manchester Radio. When you left I stuck in a CV and Mike Sharston gave me a job. Your job, in fact. I did a few years there, then a bit of telly, realised it was a mug's game and set up a little PR firm. Then it grew. And grew. We've got this office, one in Chester and a new place just opened in London. Not bad for a girl from the wrong side of Oldham. What did you used to call it? *Deliverance* country...'

'Did I say that?'

'Yes, you did.' Kate crossed her eyes, just to make the point.

'Well, I was an idiot in those days.'

'Yeah. You *were* an idiot in those days. Mind you, wrapping your car around a tree a few weeks back wasn't too clever either.'

'Can't argue with that.'

'You look different – from when I last saw you on the telly, I mean.'

'I am different. I stopped drinking for a start.'

Kate sipped her fruit tea. 'Wow. Things have changed. Mind you, we all used to drink a lot in the old days.'

'We did,' Danny agreed, smiling. 'You could pack away the pints with the best of them.'

'True. But you never seemed to take any... pleasure from it. Like it was something you had to do, rather than wanted to do. Sorry, I'm speaking out of turn. It's not my business.'

'It's fine. Not a problem.'

A pause. 'Wife, kids?' Kate asked.

'No and no. Too busy, I suppose. Too busy pratting about on the telly and getting pissed, mainly. How about you?'

Kate got up from the sofa and fetched the framed photo from her desk; she showed it to Danny. He saw the smiling face of a dark-haired boy aged about ten. 'That's my man right there: Jonathan. He's nearly eleven. He's all I need.'

'Dad not around?' Danny asked. He immediately wished he hadn't.

'Not very often. IT entrepreneur. That's what he calls himself, anyway. Lives in London. Too busy to see his son most of time. Dickhead.'

Danny felt slightly ashamed of the fact he was pleased about this bit of news. *Change the subject.* 'Jonathan? John was your dad's name. Is he...'

'Oh yes. Still with us. Couple of heart attacks, bit of cancer, a stroke, but still battling on. He always liked you.'

'I'd like to see him. Is that possible?'

'Why?' Kate asked.

Danny looked out of the window. He saw a Salford he didn't recognise. *Things have really changed. Perhaps this was a mistake,* he thought.

'Do you remember that kid that was found up at Black Moss?'

Kate face changed from puzzlement to surprise in an instant. She leant back in the sofa and put her hands to her head. 'Danny Something, you are such a walking, talking cliché! Don't tell me: *I fucked up my life in the here and now, so I want to go back and sort out the one thing that's been eating me up for years. Then everything will be all right.* Jesus Christ!'

'It's not like that...'

'What is it then?'

'Okay, it is, to some degree, like that...'

'Don't get me wrong – it's very admirable, in a way. God. I remember now... Dad didn't want me to have anything to do with it. He was dragging you here there and everywhere trying to get publicity for it. Strangeways! That was it. The only thing anyone cared about was bloody Strangeways.'

'Haven't you thought about it?' Danny asked. 'A little lad with his teeth and fingers gone, face down on the moors. All strapped up with weights ready to sink him in the Moss.'

Kate went back to her desk and carefully replaced the photo of her son in exactly the same spot where she'd taken it from. 'Weights? Christ. I don't remember that coming out.'

'It didn't. Only me and your dad knew about it. Christ, so much weird stuff went on back then,' added Danny.

'Like what?'

In a whisper – *why am I whispering?* – Danny said: 'Peter Jeffries. That stuff. The Peter fucking Jeffries' stuff.'

TWENTY-TWO

9.05 am Tuesday 17 April 1990

Danny walked into the newsroom in the middle of what appeared to be a noisy argument. News editor Mike Sharston and chief reporter Robert Crane were at the centre of it. Danny watched and listened.

He lost interest when he realised they were arguing about the best way to format a display board showing sweepstake entries for when the riot would end. There were now about a dozen prisoners left inside the jail and Manchester Radio reporters were being invited to put in a pound and guess the exact time and date the disturbance would finally come to a conclusion. Sharston seemed to favour a series of vertical columns displaying names and their corresponding guesses. Robert Crane was lobbying for a timeline, so each entry could be voided as the time of their guess elapsed. Crane had done well out of the riot: he'd been doing interviews with foreign TV and radio stations about the latest from the jail and there was talk of him getting a telly job when the incident was over. It was a case of when, not if, he'd be leaving Manchester Radio.

Danny found an empty desk just as Beth returned from the news booth. She caught Danny's eye and he pulled out a notebook and pretended to be looking for something in it as she spoke: 'Danny!' she cried, in a very loud voice. 'Message for you from a Mr Peter Jeffries, Member of Parliament for Paedophile Central.'

Robert Crane tapped the news editor on the arm and

motioned that he should listen to this. Danny turned to Beth with a polite smile as she continued. 'He says he's coming in tomorrow first thing to give you the full story on the Oldham kid case. He says – and I quote – that you should hold onto your hat, because this is the big one.'

'Paedo Pete is going to give you the big one, Danny,' cried Robert Crane. 'Thought you were a bit old for him but, any port in a storm.'

'Any *reporter* in a storm,' added Mike Shartson, with a laugh. The news editor turned to Danny. 'I thought you knew the deal with Jeffries. He's not a serious politician, he's a grandstander, a rent-a-quote. I want nothing to do with him after that Satanic business.'

Beth waved a piece of paper in their direction. 'He left a number, Danny. It's Oldham 666…'

Some of the newsroom staff were really laughing now. 'He says he's really got something on the case,' Danny protested. 'I can't stick my fingers in my ears and pretend he isn't talking. He is an actual Member of Parliament, you know.'

'Well it will need to be pretty sensational stuff for it to go on air,' said Sharston, walking back to his office. 'Sorry – correction. As well as being sensational, it will need to be *true.*'

The sports journalists had their own area at the far end of the newsroom. They were chanting 'Paedo Pete, Paedo Pete, Paedo Pete' in the style of a 'Here We Go' football chant. One was blowing kisses at Danny. *God, I hate those guys. What do you call a failed journalist? A sports reporter.*

An A4 envelope appeared in front of Danny's face. It clinked with money as Gary Keenan shook it vigorously. 'Putting a quid in, Danny boy?'

'Why not,' said Danny, fishing a pound coin from his pocket.

'You need a precise time and date for when you think the riot will be over,' explained the engineer. 'That means when the very last prisoner gives up.'

Gary had a small notebook and the stub of a pencil to

make a note of Danny's guess. As he pondered, Beth passed Danny's desk and handed him a piece of paper. 'Jeffries really is coming in tomorrow, Danny. There's his number. I'll leave it with you.'

'What time?'

'Half eleven,' she replied.

'There you go, then. Eleven thirty am, on the 18th of April. That's when I think the riot will end.' Danny put the coin into the envelope. 'And not a moment too soon.'

'Do you think he's really onto something, Danny?' asked Gary. Danny wasn't sure how to respond. Gary had shown him nothing but kindness – in his own, rude sort of way – but the sight of him out near Black Moss still unnerved him.

'I don't know, mate,' Danny said, picking up a phone and glancing up at the emergency numbers on the wall. 'But if there's a chance of moving this case on, I'll take the risk.'

TWENTY-THREE

10.20 am Monday 20 June 2016

'You honestly think that Jeffries was involved in Black Moss?' asked Kate. She was off the uncomfortable sofa now, pacing up and down her office.

'Somehow, yes.'

'Based on what?' cried Kate, waving her hands in frustration. 'He was harmless – just a colourful MP with a liking for the limelight. There's never been any evidence there was any wrongdoing. Just rumour and innuendo.'

'It'd be interesting to know what your dad thinks.'

Kate turned around, leant over the stairwell and shouted: 'Ryan! Emergency supplies! Pronto!'

One of the fashionable young men Danny had seen earlier – *not sure which, everyone under thirty looks the same to me* – came into the office having clearly run up the stairs. He handed Kate a single cigarette and a cheap plastic lighter with something approaching disapproval. 'I know, I know, Ryan. Don't give me the look. Thanks. Now piss off.'

Kate lit the cigarette and inhaled with an eye roll of pleasure. Danny was about to ask if she was allowed to smoke indoors, then remembered that it was her building. She resumed her pacing. 'Dad doesn't really like talking about that case. He never has. He'll go on about the old days with the best of them – can't shut him up – but mention Black Moss and he just clams up. Like he's ashamed of it or something.'

'He must have had concerns about Jeffries, though. Didn't

you?'

'It was so long ago, Danny. There was so much else going on at the time. I suppose it did seem weird at the time. Everything about it was weird. But maybe we didn't look hard enough. Maybe we should have gone at it harder, asked more questions. We weren't Woodward and Bernstein – we were just kids. Local reporters doing our best. I was barely twenty-three years old.'

'We were young, but we weren't stupid. The whole thing with Jeffries just stunk and we knew it. I bet your dad knew it too. He was nobody's fool, your dad – and not in the habit of being told what to do or think. If there was a bad smell around the whole Jeffries thing, then he would have known about it.'

Danny took the cigarette from her and took a drag. 'Absolutely filthy habit this. We should know better at our age.'

Kate took the cigarette back and drew the smoke in deeply. 'Fucking hellfire,' she whispered. 'Okay. When do you want to go and see Dad, then?' she asked.

TWENTY-FOUR

6.59 am Wednesday 18 April 1990

Danny's alarm came on just as the last bars of 'Strawberry Fields Forever' by Candy Flip merged into the Manchester Radio news jingle.

He'd dreamed hard during the night and his bedsheets were a damp, tangled mess – *should have had more to drink, that normally blocks it out.*

Beth started to read the news – she had her extra serious voice on. 'The news at seven o'clock, I'm Beth Hall. The flamboyant Oldham MP Peter Jeffries has died in a road traffic accident just a few miles from his home in the Alt area of the town. His car left the road and plunged forty feet into a ravine in the early hours of this morning. It's believed that no other vehicles were involved in the incident. Mr Jeffries was known for his high-profile campaigns against child sex offenders – and recently lent his voice to a campaign calling for an investigation into claims of Satanic abuse in Oldham – claims that were later revealed to have been unfounded. In other news, the Strangeways riot has entered its…'

Danny leapt from his bed. He stood very still for nearly a minute. *I've jumped out of bed like I know what to do – but I don't. What the fuck do I do? I'll ring Kate. Too early. Is it, though? Probably. Maybe the DI. Ring him. And tell him what? That the notorious, self-promoting exaggerator Peter Jeffries had the biggest scoop ever and would have been giving it to Mr Danny Johnstone later this morning… had he not died out on the moors before he could reveal all? Died. Or been killed? Come on. Grow up.*

The news was coming to end. Danny waited one minute – pulling his trousers on and finding a shirt as he counted off the time he knew it would take for Beth to get from the news booth back – and rang the Manchester Radio news desk. 'Hello, News,' she said.

'Beth, it's Danny.'

'Daniel. Thought it might be you. I take it you've heard about Jeffries?'

'Yes. Yes, I have.'

'Took a lot to knock Strangeways off the lead slot,' she admitted. 'But it finally happened. He always liked being in the news, I suppose. He would have liked it that he was the lead story.'

'He was supposed to be coming in today. To see me.'

'Here we go…'

'What does that mean?'

'Here comes the conspiracy theory.'

'He told me he had a massive story about the kid at Black Moss. Don't you think it's a *bit* of a coincidence?'

'Danny, I've been working for this radio station for five years. I've lost count of the number of times Peter Jeffries told us he had a massive story, including that time he claimed kids were being sacrificed in Satanic rituals out on the moors. It was all bollocks and Mike Sharston nearly got the boot. So, forgive me if I'm slightly sceptical about the big scoop that was coming your way.'

'But, to just swerve off the road like that for no reason…'

'Well, according to the Oldham cops, there was a perfectly sound explanation as to why he crashed,' Ruth replied, her tone was now even sharper than usual. 'He was pissed. Your mate went off the road full of booze – he literally didn't feel a thing. It's a miracle he got as far down the road as he did. Even more of a miracle that he didn't kill anyone else in the process. I know someone on the force up there – they're working on the theory he did it on purpose. Guilty conscience. Can't be a coincidence it was so close to where your dead kid was found? How's that for a theory? Unlike yours, it hasn't just been pulled from thin air. It's from a very reliable source at Oldham nick. So, forgive me Danny for not shedding a tear for dear departed Paedo Pete.'

'No, Beth. Tears were the last thing I would expect from you.'

'Glad I didn't disappoint. You aren't on shift today – you were only coming in to interview Jeffries – so we won't expect to see you.'

The line went dead.

Danny, still wearing his trousers and unbuttoned shirt, lay down on the crumpled bed sheets. He stayed still and thought for no more than fifteen seconds, then headed for the shower.

As he'd left home in the middle of rush hour, the commuter traffic meant it took Danny more than an hour and a half to get to his destination. A call to the duty sergeant at Oldham Police station had given him the location of the crash site – a fierce bend in the Huddersfield Road. Black Moss was less than a mile from the spot.

Danny parked his car in a layby close to the scene; on foot he weaved through the traffic that had built up near the bend. The road was down to one lane and temporary traffic lights were controlling the traffic as a tow truck from a local firm worked to retrieve the vintage blue Jaguar from the hefty drop on the inside of the bend. The safety barrier was split in two, the metal curled back from the impact. *He must have been going at a hell of speed to smash through there*, Danny thought. *A hell of speed driving away from Black Moss.*

There were several uniformed officers at the scene; at the centre of the activity was the smartly-suited figure of DS James Pym. He appeared to mouth the words 'fucking Nora' as Danny made his way to where he was standing.

'Hello, Mr Pym. Terrible business. An accident, do you think?'

'Yes, I fucking well *do* think that, as it happens. So, don't you come here spinning a bastard yarn saying otherwise.

We've got enough on our plates as it is without you making things worse. RTA, no other vehicle involved. End of.'

DS Pym was about to turn away from Danny, but then seemed to change his mind. 'Why? What do you know that would make me want to think any different?'

'I was due to see him this morning. He was coming into the radio station.'

DS Pym's tone and attitude changed. He stepped close to Danny. 'Why was he coming to see you?'

'I don't know, he didn't say.' Danny was getting very adept at lying to people about how much he knew. He had no intention of telling the DS anything beyond the basics at this stage.

'Then why would you think this was suspicious?' asked DS Pym, not unreasonably.

'I'm a journalist, Mr Pym. I think everything is suspicious. Do you think there's any link to the boy up at Black Moss?'

'Fuck off, Danny.' The detective turned away.

'Any witnesses, Mr Pym?'

The officer turned back. He had a slight smile on his face. 'As it happens, yes. Couldn't ask for a better one.'

DS Pym motioned towards a woman leaning against a police van parked on the other side of the hole in the road's crash barrier. Kate Smithdown was wearing a leather jacket over her pyjamas and had tartan slippers on her feet. Danny walked towards her; he'd never seen her without make-up on before. Nor had he seen her looking so upset. *She looks about twelve.* Danny wanted to put an arm around her shoulder. He didn't.

'You're the witness?' Danny said. 'What the hell were you doing out here, in your pyjamas?'

Kate turned and nodded towards a double-fronted Yorkshire stone house about a hundred yards up the road. 'That's our house.'

'You saw the whole thing?'

'Not exactly. I heard a crash and ran outside to see if I could help. I had to slide down the hillside to get to him. He was about fifteen feet away from his Jag. He'd been thrown from the car – didn't look like he was wearing a seatbelt. Classic Jeffries.'

Danny thought about what Ruth had said. 'Had he been drinking?'

Kate looked puzzled. 'How should I know? He was a mess. I've never seen a dead body before.' She looked as though she was about to cry, but quickly stopped and wiped her nose on the cuff of her pyjama top. 'Big, tough journalist, huh?'

'I'd never seen a dead body either – up until the other week,' Danny replied. 'Where's your dad? This is literally on his doorstep.'

'He's… not here. He's with my mum. She's in the hospital.'

Kate began to cry properly this time – full-on sobbing. Danny didn't know what to do. He looked around; the police and recovery team were occupied with controlling the traffic and getting Peter Jeffries' car up from its last resting place down in the roadside valley. It looked to be down to Danny to help Kate. *Why am I so shit at things like this?* 'Maybe we should get you off this road. Shall we go to your house? Pym knows where to find you if he needs you. He clearly doesn't want to speak to me.'

Kate nodded. She rubbed both her eyes with the sleeves of her jacket. She was still crying but the intensity of it was dimming slightly. They crossed the road and walked up the drive. Kate pushed the door – it wasn't locked – and threw her coat on the floor. As they went into the kitchen she pulled a portion of kitchen roll from a wall-mounted dispenser, wiped her face with it, then loudly blew her nose. 'Oh God. *Grow up, Kate.* Do you want a cup of tea Danny?'

'Yes. Sure.' He looked around the kitchen; it was all rustic woods and reassuring brickwork. There were photos on the walls and on nearly every available surface. Weddings, anniversaries, birthdays, holidays, award ceremonies, graduations – every aspect of a happy family life photographically chronicled and displayed with affection and pride. It was clear Kate was an only child and that she'd been showered with love and attention. Danny ached as he looked at the photos. *God, what a lovely family to grow up in,* he thought. It was strange to see DI Smithdown's face *smiling* out from many of the frames. Very few smiling opportunities had presented themselves in the short time that Danny had known Mr Smithdown. As well as Kate and her dad, most of the pictures featured a slim, very attractive woman; the photos charted the myriad of hairstyles and dresses that she'd worn over the years. 'Your mum looks nice,' Danny said as Kate handed him a cup of tea in an Oldham Athletic mug.

The words seemed to set Kate off crying again and another section of kitchen roll was yanked from the holder. 'Yes. She is. Very nice. She's really not well at all at the moment. That's why Dad isn't here. He's with her at hospital.'

'Which one?'

'It's quite near where you live. The Christie.'

Everything dropped neatly and unpleasantly into place. The Christie was in Withington, the next area along from where Danny lived in West Didsbury. He passed it every day when he drove to work. The Christie was one of the largest cancer care facilities in Europe. 'I see,' said Danny. 'Sorry.'

'Don't be sorry. Not your fault.'

'No, I mean I'm sorry *for* you. And your dad. Still, they say if you're going to get cancer, get it in Manchester. It's world famous...'

'It's a cancer hospital, Danny, not Lourdes,' Kate interrupted. 'They have lots of machines and plenty of medicines. But sadly, no miracles.' She sipped her tea. 'Not for Mum, anyway.'

'Is she going to be okay?' Danny asked and immediately regretted it.

'No.'

'I never realised – your dad must be worn out with it all.

No wonder he looks so tired.'

'Yes, he is. Very tired. Maybe that's why he's been so keen to get you to help on the Black Moss case. He can't do anything to help Mum – it's past that stage now. But if he can find out what happened to that kid…'

Kate started to cry again. Stepping forward, she put her head on Danny's shoulder. Again, he didn't seem to know what to do and didn't move. No arm round her, no comforting words. They stood there for half a minute. Kate lifted her head and rubbed her eyes. 'You're a cold fish, Danny Something.'

'Sorry,' he said. 'Maybe I should go.'

TWENTY-FIVE

Noon Monday 20 June 2016

'Now', was the answer that Danny gave when Kate asked when he'd like to see her father. She'd grabbed her keys, told one of the fashionable young men she was going out and she and Danny were headed for the M60 outer ring road that encircled Greater Manchester within minutes. In less than twenty minutes they'd turned off the motorway at junction 22 for Oldham. As they headed for the town, past Werneth Park, Danny saw the grey pebble-dash of the police building. 'Not changed a bit, has it?' she said as they skirted past the centre and began the uphill climb out of town.

'No,' he said. 'It really hasn't.'

Kate's car – a brand-new four-by-four that was far more expensive than the one Danny had owned before the crash – hugged the bends of the moorland roads easily and made quick work of the journey. As they got further into the hills and the moorland opened up around them, Danny noticed what he thought might be the spot where Peter Jeffries' car had left the road back in 1990. He glanced over at Kate, but she didn't respond. *Leave it,* he thought. Then they turn off the road and arrived at the detached, cottage that overlooked the moors. *Same house as in 1990. Beautiful spot. Never really noticed before.*

Kate unbuckled her seatbelt and turned to Danny. 'Let me go in first. Don't want to give him another heart attack,' she laughed. Then a pause. 'He's not what he was Danny. He had a stroke last year and it nearly finished him off. It affected his ability to speak, but he manages. He refuses to move to a care home – stubborn old bastard. I have help that comes in a few days a week. Me and Jonathan are here at weekends. We make it work.'

Kate went to the front door and let herself in. A few minutes later, she came to the door and gestured for Danny to come. She took his arm and led him through to the lounge. The photos he'd remembered from his last visit seem to have multiplied. The pictures of Kate's mother faded with age, but they were displayed just as prominently as they had ever been. John Smithdown was sitting with his back to Danny in a high-backed armchair – the kind with a sprung seat that gave you a boost when you needed to stand up. But the ex-detective remained seated. He was dressed in a pastel, v-necked jumper and an open-necked white shirt and had a blanket over his legs. He turned and smiled at Danny. It was a slightly lopsided affair; the left half of his face drooped slightly. But it was still a friendly, open smile nonetheless.

'DI Smithdown. Look at you… Lazing about in your retirement, you idle old bugger.'

John Smithdown's smile got bigger as Danny knelt down next to the older man's chair. He placed his hand on Danny's arm and lightly squeezed it.

'It's great to see you, Danny. Smashing. It really is.' There was a slight slur to his voice and the grip on Danny's arm was weak.

'Danny wants to talk about Black Moss, Dad,' said Kate. 'The boy… from all those years back. Do you remember?'

John Smithdown nodded slowly. He cocked his head slightly, indicating that Danny should lean a little closer. 'Fuckin' Strangeways,' he said.

'Dead right, Mr Smithdown. Fucking Strangeways. That's what screwed us over. Absolutely.'

The retired policeman looked at his daughter, nodded towards Danny and made a gesture with his hand close to his mouth. 'He wants to know if you're still drinking, Danny,' said Kate, slightly embarrassed..

'No, I'm not, you cheeky bastard,' Danny said. 'How about you?'

John Smithdown tilted his hand left and right as if to say, sometimes yes, sometimes no. *The old Mr Smithdown is still with us,* thought Danny. *Laid low, not quite what he was, but still there.*

The uneven smile ebbed away from John Smithdown's face. 'Black Moss,' he said, serious now. He jabbed at Danny. 'I knew. *One day.* I knew.'

Again, he pointed at Danny. 'You knew I'd come back wanting to ask about the kid, Mr Smithdown? Well *I* didn't, that's for sure.'

The retired policeman leant towards Danny and looked him in the eye. He tapped Danny on the chest and nodded. 'Nah. I knew. Always. Here, Danny. *It's in here.'*

Danny felt stinging heat behind his eyes. He wasn't going to cry – but he was pretty close to it. *He knows me better than I know myself, this bloke.*

'The thing is, it never felt right – the answers we were given at the time, I mean. The explanations – they seemed too easy, to convenient. If nothing else, it doesn't seem right that the boy was never ID'd. I've got a bit of time on my hands at the moment – you may have heard – and I thought I'd go back to the story. Look at it again with fresh eyes. What do you think, Mr Smithdown?'

'Best idea y'ever had, Danny.'

'It's a thumbs up from dad, then,' Kate said.

Danny nodded and produced his iPhone from his pocket. 'I've been looking online,' he said, flicking through some bookmarked pages. John Smithdown motioned to his daughter, who fetched a pair of glasses from the mantelpiece and gently placed them on her father's face. The old man nodded as if to say, *okay, carry on.*

'There isn't much out there on the case. It's pre-internet, obviously and I know a lot of older stuff still hasn't been archived on most local newspaper websites. But other than a few of Kate's old articles, it's mainly anniversary stuff.'

Danny showed Mr Smithdown a small item dated April 2010: *Appeal For Help To Solve Black Moss Mystery 20 Years On.* The sub-headline added: *Police ask public to 'search their consciences' over youngster's death.* 'This is straight-from-the-police-press-release stuff,' Danny said. 'All unsolved cases generate this stuff, there's nothing to it really. I wanted to know if there was anything that had surfaced over the years to identify the lad.'

John Smithdown shook his head and looked at his daughter. 'Dad knew he was always clutching at straws with the case,' she said. 'That's why he got you involved. He was desperate. No database match for a boy of that age and there was no DNA on his body. So, the only way to establish his ID was via a DNA match of someone who entered the system. That was only going to happen by a flukey bit of good luck, arresting someone who was related to him and matching them to the boy. That never happened. So... nothing.'

'Mr Smithdown...' Danny began.

'John,' said the old man, hesitantly. For the first time, Detective Inspector John Smithdown was telling Danny to use his first name.

'I'll try. No promises.' Danny had a dig into his jacket pocket and found the pad and pen he'd taken from his hotel room. 'Look, I want to track down all the officers involved in the case. Just to see if anything was missed, maybe there's some way of bringing the case back out into the open. Is there anything I could look at? Anything that seemed too weird or too difficult to examine at the time?'

John Smithdown looked questioningly at Danny and then his daughter.

'What do you mean, Danny?' Kate asked.

'I don't know. Other than you... *John*, no one seemed to care that much about the kid in 1990. I'm not saying they blocked your investigation, but you didn't get a lot of support, did you? What about your old boss, DS Pym?

Remember he bollocked you for bringing me into it?'

John Smithdown shook his head. 'DS Dickhead,' he whispered.

'Dad always felt that Pym was a career man,' said Kate. 'He had his eye on being assistant chief constable, maybe more. Pym knew the best way up the ladder was doing a good, high-profile job supporting the Strangeways situation, not digging around up at Black Moss.'

'What 'bout your lot?' asked John Smithdown. 'Where were your mates when it mattered?'

Again, Danny struggled to catch what the old man was saying. 'Dad's pointing out that the local media didn't exactly cover themselves in glory,' Kate said. 'Every journalist with a pad and pencil to their name wanted to use Strangeways to further their career. No one cared about the kid. Except maybe you.'

Smithdown nodded. Then he gestured towards one of the many framed photos on the book case. Danny went over to them and pointed at individual pictures – *so many of them* – until he got to the one that John Smithdown wanted him to bring over. It was a picture from what looked like the early nineties. It showed Kate with an oversized 'Good Luck' card. Her hair was bleached into a nineties-fashionable quiff, but it was still unmistakably her. Drinks were being raised in the direction of the camera. *A leaving party?* She was surrounded by friendly, laughing faces that were familiar to Danny. He couldn't put a name to everyone in the line-up, but he certainly recognised the majority of the people in the photo. It had clearly been taken in the newsroom of Manchester Radio, some years after Danny had left.

'It's an interesting point, Dad. Okay. Why did no one support you Danny? All that work you did and you could barely get the story on the bulletins. Who would benefit from that?'

Danny thought about seeing Gary Keenan all those years ago, driving past Black Moss. He'd given him the opportunity to explain why he was driving past the scene, but he hadn't taken it. *Why would he do that? What did he have to hide?*

'This is all getting a bit conspiracy theory for my taste,' said Kate, tucking the blanket in around her father's legs.

Slowly, John Smithdown raised his hand and pointed at Danny. He spoke. It took Danny a few seconds to decipher what he'd said. *At least one person really didn't like what you were up to, Danny boy. Remember?*

TWENTY-SIX

1.30 pm Wednesday 18 April 1990

Danny had driven home to Didsbury after he'd been to Kate's house. He listened to the Manchester Radio news as he drove. Peter Jeffries' death had been pushed into second place by the latest from Strangeways: that the jail was due to be stormed to take out the final set of protestors, whom the tabloids had dubbed *The Dirty Dozen*.

He passed the Christie hospital on the way back and wished he'd done more to comfort Kate. *Shit, what's wrong with me?*

Dropping his car off outside his flat he headed straight to the Roebuck pub nearby. He knew enough people in there to be able to stroll in and find a drinking companion or two within a matter of minutes. He drank through the afternoon, blathering and bullshitting with a changing roster of out-of-work cameramen, journalists and resting actors. He was glad of the chance to talk about nothing for a few hours; no Black Moss, no Peter Jeffries, no cancer, no Kate. *Bar room bollocks, that's all I want to talk about for the rest of today.*

By seven o'clock he was very drunk indeed. *If I don't go home sharpish I'll be too pissed to walk. Better go now.*

He managed to navigate his way out of the pub and down the road to a nearby row of takeaways. He ordered a burger and chips then took an age to find and count out the money from his pockets. He left and started on the five-minute walk back to his flat. Despite going to the toilet before he left the pub, he soon realised he needed to go again and lurched into an alleyway between two sets of Victorian terraces. It was edging towards darkness now: *no one will see me here.*

Leaning against the wall at one side of the alley, he put down his food and fumbled for his fly. The plastic bag came over his head with shocking speed and aggression; it gave him no time to protect himself. He inhaled with shock, in the process pulling the bag even tighter across his mouth. The artificial taste of the plastic made him retch. He tried to reach behind but felt nothing. He tried to twist away but that pulled the bag even tighter around his neck. He clawed at his face, but the plastic was like a second skin. There was no air in his lungs to form a shout. He kicked out but only found his takeaway food on the floor, scattering it across the ground. Slipping, he felt himself being swung to the left and his head connected violently with the wall. Once, then twice. His ears buzzed, his eyes fizzed with speckles of black and white light. *I can't fight this. Too drunk. No air. Please. Why are you doing this? Please.*

As Danny was thinking this, he was dragged to the other side of the alley and his head was banged fiercely against the right-hand wall too. This was enough to make his knees buckle and he dropped to the ground. This at least loosened the plastic bag. Instinctively, he curled into a ball just as the kicks began. None were aimed at his body. Every one of them was aimed at his head. Every one of them found its target.

A shout came from across the street and Danny heard heavy footsteps coming towards him – accompanied by another set running away. The feedback whine in his own head – as a result of the kicks and the lack of air – added to the din. More shouts. More running. The bag was pulled from his face and the air rushed into Danny's lungs as he looked around, panicking, as if expecting more blows to come his way. None came. There was, however, a man shouting at him, asking if he was alright. The man was telling Danny he was going to be okay and he should breathe slowly and steadily. Although Danny now felt surprisingly sober, he also felt very sick and turned over to threw up violently onto the ground.

'Christ, Danny,' said DI John Smithdown. 'Even by your standards, you've really upset some fucker this time.'

Then Danny was sick again. And everything went black.

When the light came back to eyes, Danny saw another figure. DC Jan Cave was also standing over him. 'He'll live, sir,' she said. 'From the smell of him he probably felt very little pain.'

'What the hell are you doing here, Mr Smithdown?' Danny slurred.

'I've been at the hospital, down the road,' he replied, quietly. Danny remembered that The Christie was barely a mile away. 'I was heading for the motorway when I saw some drunk in distress. That drunk being you. Did they get anything?'

'No. I don't know. I don't think so.' Danny looked around and saw a plastic Kwik Save bag lying on the floor. 'I don't think they were after money. I've spent it all anyway.'

The police officers pulled Danny to his feet. 'Do you want us to drive you around to Didsbury police station? It's only around the corner. I know the lads there. They could take a statement, get a description.'

'No point,' Danny said, brushing the dirt from his clothes. 'I didn't see anyone. I just want to go home.'

The DI looked at his colleague: 'DC Cave, could you possibly escort this young man to his lodgings? I need to get on my way.'

'I suppose so, sir,' she sighed, smiling slightly.

'Well you make sure you look after him DC Cave. He clearly shouldn't be out on his own – especially after he's tried to drink south Manchester dry.'

The DI nodded at Danny and headed swiftly towards his car; he'd left it double-parked with his hazard lights on and some of the other drivers were letting him know that they didn't care for this manoeuvre with their horns. 'Fuck off, I'm moving it,' Smithdown shouted and started the engine.

With a small wave to Danny and DC Cave, he was gone.

'Right then, let's get you home,' said the DC. Even off duty and out of uniform, she still looked like a police officer. Her hair was still pulled back in a stern bun and her clothes were steadfastly black and white.

'I'll be fine,' Danny said. He was still drunk, but the shock of the attack had shaken much of the alcohol out of his system. 'I'm only around the corner.'

'The boss said I was to make sure you got home okay. So that's what I intend to do.'

Danny felt his way along the alley wall and turned into the street. DC Cave walked alongside him. 'Why would someone want to put a bag on your head, Danny? Do you have any enemies around here?'

'No – apart from the people at the pub I don't really know anyone. Maybe someone doesn't like me looking at the Black Moss case.'

'That's a bit over-dramatic, isn't it? Drunk guy, walking home alone, you're fair game for someone trying to grab your wallet. I'm sure there's no more to it than that.'

'What are you doing here, anyway? Were you with the DI at the hospital?'

'No, I've got relatives nearby. I was on my way home too.'

'Terrible about Mr Smithdown's wife, isn't it?'

'Yes. Yes, it is terrible. He's got a lot on his plate at the moment. I think he should spend less time worrying about that boy at Black Moss and more time looking after his wife. And himself. But that's between you and me, okay?'

'Sure,' nodded Danny. 'Absolutely.'

'His boss, Mr Pym, is really worried about the DI – and he's worried that you're not helping the situation.'

'I get it. Of course.'

Danny crossed the road and turned into The Beeches – his flat was down a dead-end street and he and DC Cave were the only ones around. He got to the front door and fumbled for his keys.

'I think this case is getting too much for Mr Smithdown.

He's under a lot of strain. Mr Pym thinks so too. I wonder if it might be best to just leave it be for a while. Until things work themselves out with Mrs Smithdown. Do you know what I mean?'

Danny found his keys. He looked at DC Cave. She was slightly taller than he remembered – taller than him by an inch or so. She was also standing surprisingly close to him. She smelt very clean; a no-nonsense, soapy kind of smell. 'I do... I do know what you mean,' said Danny. 'It' just that I don't agree with you. I think this case might be the only thing keeping him going, actually. And I'll do anything I can to help him.'

He managed to get the key into the lock at the second attempt but didn't turn the lock. 'Thanks for the police escort, DC Cave. I'll be seeing you, yeah?'

'Absolutely, Danny,' she replied with a small smile.

He still didn't turn the lock. He waited. She took a step back from the door. 'Look after yourself, Danny. Any problems, let us know. But think about what I said, okay?'

'Will do.'

She turned, quickly took the steps down the front path and walked away. As she went, DC Cave said: 'We'll keep an eye out for you, Danny. The DC knows where you live.'

He turned the lock and quickly stepped inside. Danny ricocheted up the stairs and somehow ended up outside the door of his flat. His head felt like it was being inflated from the inside. He fell through the door, steadied himself on the other side, then locked it. His answer machine was flashing red. He pressed play and fell back onto his settee. 'Sean, it's Karen. Sorry to be the big sister, but I'm just checking in with you. Mum and Dad are worried. We've not heard from you for ages...'

'I hate it when she calls me Sean,' Danny said. He didn't hear the rest of the message. He passed out.

TWENTY-SEVEN

1.45 pm Monday 20 June 2016

Danny and Kate didn't speak much as they headed back down to Oldham and then onto the motorway back to Manchester. A few minutes after leaving the house, Kate asked: 'Why did you never mention getting attacked that night?'

'I never knew for definite it was connected to the case,' Danny replied. 'It could have just been a coincidence.'

'It becomes a bit less of a coincidence when you know it happened within hours of Jeffries' crash,' she said. Kate's voice had become louder, more insistent. 'Who knows what might have happened if Dad hadn't helped you? Christ, Danny. You could have been killed.'

'Like Jeffries was?'

'Maybe, yes. God, what else don't I know about this?'

'I think that's something you need to speak to your dad about,' Danny replied, regretting it almost immediately.

'So, there *are* things I don't know? Christ.'

'Your dad wanted you to be kept away from it at the time. He was worried something might happen to you.'

'The kind of thing that happened to you?'

'Well, yes.'

'And Jeffries...'

'I suppose. Potentially.'

'You didn't answer my question,' Kate said. 'What else don't I know?'

Danny thought for a few moments. Then he told Kate everything. The weights on the child's body; the deliberate, expert disfigurement; the concerns over Peter Jeffries and the off-the-record line from the police about how he may have killed himself wracked with guilt over the Black Moss boy; the visit to the children's home; the conversations with DI Smithdown about keeping her out of it. Everything he could remember. Everything he'd been thinking and dreaming about over the last few weeks.

After he'd finished, there was silence in the car as it cruised down the M60 towards the Salford turn-off. Danny was searching the internet on his phone. 'Sexist dickheads, the pair of you,' she finally muttered. 'I suppose I should be grateful that you were both concerned enough to lie to me. But you're still sexist dickheads.'

'Quite possibly, yes.' Conceded Danny. 'But it was such a strange time. I was completely paranoid – I thought at one stage your dad was testing me, seeing how much I'd be willing to tell you after he'd revealed something to me in confidence. I didn't know who to trust. Sorry. I thought I was doing the right thing. I still do, actually.'

By now, Kate's car was pulling into Salford Quays. More silence. They stopped close to her building. 'Okay,' she said. 'What now?'

'Well, I'm going to try the number for DS Pym that your dad gave me. In the meantime, a quick Google shows me that at least one person who used to work at Manchester Radio is still working there today. So, I'm going to pay them a visit.'

'Luckily for you, their new building is quite handy.'

Kate nodded towards a nearby converted dockside building with a red, neon MRFM logo attached to the outside wall. 'Just a brisk walk around the dock. Can you manage that, or do you need a lift?'

'No, I'll manage.'

Danny got out of the car. 'Danny?' said Kate. 'Come to my house tomorrow evening for dinner. Meet my son. Six thirty? I'll text you the address.'

'That would be really nice, thank you,' he said.

'Don't mention any of this, obviously.'

'Obviously. Got to protect the children. It's a parent's natural instinct. Your dad will tell you that.'

'Piss off, Danny,' said Kate. 'See you tomorrow.'

As he walked around the jetties and piers towards the MRFM building, Danny watched the bubble machines that aerated the water in the dock's basins. According to banners attached to the dock railings, the water was so clean these days they held swimming competitions in it. The force of the system meant that any rubbish floating in the water was pushed neatly to the corners of the basin; footballs, crisp packets, take away cartons and bits of polystyrene were all to be seen wobbling at the water's edge, waiting to be scooped out and disposed of. Danny stopped and stared at the detritus – then he realised he'd been standing there for at least five minutes.

The MRFM building was a tastefully converted dockside factory unit. Many of the old pullies and winches on and around the unit had been preserved to retain a period feel. Looking through the glass security door, Danny could see that another period feel had been maintained inside. The reception was very brightly lit – primary colours surrounded scores of framed, signed discs from recording artists and photos of the station' main presenters. *Radio stations, they never change,* he thought.

He pressed the security buzzer. 'Reception,' said a bright, young-sounding voice.

'Hi. My name's Danny. I'm here to see Gary Keenan.'

The door buzzed and Danny went in.

TWENTY-EIGHT

11 am Thursday 19 April 1990

Danny tottered over to the bathroom and looked at his face in the mirror over the sink. It was the only mirror in his flat. The right side of his face was red and scratched where the plastic bag had torn and his head had hit the wall the second time. His left eye was swollen. And he was well and truly late for work. *Fuck work*, he thought, going back to his small and sparse living room. He punched the news desk number into his phone. Beth answered. Danny wanted to talk to Mike Sharston. One of the drawbacks of working in radio is that everyone's voice is instantly recognisable to their colleagues, so there was no point in Danny pretending it wasn't him.

'Hi, Beth,' he said.

'Danny. You're so late you're in danger of missing tomorrow's shift. Sharston's in a fury.'

'I see. I'd better speak to him.'

'He's in a meeting. What shall I tell him?'

'I'd rather tell him myself.'

'You're not doing yourself any favours here.'

'Look, I got hit by a car last night. I'm in a bad way. My face is all smashed up. I'm not up to work, so that's why I'm not in.'

There was a pause. 'So, RTA with one person injured,' Beth said, in a sing-song voice that suggested she didn't particularly believe him but was writing it down anyway out of politeness. 'Did you report it to the police?'

'No. No I didn't, I just went home. I didn't realise how bad it was until this morning.'

'Are you *going* to report it to the police?' asked Beth.

'I'll be fine, Beth. Thanks for your concern though. Tell Sharston I'll be back next week. Hopefully the riot will be done with by then and we can start getting back to normal.'

'Sure. Bye, Danny.'

The phone went dead. Danny took some painkillers and went back to bed.

Danny wasn't usually in the habit of sleeping during the day, but with his face aching nearly as much as the inside of his head, it seemed like a good idea. Without the protection of alcohol, the dreams came quickly. And they came with a clarity he wasn't used to. He dreamt of that plastic bag over his head – but when he took it off there was no DI Smithdown to save him. He was in a filthy bed, the legs of which were half submerged in slate grey water. Despite the water, the bed was in a dark attic room. Rubbish floated on the water. He rolled off the bed and fell for what seemed like minutes before hitting the surface. The cold shock of it woke him.

He showered, forced down a slice of toast and headed out towards Oldham.

Danny felt odd knocking on the door of the children's home without the police being there. *This is so dodgy*, he thought. Interviewing children was a delicate matter at the best of times; children in the care of local authorities were, journalistically, completely off limits. But Danny wasn't here to interview anyone. He just wanted to talk.

He knocked. Almost immediately, the door opened and a teenage girl appeared. She'd only opened the door enough to create a slim gap. She had spiky hair wrapped in a bandana. She wore a dirty, Reynolds Girls t-shirt. She looked at Danny's swollen face and scrunched her nose in disgust. 'Brenda!' she shouted, without taking her eyes off Danny. 'It's that reporter guy. He looks all fucked up. Should I let him in?'

An older voice came from inside the house. 'All fucked up you say? He'll fit right in then. Let the poor sod in.'

The door opened a little further – just enough to let Danny squeeze through – then it was closed very quickly behind him. Danny followed the girl through to the kitchen; she turned and looked at him several times as they walked, checking on him. Brenda was sitting at the kitchen, in the same spot she'd occupied when Danny was last there. *Maybe she hasn't moved,* he thought.

'Oh dear,' Brenda said, waving Danny towards a chair. 'You really are fucked up aren't you, Mr Reporter? Who have you been annoying this time?'

'I have no idea, Brenda. But I'd like to find out.'

She laughed and popped a roll-up cigarette between her lips. Brenda lit it with a Zippo lighter, shutting the flip top lid with a loud clack. 'Well I don't think you'll find them here, love,' she said.

Danny looked around the kitchen and at the doorways to the adjoining rooms. Just as they had done last time, the home's young residents hovered and floated around the edges of the room, but they seemed closer this time. A little bolder.

'No, I don't suppose I will,' Danny conceded. 'But I'd still like to talk. Not interview – just talk.' Danny lit a cigarette. Holding it between his lips hurt his mouth. 'I'm just trying to make sense of what's going on,' he said, blowing out smoke with a sigh. 'A kid gets found dead up the road and no one knows who he is. What's more, no one seems to care. Your local MP tells me he knows what's going on and he has a car crash the night before telling me. The cops seem to suggest to my colleagues at the radio station that he killed himself in some drunken guilt trip. I'm not buying that. Then someone bounces my head off a wall. Two walls, actually. And no one gives a shit about any of it because all eyes are still firmly fucking fixed on the rioters at Strangeways. So, I'm at the stage now where I don't know who to trust, who to believe or what the fuck is actually going on. Everyone strikes me as either being a lying fucker or, at the very least, having something shitty to hide, to be honest. Apart from you lot. So, I thought I'd come here.'

Danny looked around the room. A dozen kids were now fully in the room. Some looked as though they were about ten years old. 'Sorry for the language,' he added. 'Sorry.'

'They've heard a lot worse, let me assure you,' Brenda reassured him. 'Now. You and I know you can't interview these kids. They're wards of the court. You couldn't print or broadcast what they said even if you wanted to. You'd be prosecuted. You shouldn't even be here. But, there you go. You're here. So, what is it you want to ask?'

Danny turned in his chair and looked around the room. He examined the faces of the dozen or so kids present. They were very close now – within touching distance. Some whispered to each other. Most just stared at him. Danny addressed them directly: 'Last time I was here, Brenda said that some of you were frightened – *really* frightened – about what was going on outside the home. That you'd stopped going walkabout. Why? What's got you so scared?'

The young residents said nothing. They exchanged glances but said nothing. The room was quiet, except for the thin sound of a television in another room. Then Danny heard a whisper. He turned and saw a boy of about ten with his hand cupped around his mouth, saying something into the ear of the teenage girl who'd let Danny in. Her eyes were closed, concentrating on what the child was saying. The boy's hair was very short; he wore jeans that were too small for him and a dirty white t-shirt that was too big. He spoke for about ten seconds. Then, he ran off, clumping up the stairs. One by one, the other children slipped away. Only one stayed behind: the teenage girl. She looked at Danny directly – and she didn't seem too pleased. The only people left in the kitchen were Brenda, Danny and the girl. Brenda motioned for the teenager to take a seat. She did so, but her displeasure was very clear. 'This is bollocks, this is,' she said, helping herself to Brenda's pouch of tobacco and dumping it onto a Rizla cigarette paper. Danny was going to offer her one of his, but she'd already rolled one and lit it while he was digging around in his pocket to find his packet. Danny had never seen anyone roll a cigarette so quickly or expertly. *How old is she? Fifteen, tops?*

'Honestly,' said Danny, in what he hoped was his reassuring voice. 'This is on complete confidence. I won't repeat what you tell me, I won't tell anyone you spoke to me. I was never even here.'

Danny looked at Brenda, hoping she'd provide some form of back up or reassurance. 'Up to you, Jenny. No pressure, love. Entirely up to you.'

There was a long pause. The girl stared at her cigarette. 'Something happened to Little Paul the other week,' she eventually said. 'Something horrible. Us older ones are stopping in to make sure the young 'uns are okay. If we go out, we go out together. If we stay in, we stay in together. We all look out for each other at the best of times. And the worst. This is up there with the worst.'

'Christ, Jenny, why didn't you say anything?' said Brenda, pulling her chair closer to the table.

'Because Little Paul didn't want me to, Brenda. End of.'

'I know but –'

Danny cut in. This might be his only chance. 'What happened to Paul?'

'Little Paul,' Jenny corrected. 'He likes to be called Little Paul. It avoids confusion with Big Paul, one of the other kids.'

'Fair enough,' conceded Danny. 'What happened to Little Paul?'

Jenny stubbed out her roll up and started to roll another. This time, she did it slowly. 'He was grabbed in town,' she said quietly.

'Christ almighty,' cried Brenda.

'Look, Bren. Do you want me to talk to this bloke or not?'

'Sorry,' said the older woman. 'I'll keep it zipped.'

'Who grabbed him, Jenny?' Danny asked.

'If we knew that we wouldn't be sat here wondering about it, would we, clever bollocks?'

'Sorry. I mean, what happened?'

'He was in Oldham, just dossing about, cadging fags off people coming out of the pubs. It was pretty late. Someone grabbed him from behind, took him down a side street and tried to put him in a car. He was kicking and screaming like mad. He's tough as nails is Little Paul. Anyway, whoever done it tried to tie him up, but he was making that much of a din they sacked it off and left him. Then he came back here. Shaking like a shitting dog, he was. White as a sheet. He told me not to tell anyone. Didn't want to get moved to another home if the council found out he was out and about late at night. He likes it here, does Little Paul. He likes you, Brenda. Fuck knows why.'

The older woman smiled and made as if to speak, then thought better of it and made a zipping motion across her lips.

'Does he remember anything about whoever grabbed him?' Danny said. 'Anything at all?'

'They didn't say anything. Not a word.'

'What about their faces?'

'Nope. Couldn't see 'em.'

'Why not?'

'The bastards banged a plastic bag on his head. He couldn't see nowt. Poor little shit.'

Danny tried to avoid letting that piece of information distract him. Brenda looked away. Her eyes had tears in them now, but still she kept silent. 'Does he remember anything else? A smell? A noise? Anything?'

'Just a sort of… *skrawking* noise.'

'Sorry. How do you mean?'

'Like… *skrawking*. You know. Like when you pull off a big piece of tape when you're wrapping a present and it makes that noise. Don't know what the proper word is. Maybe there isn't one.' Jenny mimed pulling out a long strip of tape.

'*Skrawk!*' she said.

'Sure,' said Danny. 'I get it.'

The room went quiet. Danny heard footsteps. Little Paul was standing at the kitchen doorway, listening in. Brenda got up and walked slowly towards the child. She knelt down and put out her arms, as if to ask if it was okay to hug him. He nodded. 'Oh, Little Paul,' she said. 'You daft sod. You lovely, daft little sod.'

Brenda held the boy tightly. 'I'd better go,' said Danny. He got up from the table, looking across at Brenda and the boy. 'I'll see myself out.'

Danny paused in the hallway. 'Thanks, Little Paul,' he said. The boy, his face buried in Brenda's jumper, said nothing. As Danny reached the front door, Jenny appeared behind him. 'Hey,' she said. 'What happens now?'

'Honestly? I'm not sure,' said Danny.

'There's no way Little Paul will talk to the police. I still can't believe he let me tell you about what happened. If he's frightened, then there must be something really scary out there. He's a tough nut, is Little Paul, but he's still just a kid.'

'Until Strangeways is finished it's hard to see how I can convince anyone that this is a really important story. So, it's down to us, I suppose.'

'No one gives a shit about us at the best of times.' Jenny scowled. 'Right now, it's like we don't even exist. Who cares if something that doesn't exist gets snatched in the street? Nobody, that's who.'

Danny pulled out his notebook and scribbled down the Manchester Radio newsroom number. Then he scribbled it out and wrote out his home number. He tore out the sheet and handed it to the girl. 'Look, if Little Paul says anything else give me a ring. In the meantime, keep doing what you're doing. Look out for each other.'

'You need to look after yourself too,' Jenny said. 'Whoever did that to your face wasn't messing about.'

'No,' said Danny. 'No, they weren't messing about, were they? Bye, Jenny.'

Danny walked to his car and drove just a few hundred yards to a corner shop nearby. He bought some cigarettes, a bag of peanuts and two overpriced bottles of Holsten Pils. *Lunch,* he thought. Slinging the bag onto the back seat of his car, he drove out towards Black Moss. When he got to the parking area he pulled a sharp right and tucked his car into the bottom corner. He was shielded from the road by a grass verge. He switched on the radio: they were playing 'Step On' by Happy Mondays. The song had become the unofficial anthem of the revitalised Manchester music scene and seemed to be currently unavoidable. Danny was already sick of the record so turned the volume down, so he could barely hear it. Using a penknife on his keyring he popped open one of the bottles and took a drink; then he waited. And watched. And waited. *What kind of person comes here?*

Sliding down low in his seat, Danny took another sip of his beer. There was a police van parked at the far end. Two officers chatted by the rear doors, closed them and made off. *Nice of them to take an interest in the dead kid,* Danny thought, taking some pleasure in the fact that he was sipping his beer in full view of the policemen. Then he watched as a couple in their 70s parked up and slowly, methodically but on their walking boots and outer layers, then pack some food into a small rucksack before setting off down the Pennine Way. They held hands as they went. *That's nice.*

He saw a group of rowdy teenagers arrive in a van; they tumbled out, laughing and joking as a harassed teacher tried to corral them into staying together. He shouted at them and made several vague threats. That seemed to work and teenagers finally formed into a group and also headed along the path. *That's going to spoil the peace for the old folks,* Danny thought.

He then watched a middle-aged man in a suit park his car, look around warily, drop a plastic bag into a bin, then leave. *That's weird.* Five minutes after he'd gone, Danny walked over to the bin to take a look. The bag had three empty vodka bottles in it. *Disgraceful.*

After finishing his second bottle of lager, Danny's eyes began to flicker and close. The sleep was light but welcome; half sleep rather than the real thing. Occasionally, Danny's eyes would open and he'd see different people arrive at the car park: a runner warming up before crossing the road and heading up the Pennine Way in the opposite direction towards Standedge. Then two people in their thirties arrived in separate cars; the woman got into the man's car. *Aye aye,* Danny said to himself. He watched their silhouettes as they spent the next ten minutes talking, kissing and embracing before the woman went back to her car. The two cars left several minutes apart but headed in the same direction. *Forbidden love in the office.*

The scenes played out before him as Danny slipped in and out of his sleep. He watched and snoozed, snoozed and watched. They he saw something that made him snap out of his restful state very quickly indeed. A white van pulled into the car park a little faster than the other vehicles; so fast a little gravel flew off as he came to a stop. The driver turned off the engine but stayed in his seat and looked out towards the moors. Danny could only see his outline, but he seemed agitated; he banged the steering wheel with the flat of his hand and bit his thumb at the point where the nail meets the skin. He looked at something out of Danny's view then stepped sharply out. Danny slid a little further down in his seat.

Gary Keenan walked over to the bin with some pieces of paper in his hand. He was tearing them into pieces as he walked. Then he put them in the bin, returned to his van and drove off.

Danny waited a good ten minutes before going to see what the engineer had put there. He looked at the pieces then pulled several out. They were photos of a young child, happy and smiling at a birthday party.

Danny took as many of the pieces as he could gather before another car pulled into the parking spot. He put them in his pocket and drove back down the hill towards Oldham

Police station.

TWENTY-NINE

2.20 pm Monday 20 June 2016

'Danny boy!' cried Gary Keenan as he opened the door behind the MRFM reception and wedged it open with his body. 'Walk this way.'

Gary's ponytailed hair was as white as chalk. He'd put on a few stones in weight since Danny had last seen him, but he appeared to be wearing exactly the same combination of jeans, grey sweatshirt and keys that he'd worn in 1990. He stuck out his hand. Danny shook it, gasping slightly at the unnecessary firmness of the engineer's grip. 'Can't Stop the Feeling!' by Justin Timberlake accompanied them down a corridor then through an open-plan office. On one side, sales staff – some wearing headsets – talked to potential clients on the phone. On the other, journalists – about four of them – silently edited digital recordings on their laptops, quietly tapping in their scripts as they went. The sound of clattering typewriters was nowhere to be heard. Nor was there any shouting and swearing. Danny was shocked at how clean the new MRFM was compared to the coffee stains and fag burns of the old station. It looked and felt more like a call centre than a radio station.

'How are you then, Danny boy?' boomed Keenan, pushing his teardrop glasses up his nose as they walked. 'I hear you've been doing a bit of landscape gardening with your motor down in London.'

'Yeah, you could say that. Thanks, as ever, for your

warmth and concern, Gary.'

'That's what I'm here for,' the engineer replied as he pushed open the door of his office. A sign on the door read: THE ANSWER'S FUCK OFF – NOW, WHAT'S THE QUESTION? Although they were in a different building in a different century, Gary's office seemed largely unchanged. There were wires, soldering irons, plastic tubs full of batteries and boxes of tiny, discarded earphones. As Gary motioned for him to take a seat, Danny's eye caught an upright pole on the engineer's desk. It was the kind normally found in a bathroom to hold multiple toilet rolls. Instead, it was stacked with rolls of different-coloured gaffa tape.

The engineer cleared away a small stack of electronics magazines and tool catalogues and gestured for Danny to take a seat. 'Don't wish to be rude, Gary,' said Danny. 'Which obviously means I'm about to say something really rude, but how the hell are you still at Manchester Radio? You should be retired by now, surely?'

'Cheeky bastard, I'm not even sixty yet. Not much older than you. I've always looked old, that's my problem. Dealing with shit from journalists for decades has aged me prematurely.'

'Sorry. It always felt like everyone was older than me back then. Like everyone knew what they were doing. And I didn't.'

'We were all just making it up as we went along, mate.' The engineer laughed. 'Still am, to be honest. Mind you, very different world now, Danny boy. No tape recorders, radio cars or razor blades any more. It's all done with iPhones, mate, by a handful of journos. Most of the bulletins are pre-recorded nowadays. So are loads of the programmes. No live reports any more, it messes with the timings. Hardly any cock-ups but equally, hardly any fun. All the mayhem has gone out of it, all the fizz and energy has disappeared. It's processed, fast-food news – McNews I call it. It's bollocks, but there you go. Anyway. What the fuck are you doing here?'

'Well, I'm kind of in between jobs at the moment – thanks to the tree remodelling you so kindly mentioned. So, I'm looking into something from the old days. Seeing if there's anything in it.'

Keenan leant forward in his chair. 'Tell me more.'

'It's a murder from 1990. A kid that was found out near a reservoir in the hills above Oldham. Nobody gave a shit at the time because everyone was too busy trying to win awards with their Strangeways coverage. Ring any bells?'

The engineer leant back in his chair and put his feet up on the cluttered table. 'Not sure. We had so many murders in those days. Which reservoir?'

Danny felt his heart beating. *Can he hear that? Can he hear how much noise it's making?* 'Black Moss.'

'It rings a bell, definitely. I know it well up there though. I've driven up and down that road many, many times. Too many bleedin' times.'

'Why's that, Gary?'

Gary looked over Danny's shoulder and checked the small window set into the door. No one was about. *What is he up to? Why so shifty?* The engineer opened a drawer on his desk. He pulled out a packet of cigarettes and offered one to Danny. 'You definitely can't smoke in here, Danny boy,' Keenan said, lighting up and offering the flame of a cheap plastic lighter to Danny. 'Sacking offence. Apparently. Like I give a shit.'

Keenan switched on a desk fan which sent a blast of air across the desk. 'Anyway. Yes. Black bloody Moss. Brings it all back.'

'Does it?'

'Yes, it most definitely does. I spent months driving up and down that road past the Moss.'

'Why?'

Keenan blew a jet of smoke straight into the fan. 'Because of the kids.'

Danny wasn't sure what he was hearing. 'What do you mean, Gary, the kids?'

'It was terrible, mate. Just the worst thing ever.'

'Gary, is there something you want to tell me?'

Gary took off his glasses and cleaned them with his sweatshirt, pinching the lenses through the material. He placed them back on his nose. 'Not especially, but it's all a very long time ago now, so I can't see the harm. I didn't tell anyone at the time. But it was the wife. Early 1990, she fucked off to Huddersfield with the kids. That's where she's from. I'd been working all the hours God sent in those days. When I wasn't in the radio station, I was in the pub. Not unlike yourself, Danny boy. She decided she'd had enough. Don't blame her wanting to be away from me. But Huddersfield? That's taking the piss. So that entailed months and months of schlepping back and forward between Manchester and Huddersfield to see the kids.'

'So that's why you were up and down the Huddersfield road?'

'Yeah. Grim it was. That MP crashed his car up there, didn't he? Dangerous bit of road, that. Then that murder. You got really involved with it, didn't you? Hang on, Danny-fucking-boy.' Gary turned off the prog rock that had been playing in his office. 'What the fuck do you think I was doing up there?'

'Sorry. Look. I saw you out at the Moss,' Danny said quietly. 'Twice. I asked you about it at the time and you said you hadn't been there. That's a bit suspicious, don't you think?'

'It was private!' Gary shouted. 'I didn't want you nosey bastard journalists knowing my business, thank you very much. I was in danger of losing contact with my kids. I didn't want anything to jeopardise that. So, I told no one. I cut down on the drinking, cut back on the long hours, sorted things out with the wife and we were back together by Christmas. Seriously, what the hell do you think I was doing up there? Come on I want to know.'

'I was a really weird time, Gary,' said Danny. 'To be honest, I didn't know what was going on or who to believe.

No one was interested in the dead kid; I was up and down to Oldham all the time and could barely get a story on air because of Strangeways. Peter Jeffries, the MP you mentioned, he died in completely bizarre circumstances. I got done over down a back alley in Didsbury after digging about in places I clearly shouldn't have been digging about in. Then I spot you up at the murder scene – twice – and you tell me you've never been there.' Danny was matching Gary for volume now. 'So, excuse me for being mildly fucking curious about what you were up to!'

There was a good twenty seconds of quiet between the two men. The strains of a song could be heard from the adjoining offices. *Is that Justin Bieber?* thought Danny. *I don't know these songs anymore. What's more, I don't care.*

'Love Yourself,' said Gary. Picking up a foam microphone cover from his desk and putting it into a drawer.

'What?'

'Love Yourself,' repeated Gary. 'The song that's playing. Justin Bieber. I fuckin' hate Justin Bieber. It's the curse of working at a radio station – all the songs burrow into your brain, regardless of how much you hate them. In the old days we had proper songs from proper bands that were from round here. The Mondays, The Roses, New Order, James –'

'Tim Booth of James is from Yorkshire, if I remember correctly,' countered Danny.

'You know what I mean. Fucking Bieber! Christ, it's like everything around here these days. Processed crap. McMusic interspersed with McNews. All safe and processed. McBollocks.'

There was quiet again. Gary opened the drawer, took out the microphone cover and put it back on his desk. 'So, Danny boy. Apart from accusing me of being a kiddie murderer, what are you actually here for?'

Danny pulled his chair a little closer to Gary's and took out the hotel notepad and pen he had in his inside jacket pocket.

THIRTY

1.15 pm Thursday 19 April 1990

Danny parked his car as close to Oldham Police station as he could and half walked, half ran inside. A collection of people whose lives weren't going quite as they'd hoped for were standing and sitting in the waiting area close to the desk. The duty officer, a harassed-looking man in his forties with his hair combed over to hide his obvious baldness, was standing behind the front desk with his hand shielding his eyes. On the other side of the chest-high counter, a young man of about nineteen wearing a multi-coloured shell suit was explaining a complex-sounding situation involving his girlfriend, another man and the other man's dog.

Danny couldn't wait for the story to unfold fully. 'I'm really sorry to interrupt, but is it possible to see DI Smithdown please?'

'Did the last bloke ya interrupted do that to ya face?' the young man asked Danny. 'Don't fookin' mind me mate – got all fookin' day, me.'

The front desk officer lifted his hand from his eyes and looked at Danny. Without speaking he held up a single finger to the shell-suit complainant, as if to say *you...wait*. He pointed at Danny and then indicated a vacant chair. He opened a door at the back of the desk area, put his head through the gap for a few seconds and returned. He put up five fingers to Danny, indicating how long he'd have to wait. Then he pointed at the shell-suit man and gestured that he should continue. The officer's hand found its original position, shielding his eyes with ease, and the young man continued his story.

Danny waited. *If it's all bollocks, DI Smithdown will know for sure,* he said to himself. *There's probably a perfectly reasonable explanation why Gary was up there. Twice. But what about those photos? That was creepy.* Danny pulled out the photos and looked at the pieces. He hadn't found them all, but there were enough to make out the faces involved.

After two minutes a side door opened – DC Jan Cave motioned for Danny to follow her. She headed down a grey corridor towards a row of offices. 'Alright, Danny. That face of yours still looks sore. Have you put anything on it?'

'Nah. I like it as it is. It's an icebreaker wherever I go. Causes a stir.'

'Yes, that's very much your thing, isn't it?'

'It's my reason for living, DC Cave.'

The Detective Constable tapped on the glass window of one of the offices. A voice half shouted, 'Come.' In they went. Behind the desk of the small office sat DS James Pym. Danny looked at DC Cave, puzzled. She closed the door behind them and stood by the door, as if standing on guard duty. 'Danny, hello. Take a seat. I hear you took a tumble last night. How are you feeling?'

'Surprisingly perky, Mr Pym, but a little confused,' he replied, lowering himself gently into the plastic chair he'd been offered. 'I was looking for DI Smithdown, is he about?'

'Not today Danny, no,' the DS replied. There was something about his manner that irritated Danny even more than usual.

'There's something I want to talk to him about. When will he be back?'

'Not for a while, Danny. Can I help?'

Danny could feel the heat of anger make his face even more painful than it already was. 'What do you mean, *not for a while?*'

'He's on leave, Danny.'

Danny stood up sharply. The chair skidded back. 'Leave?

On *leave*. What the fuck are you lot up to? Have you knobbled him now as well? Got him out of the way? Jesus Christ, you must think I'm stupid! It's almost as if you bastards don't want anyone to know what happened up at the Moss. Every time someone gets a sniff of what might be going on, something shitty happens to them. Now the DI's mysteriously gone on leave? Fuck that.'

'Danny,' said DS in a quiet and reassuring voice. 'No one is getting Mr Smithdown out of the way of anything...'

'I wouldn't be surprised if you're in on it too, you greasy bastard.'

DC Cave took a step towards him and put a hand to his arm. 'Danny, please...'

'Get the fuck off me,' he shouted, shaking free of her hand.

'Danny,' DS Pym said, quietly. 'DI Smithdown's wife died this morning. The leave he's on is compassionate leave.'

The heat Danny had felt fill his face a few moments earlier slipped away quickly, to be replaced by a cold, exposed feeling. The images of Mrs Smithdown that he'd seen in dozens of photos and the DI's house snapped into his head. He looked at DS Pym and DC Cave and returned to his seat.

'I know you've had a bit of a time of it, so we'll let this pass, shall we?' DS Pym offered. 'DI Smithdown is exactly where he should be – at home with his daughter.'

Danny couldn't look directly at either of the officers, so he looked out of the window instead. 'Sorry,' he said. 'It's all been a bit... I'm sorry.'

'It's forgotten about,' DS Pym. 'Isn't it DC Cave?'

'Absolutely. In the past already,' she added. Her voice was gentle and reassuring. Kind. It made Danny feel worse than he already did.

'Please, Danny,' said the DS. 'Leave them be, lad. We haven't even told him about the body up at the Moss. He'll be delighted, but now's not the time.'

Danny looked at the DS now. 'I don't understand,' he said. 'You've lost me.'

The senior officer took an A4 notepad from a three-tier desk tidy and turned over several pages until he found what he was looking for. 'It's been on the news already. Your radio station included. Early hours of this morning, body of a white male aged approximately thirty years, found close to Black Moss reservoir. No suspicious circumstances. I can confirm we are not looking for anyone else in connection with the find.'

DS Pym looked at Danny as if expecting him to be somehow pleased. 'Sorry, Mr Pym. You've found another body? At the Moss?'

'Indeed. Good news for all concerned.'

Danny looked at DC Cave. She was smiling. 'Another body?' he asked again.

'Yes, Danny. I was hoping I wouldn't have to spell it out. A suicide at the same spot the kid was found. Local guy. Vincent Canning. He was well known to us. Persistent nuisance, anti-social behaviour, mental health issues, that kind of thing. He'd taken himself up the Moss with a bottle of whisky. After he'd finished it he'd smashed the bottle and cut his own throat with it. Right there on the path. He left a note. Shortest one I've ever seen – and I've seen a fair few. *Sorry.* That's all it said. *Sorry.*'

'Christ. Are you sure, Mr Pym?'

'Yes, Danny. We're sure. We found items on him that linked him to the lad.'

'What kind of items?'

'Let's just say, items linked to the way the boy's body was found that only the killer could have known.'

Danny hesitated, then he said: 'Like tape? Like the gaffa tape that was used to strap weights to the little lad's body?'

DS Pym's face changed from sympathetic to annoyed very quickly indeed. He closed the pad and put it back onto the sorting tray. 'I have absolutely no comment to make about that. But at another time, when things have cooled down a little, I will make it my business to find out why you just said what you just said.'

'I know more about this case than a lot of people realise, Mr Pym,' Danny offered, leaning forward in his seat.

'Well I'm sure Mr Smithdown had nothing but good intentions in involving you – what's done is done…'

'What about Peter Jeffries? I'd heard you were blaming him at one stage.'

DS Pym looked at DC Cave. He seemed genuinely perplexed: 'That's news to me. I don't know where you heard that, but it wasn't from me and it wasn't from any of my officers. We never considered Peter Jeffries a suspect in this case. We suspected he was an old drunk who shouldn't have been driving around the moors while he was pissed up, but there's no way we thought he was connected to the boy's death. Ever. I'd like to know where that story came from… something else for me to take a look at when this has all settled down.'

'So, what happens now?' Danny asked.

'Well, the main thing is that an individual who posed a major threat to children in this area is a threat no longer,' said DS Pym, leaning back in his chair and putting his hands behind his head.

Here comes the copperspeak, thought Danny.

'Clearly Mr Canning felt that the net was closing in and that taking his own life was the only option left open to him. Tragic, in many ways. There are no winners here, Danny.'

Pure copperbollocks.

'So, beyond the inquest into Mr Canning's apparent suicide, the ongoing priority for Oldham Police will be in identifying the young victim of this terrible crime. That remains our focus.'

'So, that's it?' said Danny.

'Publicly we have to be seen to be keeping an open mind until it's official, but essentially, yes. You should be pleased, Danny. This is what it's all been about, hasn't it? Finding out the truth. Trust me, I will leave no stone unturned until we identify the young victim. We'll also be liaising with colleagues from other divisions and forces to look at other unsolved missing persons cases involving young males. We want to know if this man has struck before.'

DC Cave spoke too. Danny had forgotten she was there. 'Do you have your recording equipment with you Danny? Perhaps DS Pym could do an interview for you. Give you the scoop. You deserve it.'

'Yes. That's the least we can do. Good thinking DC Cave. More than happy to do that. I know we've had our differences, but I can't help but admire the way you've put your heart and soul into this. Very commendable. Get your gear and let's do it.'

Yeah, so you can claim the credit. 'Sure,' said Danny. 'Give me a minute. Work will be very impressed. I'm supposed to be off sick.'

Danny went to his car, retrieved his Marantz and returned to the police station. DS Pym essentially repeated the same words he'd already used in largely the same order: *Terrible crime; no stone unturned; other unsolved crimes; tragic case.*

It took just over three minutes – Manchester Radio interviews rarely stretched to any longer than that – and when it was done, Danny did as he always did: stopped and checked that the recording was okay. It was. 'Thanks very much, Mr Pym,' Danny offered. 'That's all I need. I'm not in the radio car, but I'll try to get it back in time for the three o'clock news, then see if they'll run it in full on our main news at five. It's not been easy to get stuff on air, thanks to Strangeways.'

'Well,' said DS Pym, putting his hand on Danny's shoulder. 'I hear we're on the final push there. It's nearly over. Then we can start getting back to normal.'

DS Pym put out a hand to Danny. They shook. He smelled of Paco Rabanne. 'Sorry for what I said earlier,' Danny said. 'It was way over the top. I was out of order.'

'Sure. It happens. This has been difficult for all concerned - us as well as you. So, it's no wonder that feelings boil over sometimes. Just don't make a bloody habit of it, eh?'

'As if I'd do that, Mr Pym.' Danny's smile was thin, but he

meant what he'd said. *Kind of.*

'Course not. DC Cave will see you out. Take care, Danny.'

Danny drove slowly back to Manchester. *No rush,* he thought. *Not as if they're going to lead on it. I'll be lucky if they find space for it at all.*

After he'd found a parking space on the roof, he walked slowly across the piazza towards the reception. His head still throbbed. Pauline buzzed him through the door. 'Blue Savannah' by Erasure greeted him as he stepped inside. 'Danny Johnston, what on earth has happened to you? You look like you've been hit by a bus.'

'No, just a car, Pauline. Still hurts though.' *Are you sticking with the car story? Might as well. Makes no difference now, does it?*

'You shouldn't be in work, Danny. You should be at home, resting. Or in hospital. My goodness, look at the state of you.'

Danny waved his Marantz in Pauline's direction. He felt a little unsteady on his feet. 'Got the scoop right here, Pauline,' he said.

'Is it that awful business up at Oldham? Tell me it's all over.'

'It's all over.'

'And tell me you have the scoop.'

'I have the scoop.'

'Good lad,' she smiled. 'I knew it.'

Pauline buzzed the second door. 'Please take care, Danny.'

The corridors were clogged by the usual mix of sales people, smokers and visitors. Erasure segued into 'Vogue' by Madonna. Danny's swollen face attracted glances, but not that many, considering. *Hard to surprise anyone around here,* he thought.

Inside the newsroom, heads turned as Danny entered. 'It's alive,' one of the sports reporters shouted from across the room. Chief reporter Robert Crane was editing tape at one of the Studer machines along the far wall. He pulled off his headphones; he did this carefully so as not to disrupt his hair. 'Mike!' he shouted. 'Johnston's escaped from the secure unit. And it's not a pretty sight.'

Beth Hall was at the news desk, handing over to the afternoon reader. 'Danny, my God, look at you,' she said. 'You're not even supposed to be here. Do you need first aid or are you going to tough it out?'

'I will keep going on a mixture of adrenaline and spite, Beth,' he replied.

Mike Sharston came out of his office. 'Danny. Bloody Nora, what a state. Why are you here?'

'Black Moss murder/suicide, boss. I've got an interview with the Detective Superintendent about the second body found up at Black Moss. And a good line for later about them possibly linking it to other missing kid cases.' Danny tapped his Marantz. 'It's all here.'

'Bloody good stuff, lad,' Sharston said. 'I think we'll lead with that on the next bulletin.'

Then everything went grey and white and Danny Johnston passed out cold onto the floor of the Manchester Radio newsroom.

THIRTY-ONE

3.15 pm Monday 20 June 2016

After leaving MRFM Danny called a local mini-cab firm and booked a 'wait and return' ride. The driver seemed interested as to why Danny wanted to go to a reservoir car park in the middle of nowhere, but he didn't get very far with his queries. 'I just want to take a look,' was all Danny offered.

Danny stared out of the car window as the housing estates of Salford faded into the M602 and the M60. He saw the unchanged exterior of Oldham Police station, then the town centre thinned out and the hills took over. The outlying communities seemed largely as he remembered them: grey and red estates, takeaways and mini-markets that gave way to farms and country pubs before the moors opened up and filled the horizon in all directions.

'I think we're in Yorkshire here, mate,' the driver said as the mini-cab pulled into the car park. 'That's extra.'

'No, we're not,' Danny replied. He pointed towards the Pennine Way path. 'The border's right there. Look on Google Maps if you don't believe me. I'll be back in twenty minutes.'

A few improvements here and there, but pretty much the same, he thought, as he walked quickly along the path away from the car park, past Redbrook, then out towards Black Moss. The weather was fine, the wind gentle yet warm and the sky was a blast of blue. But, as ever, Black Moss clung to its favoured grey. The water level was low, and the size and shape of the sandy area had changed considerably, but he knew he was in roughly the right spot. He thought about how cold it had been that morning; how his head had throbbed from being woken up to come to this lonely place; he thought about the young cops; he thought about that piece of plastic sheeting. *If it hadn't been caught by the wind, it would have been just another story. And I wouldn't be here now.*

Danny found his iPhone in the back pocket of his trousers and took several individual landscape photos: the path, the water, the 'beach'. Then he turned the phone upright and took a panorama shot, shuffling in a circle on the paving slabs to take in as much of the area as possible. The panorama shot looked striking, beautiful even. The area was surprisingly free of walkers – just two women on the brow of the hill, shielding their eyes from the sun to take in the view. Then they left and he was alone.

Danny retraced his steps, returned to the cab and got in the back seat. He gave the driver an address in Wythenshawe, south Manchester, a good forty-five-minute drive, more if they were to catch the rush hour traffic. 'Not another reservoir is it, mate?' the driver said, punching the details into his navigation app. 'No,' said Danny. 'No more reservoirs for today.'

He slept during the journey. He'd forgotten he'd been up most of the night. The driver woke him as they turned into a crescent-shaped street. Children played on a grassy semi-circle surrounded by identical red brick ex-council houses. Not a wealthy area, but one that clearly was well maintained by proud residents. Danny gave the driver sixty pounds – more than he was asked for – and thanked him for his patience.

He waited for the cab to go before spotting the house he wanted and walking to the door. The doorbell sounded 'The Bells of St Clements' and a woman in her late fifties answered the door. Her hair was short and grey and she was wearing a black top, leggings and slippers.

'Hi Karen,' Danny said. 'How are you?'

'I am… surprised to see you, that's how I am,' she replied.

'Sure, I don't blame you. I should have rung but I thought I'd just swing past and see if you were in. On the off-chance, you know.'

'Sure. Well, I am. In, that is.'

A man's voice came from a back room: 'Who is it, Karen?' he said.

'It's our Sean,' she shouted back.

'Who?'

'Me brother, Sean!' she shouted. She kissed Danny on the cheek as he passed. Her voice dropped to its previous level. 'Come inside, Sean. It's lovely to see you.'

THIRTY-TWO

5.40 pm Saturday 21 April 1990

Visiting hours at the Manchester Royal Infirmary didn't officially start until 6.30 pm, but DI Smithdown's police ID allowed him to smooth his way past the staff. He passed Kate off as a police colleague. As Danny saw them, he put down the magazine he'd been reading – a copy of *Q* with David Bowie on the cover – and straightened out his bed. He pushed himself up straight, smiling.

'Here he is,' the policeman said. 'I might have to arrest you for loitering – there's nothing wrong with you, lad.'

'Christ. I don't think I've ever seen you two together before. Actually being father and daughter,' Danny replied. 'Have you honestly come to see me?'

'Yes, we have, Danny.' She leant in and kissed him on the cheek. 'I've brought you these.' Kate placed a copy of *Empire* magazine and some chocolates on the table next to his bed.

'How are you, anyway?' asked the DI. He seemed genuinely concerned.

'I'm fine. Really. Mr Smithdown. I'm so sorry to hear about your wife. Truly I am. Such a difficult time for both of you, that's why I'm so surprised to see you here. I feel a bit embarrassed that you've come to check on me when you've got so much going on. It's very thoughtful. I mean it.'

Smithdown pulled up a chair and sat next to Danny's bed. 'Well, we were going a bit stir crazy at home weren't we, Kate? So, we thought we'd come and see how you're getting on. So, what's the damage?'

'Concussion, dehydration and third-degree embarrassment after passing out in the newsroom,' Danny answered.

'Dehydration? That must be a first for you, Danny lad,' said Mr Smithdown.

'If you're just here to take the piss...'

'We're here to see how you are, Danny,' said Kate.

'And take the piss, obviously,' added her father. 'Look, we won't stay too long – we told a little white lie to get in here – we were worried about you. Mainly Kate, obviously. I wasn't that worried.'

'Well, it's much appreciated. Do you mind if I ask you something, Mr Smithdown?'

'I think I can guess what it is,' the detective replied, folding his arms.

'The suicide up at Black Moss. What do you think? Honestly.'

'I've had my mind elsewhere Danny, if I'm honest,' the DI replied. 'But I've spoken to DS Pym and DC Cave and it seems pretty cut and dried. The note, the location, the items at the scene.'

'What items?' asked Kate.

'Items that connect it to the child's body, let's leave it at that, Kate,' suggested DI Smithdown to his daughter. 'This is a hospital visit, not a press conference for the *Messenger*.'

'You two – such a bloody boys' club. Why do I get the feeling I'm not wanted. Danny, can I get you anything?'

'A tea would be nice. Ask one of the auxiliary nurses. Sorry. Don't blame me, blame this guy.'

As his daughter walked away, DI Smithdown pulled his seat closer to Danny's bed. 'Make it quick, lad.'

'Yes or no – was it him?'

'I only spoke very briefly...'

'Yes or no?'

'Look.'

'I'm really sorry Mr Smithdown, I feel awful asking you at a time like this, but I'm going mad with this. Yes or no?'

'Yes. It's all there.'

'But? It sounds like there's a "but" coming.'

'But nothing. It's all there. There's nothing to suggest it wasn't him. Having said that...'

'What.'

'It's a very big leap. The suicide – Vincent Canning – he was known to the police. I had a few dealings with him over the years. Bits of this, bits of that. Nothing special. To go from being a medium-level pain in the arse to child abduction and murder, well, that's a big leap. But, that's where some of the worst crimes come from. Great big leaps.'

'So, you're not one hundred percent sure.'

'It's done with Danny,' sighed the DI. 'When you're feeling up to it and it's all goes quiet over at Strangeways, we can talk about getting some publicity aimed at identifying the lad. I think he deserves that, don't you?'

'A kid at the children's home says someone tried to snatch him too. Plastic bagged him, just like me. Are you saying your man Canning did that too?'

The DI dropped his voice to a whisper. 'I'm saying that we'll follow up on the lad from the home, but I bet you a tenner he won't talk to me. Or anyone else. The plastic bag thing might be a coincidence, or maybe the kid overheard it and use it to get attention. Or to mess you about. It wasn't Little Paul, was it? Now, there's a kid that's going to end up in Strangeways. He's a little shit is Little Paul.'

Kate returned with a cup of tea and placed it on the small table next to Danny's bed. 'When are you getting out then, Danny Something?'

'I'm just waiting for the head specialist to sign me off, then I'm away. Hopefully tonight. They've run out of tests to do on me.'

'I suppose you won't be up in Oldham quite so much,' said Kate. 'Now they've found the kid's killer.'

'No. I suppose not,' Danny conceded. 'There'll still be the inquest to cover to confirm the suicide, but we tend to pinch that kind of stuff from the local reporters. Like you.'

'Charming.'

DI Smithdown stood up from his chair. 'Danny's welcome anytime, Kate. Anytime. Can't fault the effort you've put into this, lad. You were there at the start and you got the scoop with the DS when Canning's body was found. Your bosses at the radio station must be chuffed. I see they've sent you a little something.'

DI Smithdown nodded towards the oversized, padded card on the cabinet next to the bed – a teddy bear with a thermometer sticking out of his mouth was on the front. *Sending Hugs To You To Make You Feel Better.* Some of the messages written inside were a little less wholesome: *Get off your arse and back into work, all the best Gary,* said one. *Not sure who the fuck you are but get well soon anyway. Robert C (Number One Reporter).*

'Yes,' said Danny. 'Very moving.' He took a sip of his tea. It was scalding hot; he put it to one side. There were a few beats of silence.

'I'll tell you what,' said DI Smithdown. 'The car is parked across the other side of the hospital. I'll go and get it and see you at the front reception, Kate. Okay?'

'Sure, Dad. See you in a few minutes.'

The DI shook Danny's hand: 'Ring me when you're better. Let's get that poor lad identified.'

Kate waited for her father to go – she heard him explain that *my colleague just has a few more questions* to a member of staff, then he pushed his way through the swing doors leading out of the ward. 'You don't think this Canning guy did it, do you?' she said.

'No. I don't. There's just something not right about it.'

'Fucking hell, Danny,' Kate cried. 'How come you know better than anyone else?'

'I'm not saying that. But, I know one thing. In his heart of hearts, I don't think your dad thinks that guy did it either. But his hands are tied. Mine aren't.'

'So, what's your big plan then? How do you plan to succeed where the massed ranks of Greater Manchester Police have failed?'

'I have absolutely no idea.'

She paused and looked down the corridor, checking that her father was gone. 'I'll help if I can,' she said. 'Got to go.'

Kate leant to kiss him on the cheek. She banged Danny's head slightly in the process. 'Sorry. Bye. Sorry.'

Danny watched her go. He waited a few minutes, in case she returned. Then he pulled his sheets aside slowly and swung his legs out of the bed. *Brilliant! I've always wanted to check myself out of a hospital,* he thought. *Just like in a film.*

THIRTY-THREE

3.30 pm Monday 20 June 2016

In the kitchen of Karen Doyle's house in Wythenshawe, Danny watched as his sister rattled cups and opened cupboards. 'I see you've had a bit of mither down in London, Sean,' she said, placing a teapot, two mugs and a plate of biscuits onto the small kitchen table pushed up against the wall. 'It was in the papers.'

'Yes, it was, wasn't it?' Danny's accent had changed since he walked into the house. It was broader, more nasally Mancunian. 'I don't suppose I'll ever convince you to call me Danny, will I Karen?'

'No, Sean. You won't. I've never liked that name – it doesn't suit you. Never has.'

She took a third mug into the living room. 'Alright, Sean?' came the man's raised voice through the wall. 'Came by taxi, I see. Off the road at the moment, are we?'

'For the time being Brian, yes,' Danny shouted. 'Try not to fret about it though. You take it easy. Still between jobs?'

'Thankfully, yes.'

'Good on you. Me too.'

Danny's voice dropped back to conversational level as his sister came back into the room. 'How have you been, Karen? Sorry, it's been a while.'

'A while, he says. Seven years, Sean. Maybe more. Before that, it was probably Mum's funeral. You never made it to Dad's. Sorry. I'm not having a go. I'm glad you're here. I'm glad you're safe. And I'm glad you didn't die in that bloody car crash. I'm even more glad you didn't kill anyone else while you were at it. Tell me you're not still drinking.'

'No, I'm not. I stopped after the crash.'

'Did you get help?'

'Yes. Drugs and a bit of therapy. Then I decided to come here for a bit of alternative therapy.'

'How is it going? Not drinking, I mean. Do you still think about it?'

'Yes, I do. A lot.'

'I can't bear it. Alcohol,' she said, sipping at her tea. She pushed the plate of biscuits towards her brother. He didn't take one. 'I think that's why I married Brian. 'Cos he's a teetotaller. I won't have it in the house. The smell of it makes me retch. *Looking* at it makes me retch. You went the other way, didn't you? Couldn't get enough of it. Where's the sense in that? Never understood it.'

'Do you know Karen, I'm not sure I understand it either. I was really young when we were taken into care. I don't remember much about it. It's not like we've ever really talked about it.'

'Is that why you're here then Sean, to talk about it?'

'I don't think so. But at some stage, I suppose we should.'

Karen cradled her tea with both hands. Tears looked like they were about to come. Just as quickly, she seemed to send them away. 'Yes... yes we should. Anytime, Sean. Anytime.'

'Danny. I prefer Danny.'

'I know you do. But you'll always be Sean to me. *My* Sean.' Like a gentle tide, the threat of tears came and went once again. Karen pushed a long, whistling breath out through her teeth. 'I'm not ashamed of who I am,' she said. 'Or what happened to us. I'm fine with it. Really, I am. You should try it some time.'

'Yes. You're right. I should. I *am* trying.'

She took the hands from around her mug of tea and placed them around Danny's. They felt very warm. They sat there like that for several minutes. No words, just warm hands. 'You've come so far. No one I knew growing up went to college, let alone university. But you did it. And became a famous journalist to boot. Amazing. But you've never been any use at looking after yourself. Stopping drinking – that's a start, isn't it? Progress, I'd say.'

Danny got up and emptied the remainder of his tea into the sink. He washed the cup and put it on the draining board. 'I need to be going,' he said.

'Why are you here, Sean?' Karen said after a few minutes. 'Apart from the pleasure of my company, obviously. Why have you come back after all these years?'

'There's a case I covered years back. A child murder up at Oldham. It's always bothered me. I thought I'd take a look at it again. They never identified him. It would be good to put it to rest.'

Karen joined him at the sink. She washed her mug too. 'So, it's the past you're visiting, rather than me?'

'The two aren't mutually exclusive.'

'No, you're right. They're one and the same, love. Will you come again? Come for tea. You need fattening up a bit – you look skinny.'

'Yes, of course. I've got a lot of people to see – people involved in the case – but I'll make time, definitely.'

'Please do. I'll even try to call you Danny, if that helps.'

'It's fine, Karen. Call me what you like. It's up to you.'

She placed a hand on his shoulder as they walked towards the front door. 'See you, Brian,' Danny shouted. 'Don't overdo it.'

'Not going to happen, Sean lad.'

Karen hugged him. He left. She walked to the living room front window and waved. 'What was Sean after, love?' asked her husband. He was watching snooker on TV.

'I don't think he knows, to be honest.'

'Is he back permanently?'

'Depends.'

'What on?'

'He's digging around in something from years back. I suppose it's whether he finds what he's after.'

Brian paused the television, stood up and embraced his wife. 'Never ceases to amaze me that you and him are brother and sister. You've got nothing in common.'

'That's where you're wrong, Brian. We have plenty in common. Unfortunately.'

THIRTY-FOUR

7.45 pm Saturday 22 April 1990

From the expression on her face when she walked into the Alt children's home, DC Jan Cave wasn't expecting to see Danny having a cup of tea at the kitchen table. 'Aren't you supposed to be at death's door in hospital, Danny?' she asked.

'I didn't care for their tea, DC Cave. So, I thought I'd pop round here for one.'

'Can I tempt you, officer?' said Brenda, tapping the teapot with her lighter.

'Not just now, Brenda. Thanks all the same. I'm following up on some information from, well, from Danny here, actually. Apparently one of your kids was the subject of an attempted abduction. A lad called Paul? I wanted to speak to him about it, if possible?'

'Little Paul's not here I'm afraid,' Brenda said. 'One of the older ones, Jenny, has taken him out to the pictures. *Bill and Ted's Excellent Adventure*. Have you seen it, DC Cave? It's about a couple of eejits that don't know their arses from their elbows. You might like it. Can I take a message in the meantime?'

'I'd like it if you'd could bring him down to the station, Brenda.'

'I'll do my best, but he's not overly keen on the police isn't Little Paul. Some of your lot tore him from his mammy's arms a few years back, you might recall. The vice lads didn't like the way she was providing for him and dragged social

168

services into it. She *was* providing for him – she was a great mum. Dead now, of course. Overdose. She wasn't even on drugs until Little Paul was taken off her. Terrible business, Danny.'

'It sounds like it.' Danny sipped his tea, keeping his eyes on DC Cave across the rim of the mug.

'So, sure, I'll speak to Little Paul,' Brenda offered. 'But I'd be very surprised if he would want to talk to you. Stranger things have happened, though.'

'We can't help them if the kids won't talk,' DC Cave said.

'And they won't talk if they don't trust you,' Brenda replied. 'Trust comes first, DC Cave. Every time.'

'Well, trust works both ways, doesn't it?'

'Sometimes. Sometimes. But not very often as far as these kids are concerned. I'll be in touch. You'll see yourself out, yes?'

'Definitely.'

Brenda waited for the front door to close, then shouted for a teenage boy to check that she'd gone. He looked out of the front window and confirmed that she had. Jenny and Little Paul came slowly down the stairs. 'I don't get it, Brenda,' Jenny said, taking a seat at the table. 'One minute you're all lovey dovey with the cops and the next minute we're blanking them. I wish you'd make your mind up.'

'There's cops and then there's cops, Jenny,' Brenda said. 'DI Smithdown is okay. He's sound. I don't know much about that one, old frosty arse that was just here, but her boss DS Pym is a slippery shite and I don't trust him. It's up to Little Paul who he talks to. Not you, not me.'

Little Paul, his head barely clearing the height of the table, came alongside Jenny. He put his head in her lap and looked up at Danny. 'Don't you like that copper, Little Paul?' he asked. The boy shook his head.

'Little Paul hates 'em all, don't you mate?' said Jenny, stroking the short bristles of his hair. The boy nodded. 'Every last fookin' one of them,' she added.

Brenda turned to Danny. 'So. You're not buying this whole

Black Moss thing, then? Bit too cut and dried for you is it?'

'Just doesn't feel right. Little Paul gets a plastic bag on his head, and so do I? That's a bit of a coincidence, isn't it? DI Smithdown is out of the way dealing with personal issues and a body turns up at the Moss? Life's just not like that.'

'I knew him, you know,' Brenda said. 'Canning, the poor lad up at the Moss.'

'Everyone did, didn't they Bren?' added Jenny.

'There was a lost soul if ever there was one,' Brenda agreed. 'There's one in every town just like him. Went through the care system just like this lot. When he got chucked out the other end he never found his feet. Stumbled his way through life and then ends up like this. Awful. Nice and neat for the police though. They can crack on with sucking up to the Home Office while they're dealing with the Strangeways lads. That's where the brownie points are right now.'

Jenny spoke to the boy – his head was still on her lap. 'God, Vince Canning stunk, didn't he, Little Paul? What did you used to say? *Stunk like a fookin' polecat!* Fook knows how Little Paul knows what a polecat smells like, but that's what you used to say, didn't you little man?'

'Do you think he was the one who tried to grab you, Little Paul?' Danny asked.

Little Paul shook his head. 'You would have whiffed him, wouldn't you, mate?' stated Jenny. 'No disguising that stink. He always seemed harmless to me, though. He stunk, and he was a nuisance. But harmless enough.'

'I think this whole thing still stinks,' said Danny. 'He didn't say it to me outright, but DI Smithdown didn't seem one hundred percent convinced of it either. Until they identify the boy up at the Moss and everything is sorted properly, then I think the kids should carry on being ultra-cautious. Stay in and stay out of harm's way. Especially you, Little Paul.'

The boy climbed up onto Jenny's lap. He whispered in her ear and then slid down and walked off, taking the stairs two at a time before disappearing upstairs. Jenny leaned closer to Danny. 'Little Paul says he's stopping in until you say otherwise, Danny.'

'Christ Almighty!' exclaimed Brenda. 'I've never known Little Paul to pay a blind bit of notice to anyone but Jenny here. You've a friend for life there, Danny.'

'Lost souls, Brenda,' Danny said with a smile. 'We always stick together.'

THIRTY-FIVE

11.45 pm Monday 20 June 2016

Danny finished his room service steak and chips and placed the tray out in the hallway. He lay on his bed, fully clothed. It had been a long day and he was physically exhausted, but his mind raced, leaping between all the new pieces of information he'd come across. The hotel room was a good one, with plenty of space and a view across Manchester's city centre, but something inside the room was beginning to bother him: the light buzzing sound from the mini-bar fridge underneath the flat screen TV. He got off the bed and sat cross-legged on the floor in front of it. Then he opened the door and itemised what was inside:

Four bottles of Hildon still water
Four bottles of fizzy Pellegrino water
Two small cans of Schweppes Tonic water
Two cans of Diet Coke
Two full fat Cokes
Two cans of Fanta
Two tubs of plain Pringles
One Snickers bar
One Cadbury's Dairy Milk
One Green & Black's dark chocolate bar
One Green & Black's milk chocolate bar

Then it was onto the main event:

Four bottles of Heineken
Two double measures of Bacardi
Two double measures of Johnny Walker Black Label whisky

Two double measures of Jack Daniels
Two double measures of Stolichnaya vodka
Two double measures of Bombay gin
One half bottle of white wine

Danny stared at the contents. He shook the door very gently, listening to the clank and clatter of the bottles inside. There was, he calculated, just enough to get fairly solidly drunk if he were to tackle the whole lot. *Start with the lagers, onto the wine, then work your way through the spirits, saving the Stolichnaya for last. Pringles will keep you going if you get peckish. Leave the chocolate, bit fattening.*

He pulled out one of the Heinekens and held the bottle against his cheek to test how cold it was. It was okay. *Hotel fridges never get really cold,* Danny thought. He kept it pressed against his face for twenty seconds, then returned it to its slot, closed the fridge door and put a chair in front of it. Then he found the fridge's plug and pulled it from the wall. The thrum of the fridge stopped.

When sleep came, it was a fearful business for Danny Johnston, formerly known as Sean Doyle. He was running down a path through open countryside. It was cold and dark and he wasn't wearing a shirt. The path was filled with rubbish, slowing him down. There was a gate ahead but the closer he got, the bigger the gate appeared to be. He tried to climb it, but he was too small. Or the gate was too large. Maybe both. He looked around. The fence stretched left to right as far as he could see in both directions. Something was rushing towards him from behind, shouting his name. It was coming so fast it was moving the air forwards. Danny could feel the air pressing onto the back of his neck as he turned to see what was there. It slammed into him and woke Danny up.

THIRTY-SIX

5 pm Tuesday 24 April 1990

Mike Sharston was fussing and moving papers from one area of his desk to the another when Danny walked to the doorway of his office and tapped on the frame of the open door. He'd been told to stay away for at least a week, but with the Black Moss case seemingly dealt with, he had nothing to occupy him.

Sharston's normally flushed complexion appeared to have been moving up to a purple-tinged colour chart of unhealthiness over the last few weeks; his collar seemed even more strained against his neck and his gut pushed further over his trouser belt. *A pending heart attack in a sports jacket,* thought Danny. 'Yes. Right. Come in,' Sharston said, still seemingly engrossed in his ongoing paper migration task. 'Danny. Yes. How's that head of yours?'

Danny used both hands to feel up and down his face. 'Largely intact. Sorry about the whole passing out in the newsroom thing. I feel a bit of an arse.'

'Well, we were concerned about you, weren't we Beth?' The newsreader had quietly appeared at Danny's shoulder.

'I've barely slept, Mike,' she said with a very small smile.

'Yes. Right. Steady, Beth. Try and keep those emotions in place, will you?'

'I'll do my best,' she replied. *They can't resist it,* Danny said to himself. *They're still taking the piss.*

'Look,' said Sharston. 'Joking aside, I do actually have a responsibility to protect you from yourself here. I can't have reporters getting their heads mashed in and keeling over in my newsroom. But the fact you were clearly in a mess, yet still brought in that interview about the Oldham murder-suicide speaks volumes to me. Fair play to you, Danny.'

'Thanks, Mike.' *An actual compliment. Jesus Christ.*

'Even though you're still a dickhead for coming in with a concussion,' added Beth.

'Quite. Well, don't be fooled by Beth's eternally frosty demeanour. She's been very impressed by the way you've kept at it with this kiddie murder thing. It was a thankless task, as far away from the action of Strangeways as it's possible to get. But you stuck at it without moaning.'

'He moaned quite a bit, Mike. To be fair,' Beth added.

'Alright, Beth,' said Danny. 'Mike's doing just fine, thanks.'

'Anyway,' the news editor continued. 'The post-mortem has confirmed – it was definitely suicide. So, barring the inquest to dot the i's and cross the t's, it's done with. So, when you're feeling a bit better, we should get you down to Strangeways before it all finishes. It's down to the absolute hardcore now, about seven of them, so it can't be long. Though, to be fair, I've been saying that since the start of the month.'

'I'm happy to go now, Mike, really I am,' Danny offered.

'That might be a bit premature,' the news editor said. 'Your face still looks like a dog's been at it. Maybe in a day or two.'

Beth was about to speak but she was interrupted by a shout from the other side of the newsroom. 'Mike! Lord's been snatched. It might be game on.'

Alan Lord, a convicted murderer serving a life sentence, had been seen as the second in command amongst the rioters, likely to be the last to give up after 'ringleader' Paul Taylor. If he'd gone, then the end could be very near. 'Right, who have we got?' asked the news editor. He stood up and scanned the newsroom. Three sports reporters, a cleaner, a secretary and a university placement student whose name no one could remember.

'Where the fuck is everyone?' Sharston shouted. 'I mean, seriously. This is supposed to be the biggest independent radio station newsroom outside of London. I ask again. Where the fuck is everyone?'

'Robert Crane is at the scene – has been since day one. The night time crew are asleep,' itemised Beth. 'We've got three off sick with stress, whatever that is. The day reporters have just finished and are in the pub – so at the moment, the only people free are the sports reporters and that placement student over there.'

'What's her name?'

'I have no idea,' replied Beth.

'Danny. Looks like you're on.'

Fucking hell!

THIRTY-SEVEN

11.45 am Tuesday 21 June 2016

'Mr Pym?' Danny asked as the cottage door opened. The house was small but clearly expensive and well maintained, sitting at the edge of the village of Prestbury in the Cheshire commuter belt. An equally well-maintained man in his sixties looked at Danny with a slightly annoyed expression on his face. A waft of potpourri and croissants came with him.

'It is,' confirmed the older man. 'Look, there's a sticker on the door that says we never buy anything from cold callers…'

'I'm not selling, Mr Pym. 'It's help I'm after. Your help.'

'Do I know you?'

'Hopefully, you'll remember me. My name's Danny Johnston. I'm a journalist. I used to be, anyway.'

A woman's voice came from inside the house. 'Who is it, Jim?' She approached the door and stopped just behind the former DS. She was also in her sixties and just as well turned out as her husband. 'Oh, my goodness, Daniel Johnston,' she said. 'Jim's always mentioning you, aren't you Jim? Every time he sees you on TV it's always, *I remember him when he was at Manchester Radio.*'

Danny extended a hand towards the woman. 'That was a very long time ago. It's Mrs Pym, I presume? Nice to meet you. Please call me Danny. Everyone does. Though you used to have a few other names for me, didn't you Mr Pym?'

'One or two Danny, yes. One or two. Jean, I'll take our guest to the summer house. Tea?'

'Yes. That'd be lovely… Jim.'

The ex-detective winced slightly when Danny used his first name. He led him down the side of the house to a path across an immaculately trimmed lawn. Under a willow tree was a top-of-the-line summer house. Pym produced a key and opened the door. The key, attached to an elastic fob, snapped back onto his belt once the door had been opened. Pym gestured towards a rattan armchair and Danny settled into the chair's floral cushions. He looked at the dried flowers, photos and figurines inside the summer house. 'Very nice. Retirement seems to be treating you well, Mr Pym.'

'Yes. It's nice out here. Nicer than Oldham, that's for sure.'

'They call it the Golden Triangle, don't they?' said Danny. 'Prestbury, Wilmslow and Alderley Edge. You can barely move for all the four-by-fours and footballers.'

Pym stared at Danny. 'What do you want?' he asked, quietly.

Mrs Pym arrived with a tray of tea and biscuits. She smiled at Danny as she put it on a small table between the two men. She seemed to sense her presence wasn't required and walked back towards the house. 'I often think I should have joined the police,' Danny said. 'You only need to do thirty years then you cash in your chips and retire with a lovely pension. Especially when you leave on an assistant chief constable's salary.'

'You have to put up with thirty years' worth of shit though. I'll ask again, what do you want, Danny?'

'I'm looking at an old case. One that's never been quite resolved for me.'

'And which case might that be?'

'The Black Moss kid. Remember that one, Mr Pym?'

'Yes, I do. Very much. You might find this hard to believe, but I've thought about that kid a lot over the years. I really have.'

'Can I cut to the chase?'

'Please do.'

'Why didn't you give a shit about that kid back in 1990?'

Pym poured himself a cup of tea. He didn't pour Danny one. 'That's not true, Danny. It's not true and you know it.'

'I don't. I don't know it at all, Mr Pym. It felt like me and Mr Smithdown were the only people who thought that boy was worth anything. Worth going the extra yard for. Worthy of *anything*. It seemed like that kid was an inconvenience for you while you were seen to be mopping up the mess at Strangeways. Got you that promotion you wanted, didn't it? ACC Pym. Lovely. Just what you were after.'

Danny poured himself some tea and took two biscuits. Then a third. Pym stared at him; he was leaning forward now, tense in his seat. 'Listen, I appreciate you've experienced not so much a fall from grace as a fucking skydive in recent weeks, but you've got no right coming here making accusations to try to make yourself feel better. Don't lecture me about not caring. I saw that kid laid out on slab, Danny. I saw what had been done to him. We did our best with what we had at the time. It was chaos not conspiracy. I wouldn't have put DI Smithdown and DC Cave on it if I didn't want it solving. Our best people, no question about it. Was it ideal? No, it wasn't. A combination of Strangeways, DI Smithdown's wife being so very ill and… other factors made it a very difficult case. We did our best.'

'What other factors?' asked Danny.

'DI Smithdown's decision to involve you for a kick off. He was a good cop. A great cop. But he used you, Danny. He used you to get at me. Leaking stuff to you, getting you to run stories that he knew were just guesswork on his part. Sending kites up to see if the wind would catch them. That's all it was. At the time you probably thought you were something special. He'd done it loads of times with different reporters. He'd even used his daughter, for fuck's sake. Encouraged her to become a journalist so he could undermine me. His own daughter! How low is that?'

'He's a good man. A better one than you.'

179

'Grow up, lad.'

'I'm nearly fifty, Mr Pym.'

'Then fucking act like it,' he shouted. 'Coming here with your pious act. You were as bad as him. You were trying to make a name for yourself, coming up to the hill country, giving us the benefit of your journalistic wisdom. Fuck off. You were just a kid, you didn't have a clue and it appears you still don't. If you want to do some good – and I assume that's what this is all about, trying to ease your conscience about pissing your life and what talent you had away – then try to identify that kid. Do that. Find out who that kid was and provide a bit of closure for his family.'

'The only way to ID the kid is to ID the murderer, Mr Pym.'

'We know who the fucking murderer was! That sad sack of shit they found up at the Moss with a broken bottle of whisky and a suicide note. Cut and dried. I know it might have seemed too easy from the outside, but it was bang to rights.'

'Really? At one stage you were trying to pin it on Peter Jeffries.'

'That's an outright lie, Danny. Where the fuck did you get that from?'

'One of my colleagues at the radio station said they'd been briefed, off the record, that Jeffries topped himself after killing that kid. Drove off the road on purpose. That could have only come from you.'

Pym leant even further forward. 'It. Did. Not. Come. From. Me,' he stated his finger hitting the tea tray with every punctuation point. 'Jeffries was a gobshite who loved the sound of his own voice, but he was no danger to kids. I'm sure of that. He'd been drinking that night, no question of it. But nothing suggested he was involved or that he'd crashed on purpose.'

'They why would someone smear his name after his death?'

'I have no idea. Honestly. No idea whatsoever. That's the

first I've heard of it in twenty-five years. You seem to have cooked up quite a conspiracy theory here, Danny. I don't believe in conspiracies. I really don't.'

'What do you believe in?'

'Silence, Danny. That's how bad things happen. Through silence.'

'Did you keep silent about anything connected with this, Mr Pym?'

Former Assistant Chief Constable James Pym leant back in his seat. 'No, I didn't. Did you?'

THIRTY-EIGHT

5.50 pm Tuesday 24 April 1990

Rather than wait for a cab in the rush hour, Gary Keenan volunteered to take Danny down to Strangeways. It was, the engineer said, the right time to do a gear check and swap the radio car's battery again. 'Don't want the biggest story we've ever had to go tits up at the last minute now, do we?' Gary asked as they drove at high speed though Manchester city centre.

'I'm going to treat that as a rhetorical question, Gary,' Danny said, gripping the side of the car seat as they jumped a red light, crossed the main Deansgate road and headed down Blackfriars Street towards Strangeways.

'You can treat it to a slap-up meal at the Midland Hotel as far as I'm concerned, kidder. No point in you covering the end of the riot if no one can hear you 'cos of faulty gear and a battery that's flatter than a witch's tit.'

The hoppy tang of the Boddington's brewery next door to the prison caught Danny by surprise, as did the log jam of traffic around the approach roads to the jail. Gary pulled into a side street and got out of the car. He popped the boot and lifted a new car battery out. 'Come on, soft bollocks,' he said. 'We're walking.'

'You'll get a ticket there,' Danny said, glancing at the double yellow lines Gary had parked on. 'I couldn't give a flying shit – stick it on the pile with all the others,' Gary replied, slamming the boot shut. For a big man he moved surprisingly quickly across the road towards the jail. Danny struggled to keep up. There seemed to be a general movement of people towards the prison; the word was clearly out that some kind of end point was near. Danny and Gary became part of the flow. The crowd was five deep at the perimeter fence and the pair had to push their way through to get to the radio car. Robert Crane was pacing up and down alongside the vehicle. His usually dapper appearance was no more: his suit was crumpled, his normally slicked-back hair had tumbled into his face and his eyes were underscored with dark semi-circles. He smelled of cigarettes and stale sweat. 'I think Bobby has gone feral on us,' Gary said to Danny in a stage whisper. 'He looks like a shit in a bucket.'

Crane waved to Gary, but his face clouded with disappointment when he spotted Danny. 'Are you the cavalry, then?' he asked sipping from a can of Coke.

'It would appear so,' Danny replied, glancing at the inside of the radio car and seeing the piles of drink cans, food cartons, crisp packets, sweet wrappers and newspapers that were inside. *Makes my car look like a palace.*

Gary Keenan was looking at the mess too. 'Christ, we're going to have to burn this radio car when this story is over and done with. Right, let's get this battery swapped before the seven o' clock news. You kids play nicely while I sort this out.'

The chief reporter pushed a hand through his hair and looked at Danny. 'Did you bring anything for me?' he asked.

Danny had a plastic carrier bag in one hand; the placement student whose name no one could remember had given it to him. From it he produced a new shirt, still folded and shrink-wrapped. It was dark brown with heavy black stripes and was branded with a name Danny had never heard of before. It was, by anyone's estimation, a cheap and unpleasant-looking shirt. 'Where the fuck did you get that? Shit Shirts R Us? It's a monstrosity.'

'It's what I was given. Don't shoot the shit shirt messenger,' said Danny, quietly pleased with his response.

'Christ alive,' Crane said. He pulled the wrapping away, shook out the myriad clips and pins holding it in place and held it up to the fading, early evening light. 'It'll have to do, I suppose.' Crane took off his jacket and the shirt he was wearing. He bundled up his old shirt with the remaining packaging and shoved it into the plastic bag Danny was carrying. He put it on. It looked worse on him than it did in the packet.

'So, what's the plan?' Danny asked as he looked around for a bin to put the bag into.

'The plan, young Daniel, is this,' said Crane. 'See those metal barriers over there? Any time now, some bod from the Home Office will pop out and give us an update on the situation inside. It's basically a numbers tally. Someone will ask if they plan to retake the jail by force, blah blah blah. Then we have our top line for the seven.'

'So, shall I go and wait for the Home Office bod to come out?' asked Danny.

'Will you fuck. I'm doing that. You never know, he might actually come out and say something interesting, in which case, I'm having it. You, on the other hand, will go among the crowd and vox pop them about whether they think it's all about to come to an end. After seven o'clock we have an agreement down here that all journos down tools and take a break. That way, no one scoops anyone else. We go to the Woolpack up there.' Crane pointed to an old-fashioned pub a hundred yards up the road from the jail. 'You can wait here just in case. I'll bring you back some crisps. Then, when I've had two, possibly three pints of Boddington's finest bitter, I will return, make sure all is well, use your vox pop for the eight, then I will fuck off home and you will stop here for the night. Any questions?'

'Just one.'

'Shoot.'

'Can I have nuts rather than crisps, please? And a couple of tins to see me through?'

THIRTY-NINE

1.30 pm Tuesday 21 June 2016

As the tram travelled south from Manchester city centre, Danny looked at the list of people to track down that he'd scribbled on his hotel notepad. Robert Crane was now a political lobbyist, working back in London. He was reasonably far down Danny's list of people of interest anyway. *A suit full of fuck all. Always was, always will be.* Mike Sharston had died in 2005. Heart attack. *What a shocker,* thought Danny. Brenda from the care home had passed away in 2010. *Shame, she was a lovely person.* With her gone it would be very difficult indeed to track down the likes of Jenny and Little Paul.

He got off the tram. There had been no trams in Didsbury when he'd lived here. According to Gary Keenan, Beth Hall had also been 'not too well' but she'd seemed pleased to hear from Danny via Facebook Messenger the previous night and gave him her address. She now lived in West Didsbury, not far from Danny's old flat.

He followed Google Maps and turned into Beth's road as instructed by the apps' voice. Her house was an impressive three-storey detached affair tucked into the corner of a cul-de-sac. There was a ramp fitted to the front door to allow wheelchair access and large handles were attached either side of the front door. *She must still live with her folks. They're clearly getting on a bit.*

There was a video intercom at the door; he looked up at the camera and waved. *Her folks must be very security-conscious.* Danny went to push the buzzer, but he heard Beth's distinctive voice interrupt him before he could press the button. It annoyed him a little, but it was cheerier than he remembered: 'Danny Johnston! Come in, come in.'

The door buzzed open and Danny stepped inside. He noticed a stairlift attached to the wall running up the stairs and more handles attached to door frames along the hallway. He could smell fresh baking. There was also an undercurrent of another slightly harsh, medicinal smell that he didn't care for at all. 'In the kitchen,' instructed the voice, 'come through!'

Danny did as he was asked. There was a small ramp levelling off the step into the kitchen; Beth Hall was next to the oven, setting out a plate of chocolate brownies. With a deft movement of her right hand she manoeuvred her wheelchair 180 degrees so she faced the kitchen table. 'Sit, sit,' she instructed. 'It's brownie o'clock. Tea?

'Yes please, thanks.' Her manner was bright and undeniably cheery. Danny didn't quite know how to react. She was wearing a black polo neck jumper with her hair cut into a bob – the colour was much more vivid than he remembered. Her make-up was immaculate, with her lipstick especially bright and freshly applied.

'Bet you never knew I was such a domestic goddess, did you, Danny?'

'No, Beth. You have hidden depths.'

'Don't I just? How long has it been? No, don't! It's going to be some horrendous figure that will make me feel very old, isn't it?'

'A quarter of a century, I'd say. At least.'

'Noooo! I don't want to hear it,' Beth cried, laughing as she put her hands over her ears. 'You look great, Danny. Super healthy. I heard about your problems in London. Really sorry. But maybe it was a Godsend. Is that a bad thing to say? You know what I mean, I'm sure.'

'I know exactly what you mean. It's fine. You're probably right. Crashing into a tree – best thing that ever happened to me. How about you? How have you been?'

She poured tea for them both. The mugs were earthy, handmade and fashionable. 'I've been pretty good, actually,' she replied. 'I write, I do some radio consultancy stuff, I lecture at universities; can't complain. Apart from the whole wheelchair thing – I'm perfectly capable of complaining that. Otherwise, not bad at all.'

'Can I ask about the whole wheelchair thing? Sorry. I didn't know.'

'M.S.' she said, in a business-like way. 'Comes and goes. I don't always need the chair. A crutch is fine a lot of the time. No big deal. I don't let it get to me. Much. Anyway. Have a brownie. Have two – and tell me what brings you up here. Manchester Radio's brightest star. Mr Network!'

'Yeah, well, not anymore,' Danny said.

'You had a great run,' she insisted, her eyes shiny with pride. 'Lots of people at the station in the old days thought they were going to go all the way. But you *actually did it*. All the way. A fantastic achievement.'

'I don't remember anyone thinking I was very good back then. I was the runt of the litter. Mr Invisible. You were horrible to me!' Danny was laughing now, but inside he was serious.

'I never was!' Beth protested, with a wink. 'I was harsh but fair, at all times.'

'Fairly harsh, more like.'

'Really? I thought I was the model of encouragement and understanding.'

'That must have been on my days off.'

'We were all very young and ambitious and competitive and... it was an amazing time,' she said, leaning back in her wheelchair. 'It was like we were at the centre of the news universe. Moss Side, Madchester, Gunchester, IRA bombs, all the trouble at The Haçienda club, Strangeways – everyone was looking away from London and looking at us. In Manchester. Amazing. An amazing time and amazing stories.'

'There's one story I'm still interested in, Beth. One that I want to look at again.'

'I know!' she said, putting down her mug of tea. 'The Black Moss boy. Everyone's talking about it. Amazing. What a great idea. You should do a documentary or write a book.'

'Who's talking about it?'

Beth pointed to a battered laptop that was open on the kitchen table close to Danny. He slid it over to her. A few taps and she turned the screen around, so Danny could see it. It was a Facebook page called 'I Survived Manchester Radio'. The top post was entitled 'Danny Johnston Back in Manchester'. There were forty-five comments; one stated that Danny was a 'great guy, great reporter, good to see him back on his old stomping ground'. Another was more succinct: 'Let's hope he didn't drive back – silly old piss artist'. Both had plenty of likes. The second one had also garnered a few laughing emojis. He clicked on the post – the author was Robert Crane.

'Always nice to hear from old showbiz mates,' Danny said, pushing the laptop away. 'He was always a charmer, was our Bobby.'

'He was a glory hunter, out for himself the whole time,' added Beth. 'And he was a lazy bastard, ducking out of the jobs he thought were beneath him – the poor boy at Black Moss being a prime example.'

'What do you mean?'

'That morning the boy's body was discovered. I called Robert Crane to go out there. He called you out because he didn't fancy dragging his arse up to Oldham. He wanted to stay at Strangeways – where the prizes were. Or at least, where he thought they were. Don't you remember?'

'I've been pissed for the last thirty years, Beth. I can barely remember you, let alone the finer points of what happened in 1990. That's why I'm doing this. To try to fill in the gaps.'

'Well, I'm very offended you barely remember me, Danny.'

'Just a figure of speech, Beth. I very much remember you. Though it's fair to say I remember you a bit differently. I was frightened to death of you. Back in the day, I mean.'

'I'm sure you weren't.'

'I was. I really was.'

'Well, I'm not that frightening anymore, am I?'

'No, you're not Beth.'

'So, what are you going to do with the Black Moss story?' she asked, blowing across the surface of her tea. 'A book, maybe? I think it'd make an amazing book.'

Danny nodded. 'It's definitely crossed my mind. Sure. A book. Why not?'

'If you could identify the boy,' Beth offered. 'That'd be the scoop.'

'Indeed. Tall order, though.'

'Keep me posted,' she said. 'If I can help in any way, let me know.'

After saying his goodbyes to Beth, Danny texted Kate to ask about another name on his list: DC Jan Cave. Kate had already been through her father's notebooks and found a business card with her name on: *Jan Cave – Child Protection Consultant*. She'd sent Danny a photo of it.

He thanked her via text. More messages followed:

Still ok for dinner 2nite?

Sure. What shall I bring?

Just yourself. CU 6.30 ish.

Jan Cave's card didn't have an address but a swift internet search for her name and profession via the Companies House website showed that the business was registered in Old Trafford, halfway between Didsbury and the centre of Manchester. *Perfect. I'll just swing past. If she's there, she's there. Then back to the hotel, shower up and off to Kate's.*

The red brick mill building where the former DC's offices were situated was a twenty-minute tram ride away, then just a few minutes' walk from the station. The mill had been through many lives and uses over the years. Now, according to the huge map sign at the entrance, it was divided up into hundreds of businesses of every type, from indoor climbing to Cave Consultants.

Danny made his way around the site until he got to the unit he wanted, which was tucked away close to the canal that ran alongside the mill. Climbing a small metal set of steps up to the front door, he found a panel full of buttons – many had handwritten cards signifying the business it connected to. He pressed the one next to a white card with Cave Consultants printed very neatly on it.

No reply. *Should have sent a message,* Danny thought. He pressed again. *No reply.* He turned on the steps; former DC Jan Cave was there right in front of him, her face slightly too close to his. 'Hi, Danny,' she said in a slightly amused monotone. 'Coming in or are you just going to hang around here?'

'Alright, err Jan?' Danny felt uncomfortable using her first name. *What am I supposed to call her, former DC Cave?* 'Sure. Thanks.'

Danny looked at her. She wore a smart black trouser suit and a white shirt. Her hair was still pulled back from her face – as it had always been in 1990 – but considering she must be in her late fifties, she was largely unchanged from the last time he'd seen her. 'I've been expecting you,' she stated, pressing a four-digit number into a security pad mounted next to the door. As she went in, she picked up some mail and motioned for Danny to follow her across the small hallway. There were four of five doorways; she headed to one tucked away underneath an iron stairway.

'Really?' Danny asked. 'How come?'

'They have this thing called the internet these days,' she pointed out. 'Even the police use it. You should try it sometime. We have ex-officers' forums, Facebook and WhatsApp groups – you name it. I know you've been to see Mr Pym – you got chucked out I hear. So now you're here to see me. Inevitable, really. Tea?'

'No thanks, I've had gallons today – my back teeth are floating.' Danny smiled to himself for using a Manchester expression he remembered from his childhood. He looked around the small office. It was well ordered and efficient looking. There were framed certificates on the wall and several photos, including one of her with DS Pym.

'Have a seat,' she said. Danny sat in a leather swivel chair; Jan Cave placed herself in a chair behind the modern grey desk, which dominated the tiny space.

'Do you mind if I record the conversation,' he asked, putting a hand into his inside jacket pocket. 'I'm thinking of writing a book.'

'Yes, I do mind,' she snapped. 'I don't want to obstruct you, Danny, but this is just a nonsense.'

'Oh. Okay. And why's that, then?'

She leant forward so she was even closer to him. He could smell soap. An old-fashioned, incongruous smell. 'Do you honestly think I'm going to assist you with some weird ego trip? So, you can write a book about how the police messed it all up back in 1990 and how you came to back home to save the day? John Smithdown might buy into it, but I certainly won't. This seems to have very little to do with that kid up at Black Moss and everything to do with you trying to rehabilitate your reputation at our expense.'

'No, it isn't,' he insisted, surprised at how close he was to shouting. 'It really fucking isn't... *Jan*. It really is about that kid. The kid that no one gave a shit about. The kid that your bosses didn't think would get them a promotion and put their time and effort into Strangeways instead. So, don't lecture me about being in it for myself, because you really don't get it.'

'Look,' she explained, matching him for volume. 'No one claimed to be an expert in child protection back then, but we worked hard with what we had and we did our best. That kid was almost certainly a missing from home that had the misfortune to come across a very bad person indeed. Persistent, missing-from-home kids were considered a nuisance back then. The record-keeping by the homes they were dumped in was nonexistent. No one cared about the root of the problem – that families that can't cope with the most basic things in life can't be expected to cope with the responsibility of children. Family support units – the idea of properly organised police involvement in child protection – didn't even kick in until around 1991. After the Black Moss case, I dedicated the rest of my career to trying to stop things like that ever happening again. A dead child face down by a reservoir and we can't even identify him. Why? Because no one thought it was important to keep kept track of kids like that? In 19-fucking-90? A disgrace. *That's* why I do child protection work to this day.' She moved an arm around her office, indicating the meticulously framed certificates that trumpeted her child protection qualifications. 'You're not the only one who was changed by what happened at Black Moss, Danny.'

'Okay. You said you didn't want to obstruct me. Answer me one thing. Vincent Canning. The suicide. What was he like? Tell me about him. Did he have family?'

Jan Cave, for the first time since they had sat down, leant back in her chair. 'Never met him – I only knew him by reputation. Saw him a few times through the cell peepholes at Oldham nick. He was a sad case. To be honest, looking at his record, I was surprised that he did what he did. Not that he killed himself, but that he'd snatched and kill a kid. But the evidence was there. Undeniable.'

'What about Peter Jeffries?' countered Danny. 'Your station was putting it out that he was somehow involved... ran his car off the road on purpose.'

'News to me,' she said, shaking her head. 'Who told you that?'

Danny hesitated. 'Another journalist told me that Oldham Police were actively pushing that line after the crash. True?'

'Absolutely not. Which "other journalist" was this? Kate Smithdown, girl reporter? Can't imagine where she could have gotten that theory from. Look. Her dad was an amazing copper. One of the best. But he wasn't himself during the Black Moss investigation. And he certainly isn't himself now. Poor soul.'

'One more question, Jan.'

'Okay.'

'Is there any doubt in your mind that Vincent Canning killed that little boy?'

'Do you know what? John Smithdown did an absolutely thorough job on it. Astonishing really, considering everything else he had on his plate – with his wife in The Christie and everything. He still managed to do a very professional job with Canning. I would have helped but I kept getting dragged back into other cases – and Strangeways, of course. Barely a minute went by without something to do with Strangeways needing your attention back then. So, to answer your question, I have no doubts at all about Canning's death and that he was responsible for the boy's murder. None whatsoever. The tragedy is that the chances of ID-ing the boy died up on the Moss with Canning. Cowardly bastard.'

There was silence. Jan Cave had clearly said her piece and wasn't planning to say any more. Danny thanked her and left.

FORTY-ONE

6.15 pm Tuesday 24 April 1990

After Robert Crane had received the latest head count from the Home Office and headed off in the direction of the pub, Danny went through the crowd outside Strangeways, looking for likely targets for vox pops. He hated doing vox pops. *Excuse me, sir/madam – can I garner your opinion on something completely hypothetical that you are clearly unqualified to speak about in any way, shape or form? Many thanks.*

Manchester Radio was unusually popular among the kind of people who would be hanging around Strangeways of a Tuesday evening, so it wasn't usually too difficult to get people to speak. Most were delighted at the chance of being on their favourite station. Danny looked hard at the people gathered around the jail. He quickly found a man whose friend – or at least the friend of a friend – was still inside the jail. Though he wasn't totally sure. He thought that the siege *has gotta end sometime, hannit? Can't go on forevoh, cannit?* He also asked Danny if he had any weed.

Danny then found some young women aged about twenty who were on their way into Manchester and thought they'd just take a look at what all the fuss was about before it all ended. Only one was prepared to speak – she believed the jail should have been stormed by the SAS on day one.

The Golden Rule of vox pops is that you need at least three. So, three was all that Danny had any intention of getting. He saw a woman in her forties her fingers gripping the mesh of the high-perimeter fence. She was staring at the roof. Two or three silhouettes could be seen, trotting nimbly across the roof top towards the main rotunda. Her hair, bleached white but with jet black roots, was pulled back from her face with a large elastic band. She wore an oversized black cardigan and had a clump of tissue in one hand. 'Hi,' said Danny. 'I'm sorry to bother you. I'm from Manchester Radio and I was wondering if I could ask you when you think the riot is going to finish?'

She didn't turn to look at Danny. 'Wouldn't you be better off asking how the riot started?'

'Sorry?'

'How it started,' she repeated, still looking at the jail. 'Rather than playing a stupid guessing game about when I think it will end, why not ask how it started? A prison built for nine hundred people, rammed with sixteen hundred souls. Three to a cell, shitting in a single bucket that's overflowing by morning. Locked in their cells twenty-three hours a day. Staff brutality. No grievance procedure. Food that a dog would cross the street to avoid. Why not ask about that?'

'I'm sure that will all come out once it's all over,' Danny said, slightly regretting his choice of interviewee.

'Are you sure?'

'Yes. So, when do you think the riot will finish?'

'It's not a riot. It's a protest.'

'Okay. When do you think the protest will finish?'

The woman looked at Danny. Her face was so pale it looked unreal, like she was wearing stage make-up. 'Tomorrow,' she stated and walked away before Danny could turn on his Marantz.

He watched her go, then found someone else who said they wanted it to carry on as long as possible as this was the best entertainment currently available in Manchester. Danny went back to the radio car, fed the clips back to the station and waited for Crane to return from the pub.

FORTY-TWO

6.25 pm Tuesday 21 June 2016

Danny had debated long and hard about what to bring to Kate's house for dinner. He wasn't even close to the stage where he could buy alcohol – even if it wasn't for him. He'd opted for some upmarket soft drinks from a hipster deli in Manchester city centre; overpriced ginger beer and dandelion and burdock in bottles with complex-looking opening mechanisms – and some flowers. He wanted to get something for Kate's son too, so he opted for a very large bag of Skittles from a nearby twenty-four-hour mini market. *Think I've got it covered.*

A cab took him out to Kate's address in Uppermill: *Ah. The posh part of Oldham.* It dropped him down a winding path leading to a large, detached house backing onto the Huddersfield canal. The air was warm and filled with birdsong and reassuring chugs and chatter from the canal. As Danny approached the front door a young boy with a mop of jet black curly hair came skidding down the path on a mountain bike, flinging pebbles onto the front step. 'Hi. Are you Danny?' he asked, in a clipped, not-very-Oldham-sounding accent. He stepped off the bike and laid it onto the path in one smooth movement.

'I am. You must be Jonathan.' Danny put down the carrier bag of drinks and extended his hand towards the boy. They shook.

'Are those for my mum?' Jonathan asked, nodding at the flowers in Danny's other hand.

'They are. And these are for you.' Danny pulled out the bag of Skittles and waved them gently in the boy's direction.

'I'm not allowed those,' he said in a serious voice. His face immediately broke out onto a huge smile as he quickly took them from Danny. 'Thanks a lot! Mum's in the garden. See you.'

He tucked the sweets into the panniers attached to his bike and made off at great speed. Danny made his way around the side of the house. Kate was laying out plates and serving spoons onto a wooden garden table. She was wearing white shorts and a light blue polo shirt and smiled at Danny as he approached. 'Hi. You haven't seen Jonathan, have you?'

'About ten? Dark curly hair? Carrying a massive bag of Skittles? Yeah, he's just gone off on his bike.'

'Christ, Danny. You certainly know how to please a kid and annoy a parent, don't you? I'll be scraping him off the ceiling at bedtime. I'll text him.'

'I've brought a load more sugar in liquid form too,' he said, taking the deli bottles out of the carrier bag and placing them on the table. 'And I got these for you.' He put flowers on the table too.

'Aww, thanks Danny,' said Kate. 'We'll make a viable human being of you yet. The food won't be long. What do you want to drink? I wasn't sure what you'd want, so I bought every soft drink in the local shop. How's your investigation going? Any news?'

'It's not an investigation,' he corrected. 'It's more of a refresher – and it's making things more confusing than ever, to be honest. Things just aren't as I remember them. I suppose that's what being pissed all these years does for you. Your perception of things is totally unreliable. People I thought were horrible are being really helpful. People I thought would be helpful are no use at all – no offence.'

'Quite a bit of offence taken. But, continue,' she requested, pointing at some French bread and indicating that Danny should cut it.

'I know one thing: that people are a damn sight easier to

track down now than they used to be. We used to have to go through all the Smithdowns in the Oldham phone book to find someone in the old days. Now everyone is just a social media click away.'

'And what are you planning to do with all these refreshers? You don't honestly think you can solve this and be the big hero? Put everything right?'

Danny didn't say anything. He carried on cutting bread then pushed back the top of one of the drinks he'd brought with him and took a sip. It was bitingly sweet. Kate stopped setting the table. 'You do, don't you? You think this is your ticket out of Shitsville, don't you? The redemption express.'

'It's funny – that's pretty much what the cops have said to me but it's a bit more complicated than that,' Danny said, setting aside his drink and pouring some iced war instead. 'I don't know. A book, maybe? Is it going to be like this all evening or are you just being horribly judgemental before your son returns?'

'No, I plan to be horribly judgemental without any pauses whatsoever. Ah, speak of the Devil.'

Kate's son arrived in the garden and headed straight for the table. He grabbed a chunk of bread and bit it in half. 'Jonathan! Hands washed first please, you mucky bugger.'

'I'll bet you never asked Danny if he washed his hands,' the boy answered, brightly. 'Have you washed your hands, Danny?'

'Not washed 'em for years, mate. Never found the need to. It's a myth put about by mums.'

'Hands! Now!' said Kate, pointing at Danny and making a zipping motion across her mouth with her hand. Jonathan ran through the open French windows into the kitchen, ran his hands under the tap for a matter of seconds, then ran back out, wiping his hands on his jeans. Danny winked at him as the boy grabbed another piece of bread and sat down.

'How's your grandad, Jonathan?' asked Danny. 'I knew him when he was a policeman in the olden days when dinosaurs roamed the hills above Oldham and there were no mobile phones.'

'He wanted to come, but Mum says she wouldn't get a word in edgeways if he did and that you'd ignore her. So, he got banned.'

'Pass the salad to Danny, Jonathan,' said Kate. 'Before I chuck you in the canal.'

The table seemed to have enough food on it for a dozen people, let alone two adults and a ten-year-old. Danny helped himself to spiced chicken, cous cous, corn on the cob and salad. The freshness of it shocked his taste buds – he'd been living on train and hotel food since he'd arrived back in Manchester – but there was something else: *this is the first time I've eaten with people for quite some time. God, it's so nice.*

Danny didn't say too much. He watched as Kate and her son joked with each other as they ate, gently making fun without harm or malice. Jonathan coerced Danny into a little garden football – mother and son were shocked and amused at how awful he was. Afterwards, Danny asked about Jonathan's school – a private prep nearby. In return, Jonathan asked Danny about his school; Danny told him how he'd been given money from the local council to go to a fee-paying school as he'd been identified as being very bright while at his state primary school. 'Oh, like a bursary?' asked Jonathan.

'Yes, mate. Exactly like a bursary.' Danny looked at Kate and widened his eyes, as if to say: *he's cleverer than both of us put together, this one.*

'Do you have any siblings, Danny?' Jonathan asked. 'Brothers and sisters, I mean.'

Again, Danny smiled at Kate. 'Oh right. I see what you mean. Brother and sisters. No, I don't I'm afraid. Just like you, I'm a one-off.'

'You certainly are,' added Kate. 'Right! Time to get ready for bed, Jonathan. School night and all that. Say good night to Danny.'

'Good night. You coming again, Danny?' asked the boy.

'Possibly, mate. If I'm allowed.'

'Great. See you.'

'See you, Jonathan. Say hi to your grandad for me.'

'I will. He likes you,' the boy said as he walked towards the house. 'He says... now you're off the booze, you're sound as a pound.'

'Jonathan!' exclaimed Kate. 'Bed. Now!'

Danny laughed and gave the boy a thumbs up sign. Jonathan returned it and went inside. 'What a horrendous little monster,' he told Kate. 'You must be a terrible parent – shame on you.'

'I need to start keeping him and Dad apart. I'm so sorry.'

'Not at all. As ever, your dad is spot on in his assessment of the situation.'

They sat in silence for a moment. Danny looked across the garden and watched a barge go by through the trees. On the far side of the water, a few people could be seen. Some were walking along the towpath hand in hand. Kate and Danny were happy to sit in silence for a while. 'I should be getting off, Kate. Thank you so much. It was really nice. I'll call a cab.'

'No need. I'll take you down to the station. It'll only take a few minutes and there's a train to Manchester due soon. You'll be back in your hotel before the cab gets here and you'll save yourself a fortune.'

'Sure. Great idea. What about Jonathan?'

'He'll be fine for a few minutes. Don't worry. You're not in London now – safe as houses around here. Let me grab my keys and we'll be off. Then you can tell me what your next move is in the Great Black Moss Investigation.'

'I was hoping you'd have a few ideas.'

'Maybe I do.'

They got into Kate's car and headed up the drive, towards the tree-lined path that connected the house to the road. From a vantage point close to the canal their departure was watched. Their entire evening had been watched. Watched and duly noted.

FORTY-THREE

1.30 am Wednesday 25 April 1990

Sitting in the front seat of the radio car, Danny watched as a group of young boys, aged around ten or eleven, chatted and laughed around a bonfire they'd started on wasteland close to the perimeter fence of the jail. Two of them pulled glowing batons of wood from the flames and began a play swordfight with them; sparks ricocheted around them as the swords clashed. *Kids out on their own this time of the morning. No wonder they go missing.*

Danny sipped the third of his four cans of lager. Crane had forgotten the nuts Danny had asked for, but the alcohol was keeping his hunger at bay. He was timing the cans so he could have one every hour; he'd sleep when they ran out.

He listened to the shouts and cries from the remaining prisoners on the roof as they shimmied across the rooftop. It would be strangely quiet for a while, then a shout of 'I love you!' or even 'Ken Dodd!' would cut through the night. Then quiet again. Then 'Mr Blue Sky' would start playing. While all this was going on, Green Goddess fire engines, borrowed from the army, were soaking the jail with water. The Home Office claimed it was to damp down fires started by the rioters; more streetwise observers believed it was to try to soak the inmates into submission. *I'm not surprised Crane looked like he'd just got back from the trenches – three weeks of this is enough to drive anyone mad.*

Danny decided to stretch his legs. As he stepped out of the car and locked it, he crushed the two empty cans underfoot and threw them onto the nearby bonfire as he passed. 'They won't burn, ya knobhead,' said one of the ten-year-olds.

'I'll bear that in mind, lads. Appreciate the info. Bit late to be out on a school night, isn't it?'

'Fook off!' several of them replied.

There were still about forty people milling around the jail – not including journalists. Small groups of men in their twenties went from camera crew to camera crew, volunteering to be interviewed about the latest from 'inside the jail', for fifty pounds. Sometimes, they accepted as little as ten. Danny watched as these lurid tales were spun, with the cameramen angling their shots so the interviewees faces couldn't be seen, as confident-sounding predictions were made about the occupation continuing until the end of the month. *I really hope not,* thought Danny.

He lit a cigarette as he walked around the site. The casual flow of people in and out of the area around the jail was constant. Taxis would swing past every now and then, dropping off people who wanted to take a look at *The Strangeways Rioters.* They'd stop, maybe ask someone if anything was happening. *Just the usual.* They'd hang around for a while, seemingly tire of it, then move on.

Danny did a loop of the area in front of the jail, heading back towards the radio car. As he walked up Southall Street to the right of the jail, he saw the peroxide blonde woman he'd seen earlier. She was standing at the same spot. She noticed Danny and began walking away. 'Still think it'll end today?' Danny called after her.

She turned, looked back for a few steps, nodded, then walked away. Danny watched her until she disappeared into the orangey haze of the street lights along the road. *Normally, that would be a bit weird. But not around here.*

He got back to the radio car. The two rear tyres were both flat. Crouching down to take a closer look, he noticed that both had a neat slit cut into them. He looked around. The kids around the bonfire had gone. *Little bastards.*

FORTY-FOUR

11.30 am Wednesday 22 June 2016

After Kate had dropped him off at the station the previous evening, Danny spent the train journey scanning Facebook groups that might help him find the next person he wanted to trace. He came across several sites that seemed to fit the bill: I HEART OLDHAM, OLDHAM IN THE 80s, OLDHAM MEMORIES all seemed the right kind of pages and he posted the same message on all of them.

Hi. Trying to trace anyone who remembers a local man called Vincent Canning. He was very well known in the town in the late 80s. He died in 1990. Those who were around at the time will know the circumstances – no need for me to repeat them here. I was wondering – could someone here could put me in touch with anyone who knew him or was related to him? Thanks.

Replies and comments came in very quickly. A few were recounting things that Canning had done; two mentioned Black Moss; one asked Danny how the driving lessons were going; several tagged in the same name: *Sarah Lewis was Canning.*

Danny had messaged her. She replied. She was Canning's sister and she seemed keen to talk to him. Very keen indeed.

Danny's cab dropped him off at on a steep street packed with two up/two down terraces, Glodwick just outside the town centre. The front doors of each house were separated from the street by a single, red step. The street was, he thought, how people in London imagined the whole of Manchester to look like. It certainly struck Danny as being how a lot of Manchester had looked like to him in 1990.

Sarah Lewis came to the door seconds after he knocked. From the information and photos on her Facebook page, Danny guessed that she was in her mid-forties. She looked at least ten years older. She invited him in and Danny went from the street into the living room with one step. The tiny living room floor was partially covered by carpet tiles which appeared to have come from several sources. Loud dance music thumped from an upstairs room and there were empty bottles of wine and super strength cider scattered on the floor around the furniture. There was a large brown sofa which sagged so deeply in the centre that the middle seat cushion touched the floor; the main armchair was a car seat. Sarah Lewis caught Danny's eye as he looked around the room. She looked a little ashamed. Danny felt the same and looked directly at her rather than at the surroundings. 'Thanks very much for seeing me Sarah. It must have been a little weird, me messaging you out of the blue.'

'A little bit, yeah.' Sarah pronounced little as 'lickle', an old Manchester habit that Danny hadn't heard for a very long time. 'No one's been interested in our Vinny for ages. We pretended for long enough that we wasn't even related to him. Terrible really. He were my brother – he were a fookin' nuisance at times, but I still loved him. Blood's blood innit? Do you want tea?'

'Sure. Thanks. Why did you pretend he wasn't your brother?' Danny asked, following her into the tiny kitchen.

'Why'd ya fookin' think? Because we was the child killer's family, weren't we? We had to move twice. Red paint chucked at the windows. Shit through the letterbox. All sorts. Lived over in Bolton for a few years 'til things calmed down a bit. Sorry. Dint mean to shout. Sorry.'

'No, I understand. It must have been hard for you.'

'People we thought were friends blanked us in the street. Invisible we were. Put our mum into an early grave. Speaking of which... DUANE! TURN THAT FOOKIN' MUSIC DOWN.'

Danny didn't notice any change in the volume. Sarah motioned for him to sit at the small table that was pushed up against one side of the kitchen and handed Danny some very dark tea in a mug advertising social housing helpline numbers. 'Look, Sarah, I'm not here to upset you, or pry or cause trouble...'

'Bet all three are gunna happen, though, eh?' she interrupted.

'Probably, yes,' Danny admitted. His accent had dropped several notches since he'd entered the house, mirroring the person he was talking to. *Just like the old days.* 'Do you mind if I record this on my phone? Just so I get everything right. It's not for broadcast or anything. Just for the record'

'Yeah, go on, then.'

He placed his iPhone on the table, switching on a recording app he'd downloaded. The app looked like an old-fashioned cassette player and two wheels began rotating to show Danny that it was recording. 'I was really involved in the murder of the kid up at Black Moss,' he explained. 'I saw his body the morning it was discovered. There was so much going on at the time, then when your brother's body was found, everything came to a halt. It left so many unanswered questions.'

'Tell me about it. I didn't believe what the police said at the time and I don't believe it now,' Sarah said, staring at the wheels on Danny's recording app.

'What did you tell the police at the time?'

'That no way our Vinny would do that to a kid. And that no way he'd top himself, either. No way. But they wouldn't listen. They treated me like shit, especially sending that copper round – they knew full well Vinny hated that copper.'

'Which one?'

'That DC Cave bint. She was always on our Vinny's back. Always hassling him around town. Trying to get him to act the snitch for her. He hated doing it, but sometimes he had to. She had him by the goolies. He was out of prison on licence half the time and she had the power to send him back inside just like that. He was frightened to death of her.'

Danny glanced down at his phone app to make sure the virtual wheels were still turning. They were. 'So, DC Cave knew Vinny before all the business up at Black Moss?'

'Course she fookin' did! She was on him all the time.'

'And did you tell this to the police at the time?'

'Yep. But who do you think they sent 'round to take me statement when Vinny's body was discovered? I said I didn't want to talk to her, but she reckoned she was the only one available. Short-staffed 'cos of Strangeways. She had shit on me as well. I never claimed I were an angel. Neither were our Vinny. But she told me if I kicked up a fuss I'd be inside again. So, I kept quiet. Fat lot of difference it would have made, anyhow. I even tried the local paper – they didn't wanna know either. That's the way it works, innit? No fooker listens to the likes of us. Not the police. Not nobody.'

'Well, I'm listening, Sarah. I really am. What do you think happened to Vinny?'

She lit another cigarette. 'You'll think I'm barmy. Everyone round here does.'

'I know the feeling. I won't think that. Not in the slightest.'

She sighed, exhaling smoke at the same time. 'The police. That MP up the hill who died in the crash. All powerful people, aren't they? All in it together. Looking after their own. Scratching each other's backs. I reckon our Vinny saw something he shouldn't have saw. Heard something he shouldn't have heard. And some fooker thought, "No one will miss this scrote. Let's get rid. But hang on a minute. Maybe he could be useful for one last thing. I can kill two birds with one stone here: sort out Vinny Canning and blame the death of that kid on him at the same time." And that's what did for our Vinny.'

'Do you have any proof of this, Sarah?'

'Absolutely none whatso-fookin-ever. But Vinny was scared before he died. Scared the cops were out to get him. Scared he was going to get the blame for something he didn't do. People thought Vinny was mad. Maybe he was, but he wasn't daft. You think I'm mad too, don't you?

Danny thought about Jan Cave's clear denial about knowing Vinny Canning. *She looked me in the eye and lied. It's happened. The first out and out lie. Right there.* 'No, Sarah, I don't think you're mad in the slightest.'

FORTY-FIVE

5.40 pm Wednesday 25 April 1990

Danny had been outside Strangeways' prison for nearly twenty-four hours. Throughout the day, he'd been fully expecting Robert Crane to return so he could take a break, but so far, nothing. *I am in serious danger of entering into the hallowed halls of the Twenty-four-Hour Club, here,* he thought. *It would be just like that bastard Crane to turn up at the last minute to make sure I don't.*

He scribbled notes, preparing for the package he had been asked to do for the six o'clock news. He'd been doing items on the hour throughout the day, many of them live. Doing that many live reports had certainly cured him of any lingering nerves he had about speaking off the cuff. *Work out the first and last things you're going to say, plot three key points to make in the middle, then join them up – easy.*

As he wrote, he spotted Gary Keenan approaching in the rearview mirror. He was rolling two tyres up the street, had a Marantz tape recorder over one shoulder and a cigarette dangling from his lips. Danny got out. 'Danny boy!' the engineer cried. 'You read my mind. I'd rather not jack this car up with you still inside, if that's all the same. The local scrotes have been out again, have they? This is the third fresh pair of tyres since this started.'

Gary handed Danny the tape recorder: 'Got you a fresh Marantz too. Figure your one would be knackered.'

'Well, I have it on good authority that it's all going to end today, Gary.'

'Is that right?' said the engineer, spitting out his cigarettes and jacking up the radio to change the first tyre. Well if it does, you're on strict instructions to let Robert Crane know asap.'

'Strict instructions from who?' Danny asked.

'From Robert Crane, you dick. You don't think he wants you to get any of the glory for this, do you? They've put him in a hotel down the road to rest up, but it's only five minutes away, so he can dash over if it all kicks off and do the final report. You must contact him on pain of death, got that?'

'Got it, Gary.'

'Grand. You doing something for the six?'

'Yup.'

'You'd better crack on then.'

Danny took the cassette from his old Marantz and put it into the fresh recorder Gary Keenan had brought with him. He lined up a clip from an interview he'd done earlier in the day with a solicitor who represented several men who had been in the jail. The man had sought Danny out – the radio car was a giveaway – telling him his clients had asked him to put out their message about conditions in the jail via Manchester Radio. Standing next to the car as Gary worked on the tyres, Danny made a note of where the start of the clip was on the four-digit counter on the face of the Marantz. Then he did the same with some atmospheric sounds he'd recorded earlier in the afternoon – the noise of sirens and music being blasted at the remaining rioters. He fed the clips back to the radio station and prepared to feed his own voice down the line too. At ten minutes to six, he rang the newsroom. Mike Sharston answered. *Christ, we are short-staffed if Sharston's come out of his cave.*

'Hi, Mike. Piece for the six. Right, here's the cue,' he said. 'Ready? Okay.'

Danny said the words of the cue slowly so Sharston could type then: *The 24th day of the stand-off at Strangeways' Jail is drawing to a close with the authorities seemingly no closer to ending the longest prison disturbance this country has ever seen.*

Meanwhile, a solicitor for some of the inmates who've already given themselves up says he believes there's now just five rioters left inside the prison. Danny Johnston is outside the jail and sends this report.

'Okay? So, mix in a bit of the atmos at the start then bring in my voice after two seconds. Here we go. Three, two, one:

Day 24 of the riot has seen more sirens and more music blasted at the remaining inmates, neither of which seems to have made the slightest bit of difference to their resolve. They're still on the roof, still shouting defiant messages and still showing no signs of giving up their protest – despite the loss of a key figure, Alan Lord. He was snatched by prison officers yesterday. Mark Tarporley, a Manchester solicitor representing several men involved in the disturbances, says he believes just five inmates are left, including the so-called ringleader of the riot, Paul Taylor.'

Danny paused and said: 'Right, so the clip of the Tarporley goes there; end it when he says, "my information is that the number is just five," then I'll round it up. Three, two, one:

It's hard to believe that just five men are still in control of Strangeways – what's even more incredible is that there doesn't seem to be a thing that the prison authorities, the Home Office or the British Government can do about it… other than wait. This is Danny Johnston, for Manchester Radio News, at Strangeways Jail.'

Danny waited a few seconds and then said: 'Okay, I'll assume that's fine unless I hear otherwise.'

The line went dead. He lit a cigarette and flicked on the radio. 'All I Wanna Do Is Make Love To You' by Heart segued into the news jingle, followed by the news and Danny's report. *I'm finally starting to enjoy this job.*

Danny watched as the TV reporters started and finished their live reports for their six o'clock bulletins. *I could do that. Might need a haircut and some better clothes. But, yeah. Why not?*

The radio car dropped slowly to its normal height as Gary loosened the jack. 'Very good that, Danny boy. Nice to hear a fresh voice on this. Getting sick of Crane saying the same things in a different order all day long.'

'Thanks Gary,' Danny replied, offering the engineer a cigarette with a smile. 'But, as I've pointed out before, I'm very much straight.'

'You may be straight, but you're not very observant.'

'How do you mean?'

'Look.'

Gary nodded towards the roof of the jail. The five remaining rioters were gathering at the left side of the roof. As they did so, a cherry picker rose slowly to meet them. There was a wave of raised voices across the site. 'Fuck me, it's ending,' shouted Danny. 'It's actually ending.'

'Right,' said Gary. 'You ring the news desk. I'll check the signal ready to go live and line up some extra cable in case you have to go walkabout. This is your big chance, Danny. Don't fuck it up.'

'But what about Crane? Strict instructions to call him, you said.'

The engineer opened the boot of the radio car and pulled out a large reel of microphone cable. 'Fuck him, Danny! There's no time. Go, go, go!'

Danny rang the news desk. A young woman answered. 'Err. Hello. Sorry. Manchester Radio newsroom, can I help you?'

'Hi, it's Danny at Strangeways. Who's that?'

'It's Michaela.'

Danny was thrown: 'Who?'

'Michaela. The work placement student.'

So THAT'S her name. 'Right, of course. Michaela, who else is there?'

'No one. They've gone to the pub.'

'What?' Danny couldn't believe what he was hearing. 'Shit me. Really?'

'Yes. Is anything wrong?'

'The riot. It's ending. Right now. I need you to ring Sharston, get him back here and tell whoever's on air that they need to be ready to take a live feed from the jail as soon as possible.'

'FUCK SHARSTON, DANNY!' shouted Gary. 'GO LIVE NOW!'

'But the protocol to break into the schedule is for it to be okayed by Sharston.'

'NOW, YOU TWAT, NOW!'

'Michaela,' said Danny. 'Patch a talkback feed up to the studio.'

'What?' the young woman said. 'I have no idea what you're talking about.'

'Shit. Okay. Forget it. Tell the presenter to take the outside broadcast feed in exactly thirty seconds. Start counting backwards from thirty in your head slowly. Keep the phone line open and run to the studio and keep counting. When you get to zero, tell him to slide up the OB fader. Whatever he says, don't take no for an answer. In thirty seconds. Add one-thousands to get real seconds. 1030, 1029, like that. Got it?'

'Yes.'

'Great Michaela. Now, start…'

'*Okay… 1030, 1029…*'

Danny listened as Michaela's voice faded away. He was counting too. The studio was fifteen seconds away, giving her another fifteen to convince the presenter to do as they were told. Tight. *But do-able.*

Gary Keenan handed Danny a set of headphones and a microphone as he unravelled a looped pile of cable at their feet. 'Slick idea that, Danny boy. Like your style.'

Danny nodded as he continued a whispered count.

'*…1022, 1021, 1020…*'

'Might, work, might not. Depends how thick the presenter is. Knowing our presenters, pretty thick…'

'Shut the fuck up Gary… *1015, 1014, 1013…*'

'Don't start turning into a diva on me. Ready?'

Danny put on the headphones but left one ear uncovered so he could hear what was going on around him. He could hear the station output: 'Dirty Cash' by The Adventures of Stevie V. He gave Gary a thumbs up.

'Good luck, our kid,' said Gary.

Danny watched as the first of the final five rioters on the

roof of Strangeways jail reached out towards the cherry picker cradle.

'1005, 1004, 1003, 1002, 1001…'

FORTY-SIX

4.30 pm Wednesday 22 June 2016

'She lied, Kate. Right to my face. I checked back with Canning's sister. Rang her and went through the whole thing a second time. Cave told me she didn't know Vincent Canning, yet his sister says he was her snitch and he was terrified of her. Why would she do that?'

Kate gestured for Danny to sit down, but instead he kept pacing across the open area of her office. 'I don't know,' she said. 'I really don't.'

'You must have come across her back in the day. Did Cave seem straight to you?'

'Too bloody straight. Never got so much of a sentence out of her for the paper. She played things absolutely by the book. She never seemed to have the common touch, could never connect with people like Dad could. But he won't have a word said against her. So, yeah, I don't know why she'd do that.'

'What about Canning's sister? She said she tried to get the local paper to look into it. Was that the *Messenger?*'

'I'm afraid it might very well have been, yes,' Kate confirmed, looking at the floor rather than at Danny.

'So, the paper knew there were questions about Canning's suicide and did nothing? They ignored her?'

'She'd turn up at the front desk, off her head, shouting and screaming,' admitted Kate. 'Every newsroom has them, Danny, you know that. Nutters claiming cover up this and conspiracy that. Whoever is the most junior in the office

214

normally gets sent out to speak to them. I'd moved up the ranks by then, so it never fell to me.'

'And you didn't think to tell me?'

'It's was a bloody long time ago, Danny! You've haven't exactly got a photographic memory about this yourself, have you? You were pissed most of the time, I believe.'

'Great. Thanks for that, Kate.'

'Sorry. That was out of line. Apologies.'

'Forget it. Look... I really need to speak to your dad, Kate. Something isn't right about this. Is it okay if we ring him?'

'Of course. He's got Jonathan with him at his house. Mutual babysitting.'

Kate speed dialled the number on her desk phone and put it on loudspeaker. Jonathan answered. 'Hi, Johnny. How was school?'

'Fine, thanks. Can I have some biscuits? Grandad's got some Hobnobs and he says they are the greatest biscuits ever made.'

'He's probably right. Can you put Grandad on the phone please? Hold the receiver to his ear, it's easier for him.' A pause.

'Dad, it's me,' she said. 'I've got Danny with me and you're on the loudspeaker, so don't say anything libellous, okay?'

'Spoilsport,' said the former detective, eliciting a small smile from both Danny and Kate.

'Jim, it's Danny. Vincent Canning – the suicide up at Black Moss – I've been talking to his sister. Did you know he was a regular informant for Jan Cave?'

'No. No, I didn't. But cops kept grasses to themselves in those days.'

'His sister says that he was scared of DC Cave,' Danny continued. 'Frightened to death was the expression she used. Yet she was sent to get a statement from his sister when he died and there was no disclosure that DC Cave knew him at the time. That's not usual, is it?'

'Not usual. No. Didn't even know he had a sister.'

'I spoke to Cave about this and she denied ever knowing

Canning. Yet his sister says she was on him constantly. Why would she do that?'

'Haven't got a clue, Danny. It was a very bad time, as you know. As Kate knows, too. Very bad.'

Danny looked at Kate and she indicated that he should carry on with his questions. 'I know Jim. I'm so sorry. You had so much to deal with – with your wife being so ill and having the Black Moss boy to investigate and then Canning's suicide.'

There was silence from the speakerphone. 'Not me, Danny.'

'How do you mean?' asked Danny.

'Dad had nothing to do with the Canning case,' said Kate. 'By the time Mum had died and he'd been given compassionate leave, it was all sorted.'

'Who sorted it?' Danny asked.

'DC Cave,' came the crackly reply from the speaker. 'I was very...' The old man struggled to get the words out. '... grateful at the time.'

'Of course, Jim. Completely understand. Listen, thanks very much. I'll speak to you later.'

'Okay Danny. Take care.'

Kate leant close to the speaker: 'I'll talk to you later, Dad,' she said and returned the phone to its normal setting. 'Okay. That's really, really strange,' she said.

'Cave told me your dad did all the work on the Canning case. He says he didn't. Well, I know who I believe. Cave said she didn't know Canning, but his sister says she definitely did. Again, my money is not on DC Cave. It's smells like shit to me.'

'You're not going to do anything weird, are you Danny?'

'No. I'm going to go back to the hotel and think it through. Don't worry. I just need to get my head around it... doesn't make sense.'

'Okay, I'll be picking Jonathan up from Dad's then heading home; call me later.' Kate stood up and gave Danny a hug.

'I will.'

'No weird stuff, Danny Something, okay?'

'No weird stuff, Kate.'

'Promise?'

'Promise.'

Danny made his way down the stairs. When he was out of earshot he made a call on his mobile: 'Gary? It's Danny. Great, mate. Listen… you're the master of all things electronic, aren't you? How easy is it to get into an office protected by a keycode, when you haven't actually got the keycode?'

FORTY-SEVEN

6.45 pm Wednesday 25 April 1990

Danny talked live on air for more than twenty minutes as Glynn Williams, Martin Brian, John Murray, Mark Williams and Paul Taylor came down from the roof of Strangeways jail. The words flowed out of him and he decided he wouldn't stop until someone told him to. Eventually, a call came through to the radio car mobile phone from the studio. Gary took it, nodded and made a thumbs up sign, then made a cutthroat sign to Danny, who brought his live report to a close: *Tomorrow morning – or maybe even tonight – the clean-up operation will begin at Strangeways jail. As that's happening, so will another task: that of finding out how this happened and most importantly, why it happened. This is Danny Johnston for Manchester Radio News at Strangeways jail in Manchester.'*

Danny waited a few beats, got the all clear and took off his headphones. Gary Keenan shoved a cigarette between Danny's lips and lit it for him. 'Well done, our kid,' said the engineer. 'Amazing.'

'Cheers, Gary. Don't know where it all came from. Doubt I could do it again if you paid me.'

'That was Sharston on the phone, by the way. He came out of the pub sharpish when he heard. Don't worry. He's cock-a-hoop. Says you were right to go straight to air; he loved the countdown bit with whassername the student...'

'Michaela, apparently.'

'I'll take your word for it. And he says it was the right call to go for it rather than wait for Bobby Crane. Which might prove helpful as I can see Bobby heading this way and he has a face on him like a tropical fucking thunderstorm…'

Danny turned just as Robert Crane pushed his forearm across his chest and forced Danny backwards against the side of the radio car. 'You sly little twat. You knew fucking well you were supposed to call me if it all went off and you deliberately took the tale for yourself.'

'It wasn't like that, mate,' countered Danny. 'Seriously.'

Gary Keenan grabbed Crane, spun him around and pushed him away with little visible effort. 'He did the right thing,' the engineer shouted. 'If he'd waited we'd have got nothing. And Shartson agrees. So, stop being a prick and calm the fuck down. Danny's got it covered for the seven, haven't you mate?'

'Yes, I do, Gary. Thanks.' Danny glanced up the road and saw prison officials putting up crash barriers. Journalists and camera crews rushed to get a good spot. The final government statement of the riot was about to be made. 'Look, the Home Office bod is coming out,' Danny said to Crane. 'This is it. The end. Robert, do you want to get the audio for that while I prep a piece for the seven? It can be a co-production – you and me - how about that?'

'Three and a half fucking weeks I've been here,' Crane muttered as he pulled a microphone out of his pocket, tested the Marantz and half walked, half ran towards the barriers.

'The mighty Robert Crane,' Gary said, shaking his head. 'Reduced to being your audio bitch. Why not get him to knock off a few vox pops while he's at it? Just to plunge the knife in even deeper?'

'Not a bad idea that, Gary. Will you tell him, or shall I?'

'Please, please! Can I? This has been a long time coming. Arrogant bastard deserves this. Very important lesson, Danny boy. Try not to be a twat to anyone on your way up. They're very likely to remember it on your way down.'

The engineer walked towards where Robert Crane was caught in a scrum with other reporters, surrounding an official from the Home Office, who was shaking his head a great deal. 'Gary?' Danny shouted after him. 'Thanks very much.'

'No worries, mate. Seize the day and all that.'

The statement from the Home Office to mark the end of the riot was clearly short and sweet. Robert Crane was already heading back towards them, checking the audio on his recorder. 'Oi, Bobby!' shouted Gary. 'While you've got your Marantz out, one more thing...'

FORTY-EIGHT

10.40 pm Wednesday 22 June 2016

Danny had arranged to meet Gary in a side street across the road from the mill that housed Jan Cave's office. He'd walked there from the hotel rather than take a cab or a tram; although he wasn't in the habit of breaking and entering, he figured the less indication that he'd been anywhere near the site, the better. He'd also decided it would be best to meet away from the site to avoid any CCTV cameras around the mill.

Gary pulled up in a white van that looked remarkably similar to the one Danny remembered him driving in 1990. He'd advised Danny to wear nondescript clothes; not a problem for Gary as he was wearing the same jeans and grey sweatshirt combo he always wore. The night was warm and clear. The main road dividing them from the mill was busy with traffic heading into Manchester. 'Alright, Danny boy? Bit different for a Wednesday night out this, innit?'

'Gary, you don't have to do this if you don't want to – I'd completely understand.'

'Don't be daft. It's great, this is. Look. The kids are all grown up. The wife barely talks to me. I'm long past my sell-by date at work… this is the closest thing to excitement that's come my way for years. Bring it on.'

'As long as you're sure. Okay, this is what I know so far…'

The engineer held up a hand. His fingers were calloused, and the palm was peppered with tiny cuts and burns. 'I rather suspect that the less I know, the better, Danny boy.

Has someone who might be bad 'un been lying to you?'

'Yes.'

'Might there be a few answers in this office that might catch aforementioned bad 'un?'

'Yes.'

'Then that's all I need to know – let's crack on, then.'

The inside of Gary's van was essentially a mobile version of his office at MRFM. It was awash with tools, electronica and a rainbow of electrical tape. Gary took a utility belt that bulged with small-scale tools and gadgets and wrapped it around his waist. He also produced a couple of old baseball caps, banging them against his leg to remove the dust. 'Put this on and pull it down over your face,' he advised Danny, who took the cap and glanced at the small logo on the front. 'Blue? The boy band, Blue? What kind of baseball cap is this?' he asked.

'A free one. Now shut the fuck up, turn it inside out, put it on and let's go.'

The two men crossed the road and walked around the outer edge of the mill car park, which was dotted with just a few cars. Danny led the way, showing the engineer the office entrance. 'Don't be tempted to look for cameras,' Gary said. 'There will definitely be cameras. Just keep your head down and your cap pulled low and keep going.'

They got to the front door. 'Just see if there's any security blokes about,' instructed Gary. 'These places share one bloke between several sites. They only come around every few hours. Just take a peek, will you?'

Danny turned on the step and looked around from under the rim of his cap. He heard a double clink, followed by a beeping noise and turned to see that Gary had already opened the main door. 'Christ, Gary. You don't mess about do you? Where did you learn to do that?'

'Lost count of the number of times I've had to break into the radio station over the years because the security system has ballsed up. It's simple enough. You just need to know how to do it.'

'Okay. How *do* you do it?'

'Never you mind. Where's the next door?'

As they headed towards the second door, Gary put a small LED torch into his mouth. 'I think I heard something,' Gary whispered.

Danny turned towards the outer door, looked around and saw it was all clear. Again, he heard a double clink and a beep. 'I fell for it again, didn't I?' Danny asked, rhetorically.

'You certainly did, Danny boy,' Gary replied, talking around the torch in his mouth as he pushed open the inner door. 'Now, let's not fuck about, please. In and out, okay? It might be helpful to know what we're actually looking for.'

'Yes, it would, wouldn't it?' Danny agreed, stepping gingerly into the small office and switching on the torch setting on his iPhone. Jan Cave's office was as neat and frugal as he remembered. A desk with minimal stationery – no computer – two chairs, a printer, framed certificates on the walls and a double-fronted metal cupboard; that was the full extant of *Jan Cave – Child Protection Consultant.* Danny and Gary looked at the cupboard, then at each other.

'I've been asked to open more metal filing cabinets by more radio station managers than you've had liquid lunches, Danny boy. So, yes, I can open it.' The older man took a small, sharp metal tool like a dentist's pick and applied it to the cupboard's padlock, which snapped open almost instantly. The pair shone their lights inside.

'She really likes stationery, doesn't she?' the engineer said, taking the torch from his mouth and casting its beam across neat shelves of sticky notes, pens, pencils, A4 sheaves of paper and highlighter pens. Beneath them were drop files filled with child protection consultancy cases going back to the early 2000s. Danny flicked through them: schools, sports clubs, youth organisations, dance schools and virtually every local council social services department in the area were represented.

'And she's been very busy since she cashed in her thirty-year ticket from the police,' added Danny. 'Very busy indeed.'

At the bottom of the cupboard was a large metal box. It looked old and out of place; it was also padlocked. The two men knelt down to take a closer look. Gary's joints clicked and cracked with the effort. 'Last peep, Danny boy, then we need to be on our way. We're pushing our luck, here. Not to mention the damage it's doing to my old bones.'

Gary popped the lock with the same ease he'd done previously. He pushed himself up from the floor and put his torch back in his mouth as he put away his lock-picking tool. A perfect circle of LED illumination wobbled and wavered across the box. Danny flipped up the hook-and-eye clasp that held it shut, then opened the lid and looked inside.

FORTY-NINE

10.15 pm Friday 27 April 1990

'The free bar doesn't look like it's going to run out anytime soon, does it?' Danny was on his tip toes as he shouted into Gary Keenan's ear over the loud music being blasted out across the packed upstairs room of the city centre pub.

'There's a very good reason for that, Danny boy,' Gary replied. 'See Mike Sharston over there?' Danny glanced over at the head of news, who had an arm around Robert Crane's shoulders and was animatedly waving a bottle of beer in the air as he spoke. 'He's got a blank cheque in his pocket – literally, a blank cheque from management – to pay for us to get battered into next week. And it's largely thanks to you. So, drink up, mate, 'cos it'll never happen again.'

'Will do, Gary, will do.'

Danny ordered 'two very large vodka and oranges, please,' from one of the harassed-looking bar staff.

'Do you mean a double, sir?' she asked.

'No, he said a VERY large one,' clarified Gary.

Two triple vodka and oranges were delivered – no money changed hands and the two looked across the room. Around the edges of the room, two dozen people were shouting, screaming, laughing and arguing as a DJ played music at teeth-rattling volume. Beth Hall was dancing with one of the sports reporters, grinding her backside against him to De La Soul's 'The Magic Number' as several other journalists cheered them on. Pauline the receptionist was dancing on her own with a half-empty bottle of wine in one hand, until one of the studio producers began to do some grinding of his own against her. Pauline dropped her bottle and it smashed on the hardwood surface of the dance floor. A cheer went up.

'Things are about to go downhill very, very rapidly,' Danny offered.

'I know. Fucking great, isn't it?' added Gary, clinking his glass against Danny's and heading off into the fray.

Danny leant on the bar, not wanting to lose his prime place as order after order came at the staff from those present. A woman, aged about twenty-one wearing a baggy 'Cool As Fuck' t-shirt, jeans and Doc Martens approached him with a huge vase-like glass of white wine. A hefty blob of wine seemed to spill over the rim with every step. 'Daaaaaanny!' she cried, giving him a hug and spilling more wine down the back of his shirt. 'Daaaaaanny The Champion of the World! Have you heard? I've been offered a job at the station. Newsroom assistant! Can you believe it? All because I could count to thirty backwards!'

'But more importantly, it's because you refused to take no for an answer,' he shouted. 'You convinced that presenter to do your bidding and slide up that fader with the power of your personality. That's what it's all about. Good for you.'

The music changed to 'Put Your Hands Together' by DMob. 'Come and have a dance,' Michaela shouted, tugging at the sleeve of Danny's shirt.

'Maybe later. Just finishing my drink,' he said, tapping his glass and smiling. She shrugged as if to say: *you're loss…* and tottered off towards the dance floor. As she went away, Danny saw that Mike Sharston and Beth Hall were heading his way. The news editor put a hand on Danny's shoulder and pointed in the direction of the exit. The three walked through the crowd. Sharston pushed open the function room door and walked through onto a landing. The noise level dropped significantly. The news editor put his pint glass onto a cigarette machine that was pushed up against a wall next to the toilets and Danny did the same. Beth stood next

Sharston, leaning slightly against his shoulder to steady herself.

'I'm not in trouble already, am I?' Danny asked, swaying slightly and making a mental note to buy some cigarettes when they were done.

'No, Danny. Definitely not,' said Sharston. 'Your stock is still very high. Too high, if anything.'

'I've no idea what that means, but if I'm not in the shit, that's good enough for me.' Danny made another mental note: *be careful... he's still your boss and you're really quite drunk.*

Beth spoke next: 'It means you were a bit *too* good at Strangeways the other night.'

'Still no idea what you're talking about, Beth,' said Danny. 'But it sounds vaguely like a compliment, so I shall give it a good home.'

'Listen, Danny,' said the news editor. 'You know that the TV guys are always sniffing around our reporters, picking off the best talent. It's happened for years. There's not a lot I can do about it, other than get something in return. For the last few years I've had a deal with ITV and the BBC: if you want reporters, don't go behind my back – come to me first. I'll tell you who's worth having and who's to be avoided.'

There's was a loud crash as Robert Crane came through the function room door. Danny gave him a smile; Crane gave him the finger.

'Danny, your contract's coming up...'

Oh, hello. Here we go...

'... and Beth has been telling me about how you've put everything into this dead kid out on the moors,' Sharston continued. An unpleasant thought snapped into Danny's head: *shit! What's wrong with me? I've barely given it a moment's thought since I was called out to Strangeways.*

'... doing stuff in your own time. Getting friendly with the local cops. Even carrying on with it after you got your face bashed in. Fair play.'

'I'm still baffled, Mike, to be honest...'

'We're letting you go, Danny,' interrupted Beth. She

winked at Danny as she said it.

'What?'

'Letting you go to ITN. They're after fresh blood, and having spoken to Beth, we think they should go for you. We'd already decided, but this Strangeways thing put a cherry on it. We broke the story first because of your quick thinking. In fact, it made me want to keep hold of you... but that wouldn't be fair.'

Robert Crane came back into view at the other end of the hallway. Two other journalists were pushing him through the door back into the function room. He was pointing at Danny and shouting. 'Love Shack' by the B-52s drowned out what he was actually saying, but Danny felt he could still get a sense of it.

'So, it's down to you, Danny,' said Beth, ignoring the commotion. 'Do you want a job in network telly, or not?'

FIFTY

10.54 pm Wednesday 22 June 2016

'It's just a load of crap, mate, let's go,' Gary said, pointing the beam of his torch directly into Danny's face after they'd seen the contents of the locked box.

'Shine the light back on the box, Gary,' said Danny. 'Let me give it a proper looking at, then we can go.'

The cold LED circle flicked back to the bottom of the cupboard. Danny sat on the floor and looked at the contents. There were old copies of the *Manchester Evening News* and other local and regional newspapers, some going back nearly thirty years. Tucked in the top right corner was a shoe box. Danny opened it; inside were old cassette tapes. The brands were ones that Danny hadn't seen for a long time: AGFA, Memorex and even some with Boots logos on them. Each had an initial and a date on them, nothing else. 'Time's up, let's go,' whispered Gary.

Alongside the newspapers and the shoe box full of cassettes was a padded, fawn-coloured jewellery box. It had a tiny gold-coloured clasp on it holding down the lid. Danny opened the clasp and a ballerina on a spring popped up and did a slight turn, accompanied by a few plinking notes of music. Both were enough to startle him into dropping the musical box. 'You big soft arse, Danny. Out, now!'

Danny turned to Gary and grabbed his hand, guiding the beam of the light into the overturned music box. It had a false bottom underneath the ballerina mechanism. Inside it were a dozen or so tiny teeth, yellow and flecked with brown dots and smears.

'Jesus fuck, Danny!'

'I know, I know. Out!'

In a blur of movement, Danny shoved the lid back on the musical box, refitted the clasp and closed the lid of the metal box. At the same moment, a yowling, deafening alarm went off. 'What have you done?' Gary shouted over the din.

'Nothing,' Danny yelled back. 'Finish up and let's go.'

Gary clicked shut the padlocks and the two men made their way out of the office, closing the door behind them. They did the same at the outer door. The alarm was even louder outside the office. Instinctively, Danny glanced around, and his eye caught the security camera tucked in the corner between the wall and the ceiling. He paused a beat, then took off his baseball cap, stared at the camera and gave it the middle finger.

FIFTY-ONE

10.15 pm Friday 4 May 1990

Management at Manchester Radio quickly discovered that since joining the station in October of the previous year, Danny hadn't taken a single day of annual leave. There was no way they were going to pay him for the time he was owed, so the only solution was to reduce his four weeks' notice to five working days. Seven days after being told he'd been offered a job, he was gone.

One week after the post-Strangeways party, a smaller, quieter send-off was held for Danny at the same venue. No function room was required this time, just a low-key corner of the radio station's favoured pub. There'd been a few swift words from Mike Sharston, some gifts – a dictionary signed by everyone at the station plus a twelve-bottle case of red wine – and the usual cheery words of good luck and promises to stay in touch. Pauline the receptionist told everyone who would listen that she'd always believed in Danny; Michaela the former placement student got drunk quickly and became a bit teary, vowing that she would never, ever forget Danny; Beth was very complimentary and even given him a hug and a swift kiss on the cheek. Robert Crane was the only person not to show a face.

In ones and twos, people drifted away; before too long, Danny and Gary Keenan were the only ones left. Eking out a pair of expensive and large whiskies that Gary had bought for them, they sat on stools at the end of the bar. Despite it being Friday night, the pub was nearly empty. Danny looked around at the tired, dated fixtures and fittings. 'Why do we use this pub?' he asked Gary.

'It's the only place that'll have us. You should have seen the mess in the upstairs function room after last week. Jesus wept. Anywhere else would have barred us for life.'

'I won't miss it, if I'm honest,' Danny offered.

'Don't give it a backward glance, mate,' the engineer said. 'Get yourself off to London and do your thing. You deserve it.'

'I don't know how you lot will survive without me, Gary.'

'We always do. They come and go, but the station always survives.'

'Ah. But they'll always remember me.'

'Course we will.' Gary drank the last of his malt and stepped down unsteadily from his stool. 'Here's one: Knock, knock…'

'What?'

'Try again. Knock, knock…'

'Who's there?' Danny asked with a sigh.

'Danny.'

'Danny who?'

'That's showbusiness, mate. See you sometime.'

Gary waved as he went but didn't turn around. Danny asked the landlord to call him a taxi and cradled his whisky until the driver came to the pub door. 'Taxi for Danny,' the driver shouted.

'Yeah,' Danny confirmed. 'Taxi for Danny.' He drained his glass and left.

When he got home, Danny's flat was even emptier than usual. The minimal possessions Danny owned were already boxed and ready to be driven south the following morning. His answer machine had yet to be packed away though, and the red light flashed to show he had messages. The digital display showed there were three of them.

Message One: *Danny. John Smithdown. Hello. Just a belated thank you for your help with the Black Moss case. Obviously, I've had a lot on my plate with the funeral and everything, but DC Cave seems* to have had things under control. I hear you finally managed to get yourself to Strangeways. Anyway, let's have a pint in my local, maybe even a curry.

Message Two: 'Danny Something! Pick up, pick up. It's Kate here. Remember me? I know you're Lord Scoop of Strangeways now, but give me a call. We've got a real opportunity to do a proper job on the Black Moss kid, get him identified, but I need your help. Someone said you'd left Manchester Radio. That can't be right, can it? No, it can't be. Anyway. Call me back.'

Message Three: 'Danny, it's Brenda from the kids' home. Hi. Look, I wanted to let you know that Little Paul has gone AWOL. He seemed to have taken a shine to you and I was wondering if you'd heard anything. Let me know as soon as poss.'

Danny thought for a few moments. Then he deleted all three messages and went to bed. The next day he moved to London, leaving everything behind him.

PART III

FIFTY-TWO

12.05 am Thursday 23 June 2016

Gary Keenan was sitting on the floor of Danny's hotel room with his head inside the mini-bar fridge. He came out with a bottle of lager, a whisky miniature and a can of Coke. Tossing the Coke to Danny he popped the top of the lager with a fitting on the Swiss Army knife attached to his belt. Half the lager went in one tilt. 'Mini-bar lager... it's never quite cold enough,' he muttered. The second half of the lager went as quickly as the first. The whisky followed it at the same pace.

Danny slid down the side of the bed and joined Gary on the floor, watching enviously as the engineer reached for a second lager. Danny opened his Coke and took a half-hearted sip.

'So, Gary,' he said.

'So, Danny.'

There was silence. 'I suppose we should talk about the whole teeth-in-the-box thing,' Danny said.

'It would seem sensible, yes. Might also be worth touching on something else while we're at it. That being... WHY THE FUCK YOU GAVE A FULL-FRONTAL FINGER TO THE SECURITY CAMERA!'

'I think it was pretty obvious that we were there anyway,' Danny offered. 'We didn't exactly cover our tracks like ninjas did we. Christ. It was creepy as fuck. Never heard a bloke scream like you did back there, Gary.'

'Is that what you journalists call gallows humour? Because

it isn't funny. Not in the slightest.'

Silence again. Gary scraped at the label of his beer bottle with his thumbnail. 'I've seen some weird shit in my time, but that took the biscuit,' said the engineer. 'Souvenir teeth? That's trophy shit, that is. *Weird* trophy shit. What the fuck is this all about, Danny?'

'When I was first out on the moors in 1990,' Danny explained. 'That kid's body was out there in the sand. The cops were trying to hold a sheet up in the wind, trying to stop people from seeing what was going on. They seemed more concerned that people would notice what a mess they were making of it – more concerned about that than they were about the kid. It feels like that all over again. *That's* what the fuck this is all about, Gary. I always felt like they fucked up – now it feels worse than that. It's pretty clear the police have been covering something up all along. The only people involved in this – the only ones whose stories don't match up – are the cops. But what am I supposed to do about it – go to the police? How much good will that do, apart from *no* fucking good?'

The engineer finished his second beer and threw it into the bin, rattling it so hard it nearly toppled over. 'Understood, Danny boy. But prancing about in front of the camera wasn't perhaps the subtlest move you could have made at this stage of the game, was it?'

'Yeah, I know,' Danny conceded. 'I just wanted to let them know that I know they're lying and I'm not going anywhere. Not this time. It was fishy as shit back in 1990; it stinks even worse now. Keeping a box of teeth inside a locked cupboard – who the fuck does that?'

'I can honestly say, I don't know anyone who does that,' Gary conceded. 'So, what's the plan?'

'First thing in the morning, we're back to that office. If she's there, confront her. If she isn't, we'll break back in and take a few things from that cupboard.'

'Thought you might say that. Then what?'

Danny stared at the writing on his can of Coke. He

thought for a few moments: 'Fucked if I know.'

'It's a work in progress, then,' Gary said, trying to sound positive. 'Right you are. Mind if I crash here?'

'Sure.'

'No funny stuff though, right?'

'I think it's fair to say I'm not especially in the mood for any funny stuff, Gary.'

'Be like that then,' smiled the engineer. He got up, took a spare blanket from the wardrobe and grabbed the suitcase stand from the other side of the room, putting it in front of the armchair tucked into the corner. He sat down, stretched his legs out across the stand, covered himself with the blanket and closed his eyes. Within two minutes the engineer was asleep.

Danny stayed awake for quite some time. It wasn't Gary's snoring that stopped him from sleeping – though it didn't help – it was the thought of the teeth. And how small they were.

At 7.30 am, Danny nudged Gary awake. He put a cup of tea into one of the engineer's hands and a pastry he'd taken from the hotel restaurant into the other. 'Come on, lazy arse. Let's be having you. We've got weird shit to sort out.'

After paying £28 to have Gary's van released from the hotel's underground car park – *I'll pay it Gary, stop fucking moaning'* – they headed back towards the mill and Jan Cave's office.

No side streets and baseball caps this time; the two men parked in front of the office, close to a double set of industrial bins. A security guard was there, looking at the keypad system. His stomach bulged under a dark blue jumper that was too small for him. He looked tired and was distractedly rubbing his shaven head: 'You the locksmiths?' he asked as Danny and Gary walked towards the front door.

'Yes indeed,' replied Gary, surprising Danny with the swiftness of his answer and the effectiveness of his lie. 'We've just come to assess it first and then we'll put a quote together.'

'Not sure how they got in,' offered the guard, 'but the system needs resetting or replacing, one or the other.'

Gary looked sagely at the keypad. 'Right. Well, whoever broke in knew exactly what they were doing. Professionals. No question about it. But, yeah, you need a whole new system here, mate. It's so old the bloke who installed it was probably wearing a powdered wig. Get it updated and keep the scrotes out, that's what I reckon.' Gary turned to face Danny. 'You go and look at the internals and I'll get this priced up.'

Danny nodded and walked past the security guard. As he did, Gary asked the guard: 'Don't suppose there's any chance of a brew, is there, mate?'

While Gary distracted the guard, Danny headed straight for Jan Cave's office. The door was open. Everything was gone. Other than the carpet – which appeared to have been hoovered – and a cream-coloured lampshade on the light fitting, the office was completely bare. Gary joined him at the door. 'Well either someone burgled the place after we left, or your mate the ex-policewoman has cleaned up and moved out,' he said, quietly. 'She's very efficient I'll give her that. I'll bet there was a CCTV link to her house. She was probably watching us all the time – especially your one-fingered salute at the end. Don't suppose she's left a tooth or two behind, has she?'

'Not as such, Gary, no.'

'Too much to hope for, I suppose. What now, Danny boy?'

'I don't know. Let me think.'

The security guard arrived with two cups of very dark tea. 'Nice one,' said Gary, taking the less chipped of the two mugs. 'What's your name, mate?' he asked the guard.

'Tariq.'

'Listen, Tariq,' Gary said. 'This is going to be a bigger job than expected. Have you got any contact details for the occupant? Our boss is out and about and we need to contact them asap so we can okay the work and get this office secure.'

'So sorry, no,' replied the guard. 'I'm just a temp for the firm with the contract; we've got several sites around here. I don't know any of the businesses at all.'

'Could you ask, please, Tariq?' Danny said. 'It'd be a massive help.'

The guard walked away from them, tugging at the walkie talkie attached to his belt. As he went, Danny motioned for Gary to follow him out of the building and he headed straight for the bins near their van. They were gunmetal grey, with twin plastic lids on and were easily six feet tall. 'Give me your penknife a minute,' Danny said to Gary. 'And then give me a leg up.'

Gary easily hoisted Danny up the side and into the first metal container. Along with various broken lamps and bits of chipboard, there were a dozen tied black bin liners. He pulled out the main blade of the penknife and sliced a bag; it was filled with paper coffee cups, takeaway cartons and some mail. The second was filled for a sports trophy company. The next bag was full of fishing magazines. The third was office stationery – much of it still sealed and unused – and junk mail, addressed to Jan Cave Consulting. Danny threw the bag out of the bin, climbed out and upended it in the car park. He began kicking at the various items of post, office waste and food wrappers. 'Here we go,' Danny said, picking up an envelope that looked different to the others. It wasn't a letter that had been sent to the office – it was one that was ready to be posted, but the envelope had been torn in two. Danny looked inside. There were two halves of a newspaper cutting inside. There were also two halves of a compliments slip; on it was written: 'Danny J's an accident waiting to happen. Will you tell him, or shall I?' It was signed 'Jan'.

Danny walked away and read the cutting with his back to Gary. He was silent for several minutes. Then he walked back, showing Gary the two envelope halves. 'I know this address,' said Danny. 'Let's go.'

Danny tucked the torn envelope into the inside pocket of his jacket. 'You okay, Danny?' queried the engineer. 'You look a bit weirded out.'

'I *am* a bit weirded out,' Danny confirmed.

The security guard came back across the car park as they got into the van. 'It's all good, Tariq,' Gary said, cheerily. 'We've found an alternative address. In fact, we'll pop round there right now in person. Don't worry. We'll tidy this lot up later.'

'I've got to hand it to you lads,' Tariq said. 'You are the most conscientious locksmiths I've ever come cross. Definitely, definitely recommending you next time there's a break in.'

'Cheers, Tariq!' Gary cried with a wave, as they drove out of the car park. They headed though Salford towards the motorway.

'So, where are we headed?' asked Gary.

'Oldham,' Danny replied, putting the postcode into Google Maps and letting the app guide the engineer to their destination.

'Lovely,' sighed Gary. 'Fucking lovely.'

They drove against the tide of the worsening rush hour traffic heading towards Manchester, heading for the ring road, then north west, away from the city centre, towards Oldham. 'Can't Stop the Feeling!' by Justin Timberlake was the soundtrack as they passed the police station. 'My ears just popped, then,' said Gary as the countryside opened out and they reached higher grounded. Danny said nothing. He was thinking about the cutting in his jacket pocket – more than that, he was thinking about Jan Cave's note attached to it.

'So, Danny boy,' Gary asked. 'Remember, I'm just a thick old radio engineer. Are we heading for the address on that envelope?'

'Yes, we are,' Danny confirmed. 'It was the only bit of mail in the bin bag that didn't have the office address on it. It was outgoing mail – due to be sent but it never got posted. She clearly changed her mind.'

The female Google Maps' voice told Gary that their destination was coming up on the left. Danny saw Kate hurrying her son into the car parked in the driveway of her father's house. She was surprised to see him. 'Danny? Bit early, isn't it?'

Jonathan ran over to Danny's side of the van. He opened his smart school blazer on one side, showing Danny the bag of Skittles poking out of his inside pocket. He put his finger to his lips, urging Danny not to say anything to his mum. 'Ah, the breakfast of champions,' Danny whispered. 'Your secret's safe with me, mate.'

'Grandad's inside, Danny,' Jonathan shouted as he raced back to the car. 'See you later.'

'Oh wow, Gary Keenan!' Kate said. 'Christ, haven't seen you for years. Double surprise. Danny, I can't stop, I've got to get Jonathan to school. Is everything okay?'

'Sure, Kate,' Danny said in his most reassuring voice. 'All Good. Speak later.' As he stepped out of the van, Danny went around to the driver's window and spoke quietly to the engineer: 'Gary. Just drop me off. I've got stuff to sort out here. I'll ring you later.'

'Okay, Danny boy. Fucked if I know what's going on, but I'm sure you'll tell me in the fullness of time. Or not.' His voiced changed from a whisper to a shout: 'Bye, Kate. Looking more sensational than ever.'

Gary drove off and Kate pulled away in her car too; Jonathan waved from the back seat. Danny walked inside John Smithdown's house. He watched as the older man shuffled across the living room to his favourite chair. Each step was a measured effort. Danny knew better than to offer help. He waited until the older man lowered himself slowly into the chair, then made himself known. 'Danny!' Smithdown said. 'What you doing here?'

Danny pulled a chair next to the retired detective and pulled the torn envelope from his pocket. He took out the two ripped pieces of the newspaper article, placed them on the arm of John Smithdown's chair and pushed them together, smoothing them out as best he could. The clipping had been well kept and showed little sign of age or damage – up until being torn in two at Jan Cave's office. It had been cut carefully from a paper as if in preparation for a scrapbook or archive. It had *'Manchester Evening News* library copy, please return' stamped on it and was dated Saturday 3 February 1973. The headline read:

CHILDREN RESCUED FROM 'HORROR HOUSE'

Danny placed a third piece of paper next to them: the compliment slip with Jan Cave's neat writing on it. Danny looked at Smithdown – his gaze wasn't returned. 'John. You've never, ever shitted me. Please don't shit me now. I've a lot of things to ask you about, but this one goes first. What the fuck is this?'

The old man continued looking at the torn article. There was a slight gap between the two pieces. With a shaking hand he touched one half of the cutting and pushed it, so it touched the other half. Finally, he looked at Danny. Former DI John Smithdown's eyes were wet, but he blinked the tears away. Danny read the cutting out loud. His voice was just a whisper.

A boy and girl were rescued yesterday from what police are describing as a 'house of horror' in Salford.

The children, a girl aged nine and a boy of six, are thought to be brother and sister and were found tied to their beds in squalid conditions at an address in the Weaste area of the city. Police have asked that the exact address be kept secret to avoid identifying the youngsters.

A man and woman, thought to be their parents, have been arrested on suspicion of child cruelty. Police broke down the door of the house after a tip off from neighbours. One woman who lives on the street, who asked not to be named said: 'The mum and dad are notorious around here. Drunk all the time and screaming and shouting at those kids. Sometimes you'd hear the boy and girl crying too. You never saw them out and about. They never played out like the other kids do. It's just awful.'

The photo accompanying the story showed a police officer with two children, their backs to the camera. The policeman was holding his helmet in one hand; his other arm was around the boy and girl. The side view of the young policeman's face showed how handsome he was. His hair was dark, cut short yet curly. There was a look of pure anger on the PC's face. The photo caption read: *PC John Smithdown comforts the two crying children taken from the so called 'house of horror'.*

'I'd only been on the job a few months when we were called to that house...*your* house,' Smithdown said, looking at the clipping. 'I'll never forget it as long as I live. The stink of the place. Piled high with shit and rubbish. You and your sister tied up like dogs, so thirsty you were drinking dregs from beer cans. We got you out late morning and waited for them to return. I was there until half eleven at night. The bastards had been out all day and half the night drinking.'

'What's my name, John? Tell me. Do you know? What's my real name?'

'Sean,' the older man said. 'Your name is Sean Hargreaves. I'm so sorry that you had to find out like this.'

Danny chose his words carefully. 'I always knew things were bad before we were adopted. Really bad. But I'd always pushed it away. My sister, she always dealt with it better. I wanted nothing to do with the past. I even used to tell people I didn't have a sister – as if that would help cut the ties. But it's not that easy, is it?'

'No, Danny. It really isn't. I wish it was. How is your sister?'

'She lives down in Wythenshawe. Married to a nice bloke. Bone idle, but nice. Decent people.'

Smithdown squeezed Danny's arm. 'You're decent people too, Danny. I mean it.'

Danny touched the newspaper pieces, pushing them slightly apart. 'Years ago, John, you said something to me... something about feeling bad for involving me in Black Moss, didn't you?'

John Smithdown nodded.

'Did you know, John? In 1990... did you know me and the

kid in the photo were one and the same?'

'Not at first, Danny, no. But there was something about you... so I did some digging. By the time I'd put two and two together, I'd already involved you. *You'd already involved yourself.* I thought... perhaps you were using it to try to wipe the slate clean. Trying to do right by that little lad at the Moss. I didn't want to pry. Maybe I should have. I'm sorry.'

Danny leant in close. 'I found teeth John, *fucking teeth,* at Jan Cave's office. Now the place has been cleaned out and she's disappeared.'

'I don't get it, Danny. I swear I don't. She was the best cop I ever knew. So hard working. She took over everything to do with Black Moss when my wife died. Everything. Now she's a child protection expert – that's not the CV of someone who means harm to children.'

'She's the only person involved in this case who isn't telling the truth,' Danny pointed out. 'Plus, she's the only one with a box full of kids' teeth.'

Smithdown shifted into ex-cop mode: 'Did you get any evidence of this Danny – a photo or anything?'

'No. No, I didn't. Jan Cave is trying to make out that I'm not to be trusted because of this.' Danny jabbed at the cuttings. 'That I'm round the twist. Who'd believe a drunk old journo like me? What's more, he's all fucked up because of his childhood. Perfect, isn't it? Your address is on the envelope. But she never posted it to you. Why's that?'

John Smithdown pulled a similar envelope from the pocket of his cardigan. 'Because she sent me this one instead,' he replied. 'It arrived this morning. It had been pushed through my letterbox.'

The cutting was again from the *Manchester Evening News* and the photo of John Smithdown was featured alongside two police mugshots of Danny's biological parents. *'HOUSE OF HORROR' MUM AND DAD JAILED FOR SICK ABUSE* said the headline. Jan Cave had written an identical message across the cutting as she had on her previous effort. 'She obviously thought that this one would drive her point home a bit harder,' Danny said, looking at the story but trying not to take too much of it on board. 'You know...*Danny's not right, he's not to be trusted.*'

'What now?' asked the older man. 'My connections with the force are long gone – most of my ex-colleagues are either dead or in care homes, Danny. What are you going to do?'

Danny thought for a moment. 'I'm going to walk into Oldham nick and tell them what I know. I had someone with me at her office – they can do the same. But before that, I'm going to stop and see someone.'

'Who's that, Danny?'

'My sister.' Danny pointed at John Smithdown's cutting. 'Can I have that?'

'Of course.' He handed Danny his cutting, then carefully scooped up the two halves of the other one. He looked at Danny as he passed it to him.

Danny put all the cuttings into one envelope and patted the ex-detective on the arm. 'Bye, John. I'll ring later. Don't tell Kate. No point in worrying her at this stage.'

'Sure, Danny. Story of my life, that is.'

Danny headed for the door. John Smithdown spoke: 'Danny?'

'Yes, mate,'

'I'm so sorry.'

'You saved us, John. *Saved us.* So, don't be so fucking stupid.'

Danny walked down the steep slope from the Smithdown's home, calling a local cab as he went. He wanted to walk for a while. Wanted to think, so he gave the firm a description of what he looked like and set off down the road towards Diggle.

Within minutes he reached a spot he recognised: the bend in the road where Peter Jeffries had crashed his car all those years ago. It looked safer now than it had then. More robust. Danny stood a moment and tried to remember the scene of the accident. As he waited a lone car went past, down the hill away from Black Moss. It was travelling too fast and there was a squeak as the driver pushed on his brakes a little too hard, panicking that they'd connect with the barrier on the outside of the bend. Danny watched as the car drove away. *But Jeffries' car didn't go through the barrier on the outside of the bend. It crossed into the wrong side of the road and crashed into the inside of the bend. Like he was trying to avoid something. Or he'd been sent in the wrong direction. Or both.*

Danny must have standing on the bend for some time when he was snatched away from his thoughts by the beeping horn of the taxi driver, who'd pulled into a layby a few yards from where Danny was standing. Danny got into the cab and gave the driver his sister's address in Wythenshawe.

FIFTY-THREE

11.55 am Thursday 23 June 2016

Treating them like precious artefacts, Danny placed the newspaper cuttings onto his sister's kitchen table. Karen didn't look at them. She looked at her brother instead. 'I've seen them,' she said, smiling and crying at the same time. 'Got copies upstairs. I know them off by heart. I wish I was more like you; young enough at the time to forget or at least, not fully understand.'

Danny looked around the kitchen, as if he'd find the words he was looking forward. After a few moments, he did: 'It's like I *knew*... but *didn't* know. Remembered... but didn't really want to remember. The memory was there but it was easier to just not access it. That sounds like psychobollocks, I know, but it's true. What do you remember, Karen?'

Karen Hargreaves looked at her brother: 'They beat us. They left us tied up in our own filth. The only time they washed us was when they wanted to touch us. Or let someone else touch us. How long have you got, our Sean? How much do you *want* to know?'

'I've got all the time in the world, Karen. Not today, maybe. There's a *lot* going on today. But after today. Definitely. It's time.'

Karen looked at the clippings. Her eyes lingered on the story that showed the two mug shots. Their real parents. The man's eyes were downcast, reluctant to meet the camera lens. The woman was different – defiant and angry-looking. 'They must have had a terrible life before they had us,' Karen said quietly. 'Terrible.'

'They treated us like *animals*, Karen. How can you feel sorry for them?'

'I didn't say I felt sorry for them. I said something terrible must have happened to make them that way.'

She got up from the table and took down a framed photo from a shelf cluttered with mementos, letters, postcards and children's drawings. The instamatic tones and colours identified it as being from the 1970s or early 80s. In the photo, a couple smiled, their arms linked. He was around forty, dressed in a chunky brown jumper and jeans. He was broad and looked like he knew what a hard day's work meant. She was younger, wearing a lime green dress; she had blonde hair that looked like it had just had a shampoo and set. Karen took the photo and placed it on top of the cuttings. 'These people who took us in and raised us, the Johnstons. They were our real mum and dad.' She prodded the press clippings: 'Not these monsters.'

Danny took the photo from her hands. 'I never really appreciated them. Never really thanked them for what they did – they treated us so well, got me into a good school, pushed me, encouraged me. First thing I did when I got that newspaper job after college was move out and then I barely contacted them. Then they were gone.'

She reached out, putting her hands around his as he held the photo. 'They didn't blame you. They understood. They kept in touch via me. It made them sad, but they understood.'

They sat in silence at the kitchen table. Danny pushed the photo to one side and pointed at the newspaper picture of John Smithdown. 'I know him – PC Smithdown, there – I know him really well. He turned into a great cop – a detective. One of the best. He's helping me look at an old case – a child murder from when I was at the radio station.'

'Why wasn't it solved at the time?'

'Because no one cared.'

'That's when bad things happen, Sean.'

'Yeah. I know.'

'So, what are you going to do about it?' Karen asked.

'I think I've found the person who knows what really happened. I'm going to the police today. Right now, in fact. And I'm going to get them arrested.'

'Sounds like a plan,' Karen said.

Danny's text alert went off. *Hi Danny, it's Beth. Some mental ex-copper woman just turned up at my door, looking for you. She was screaming and shouting. I didn't let her in… but she was scary as hell. She says she's coming back. Come ASAP please!!*

'Change of plan,' said Danny. 'I've got to go. I'll let you know how I get on.'

Danny stood up and hugged his sister. Then she looked at him. 'I don't really know what you're up to but promise me you'll take care.'

'Of course.'

'Promise?'

'Promise.'

FIFTY-FOUR

3.10 pm Thursday 23 June 2016

It occurred to Danny that he might need to make his approach in a low-key way, so he asked the driver to stop a few streets away from Beth's house.

Although only a few miles from his sister's house, Didsbury was a far more upmarket affair, even more so than when Danny had lived there in 1990. The main road running adjacent to the cul-de-sac where Beth lived was peppered with a few cars, cyclists and pushchair-wielding parents, making Danny self-conscious about the way he was stealthily walking too slowly along the pavement. He made an effort to walk in a more normal fashion, which only made him feel even more self-aware of the strangeness of the situation. *What the fuck are you doing? This is mad.*

As he turned the corner into Beth's street, he noticed her front door was open – only slightly – but open nonetheless. *That's not right. She's so security minded.* No way would she leave the door open. That's not right at all. Fuck, fuck, fuck.*

Danny picked up his pace as he approached the front door. He looked around. The dead-end street had six houses on either side. Beth's was tucked into the corner on its own. No one was around. He'd had plenty of doorstep encounters in his TV days, but they were always with a camera crew and a producer. Never on his own. Danny felt very exposed without the bravado that being in a group of people – especially one carrying a camera – can provide. He quietly took the three steps up to the front door and looked through the gap. And listened. 'Beth?' he asked. Then again. Louder this time. 'Beth? It's Danny. Is everything okay?'

He gently pushed the door wider and saw Beth's empty wheelchair in the hallway. Stepping inside the dark hallway and squeezing past the wheelchair, he heard a radio from what sounded like the kitchen. He made his way towards the only sound in Beth's house – the radio. 'Beth,' he said again. 'Don't freak out, it's just Danny. I got your message and was worried. You alright?'

He turned into the kitchen and saw Beth lying face down on the smooth lino floor. Her eyes were closed, and she looked so still, she didn't appear to be breathing. Danny took several quick steps towards her and bent down. As he did so, a strong arm slipped around his neck; a hand clamped onto the back of his head, locking him into a shockingly powerful choke hold. He felt the weight of the attacker's body force him to the ground, knocking what little breath he had in his lungs out of him. The side of his face was pressed hard onto the cold kitchen flooring as he struggled. He tried to push himself upwards, but the fight was draining out of him. Danny remembered a TV piece he'd done about self-defence. An expert had told him that trying to knock someone out by hitting them over the back of the head was a piece of Hollywood nonsense. You're more likely to enrage them – or even kill them outright. The chances of getting it just right were minimal. No. The best way to put someone into unconsciousness was a choke hold. *Good to know,* he thought.

Still struggling, Danny caught the shortest of breaths and the medicinal smell of soap rushed into his nostrils. The only part of his attacker he could see was their elbow, clad in a crisp, white shirt. *Fuck this.*

His face was close to Beth's on the kitchen floor. She opened her eyes and looked directly at Danny. And winked. As he whited-out into unconsciousness, Danny heard Beth speak. It was the same tone she'd used to him back in the Manchester Radio days: sneery, aloof and sarcastic. Very different to the cheery voice he'd heard her use two days earlier. She said: 'Danny Johnston. You are, without doubt, the stupidest cunt I have ever had the misfortune to come across.'

FIFTY-FIVE

5.30 am Friday 6 April 1990

'Yeah? Umm... Hello?'

'Danny, it's Beth.'

'Oh, hi. Right. Hi. I haven't overslept, have I?'

'No. It's fine. We've got a suspicious body out near Oldham. It's the absolute back of beyond but you're the next reporter on shift. Sharston wants you to go and check it out. Please tell me you have a Marantz?'

'Right. Okay. Yes, I do. That couldn't be further away from where I live if you tried. It'll take ages to get there. Aren't there any reporters that live nearer? Robert Crane lives in Middleton, doesn't he? That's much nearer.'

'Two words Danny: STRANGE, WAYS,' Beth shouted. 'Robert and the rest of the good journalists are down at the jail and will be for some time. It's down to you.'

'Right. Sorry. I wasn't being unwilling – just thinking of the practicalities, that's all. Right. Have you got an address?'

'Yes, I have,' Beth confirmed. 'It's a bit of a weird one... It's Black Moss reservoir. I've got some directions. Got a pen? Right. Take the A62 out of Oldham. Pass through Diggle. Stop at Brun Clough Reservoir car park. No, not Burn, Brun. Clough as in Brian. There's a Pennine Way sign on your right. Walk the Pennine Way path until you reach a second reservoir, that's Redbrook. The next one is called Back Moss. There's a smaller reservoir next to it called Little Black Moss. Then look for a beach and police activity.'

'Beach?' queried Danny.

'Yes. Apparently, there's a beach there. Probably just the low water level exposing the sand around the reservoir. I don't know. Do I sound as if I work for the water board? That's the information that's come through.'

'Okay. Probably take me an hour to get there, if I get out sharpish.'

'Then you'd better get out sharpish then, hadn't you?' said Beth.

'Right you are.'

'Danny?'

'Yeah?'

'Don't fuck it up.'

FIFTY-SIX

3.40 pm Thursday 23 June 2016

There was a lot to take in for Danny as he came to in an alleyway close to Beth's house. Yes, there was the thumping, swollen feeling in his head as he regained consciousness and realised where he was. There was also the sight of two young police community support officers looking down at him: 'You alright, sir?' one said in the overly-loud, overly-slow way that someone might speak to an elderly relative. He was in his mid-twenties with a light beard and seemed very wary of the situation.

'Bit early for it sir, don't you think?' said the other, a woman who looked very disapproving indeed of Danny lying in an alleyway on a Thursday afternoon.

But the number one source of confusion was the explosive, orangey and utterly forbidden taste of vodka that filled his mouth and was busily setting fire to the inside of his chest. There was barely enough to wet the inside of his mouth, but it was mixing with his saliva and Danny had swallowed it as a reflex action. There was barely a shot's worth, but it was enough to knock his senses sideways.

As Danny sat upright, he noticed his light black t-shirt was wet through, so much so he could feel moisture seeping into his trousers and underwear. He *reeked* of alcohol. The smell of it, the taste of it, the feel of it against his skin, thrilled and shocked him in equal measure.

'We've had a complaint, sir,' PCSO number one said.

'Been causing a nuisance, have we?'

'*She* fucking sent me out there!' shouted Danny. 'Sent me out to the Moss, all those years ago. She's right – I am stupid! A stupid, stupid cunt. Jesus Christ Almighty what a mug.'

Danny tried to get to his feet but lurched sideways, leaning heavily into a hedge running down one side of the ally. 'Take it easy, sir,' said PCSO number two. 'And tone down the language – there's a police station just around the corner on Elizabeth Slinger Road. I'm sure our friends there would be happy to accommodate you if you persist in causing a public nuisance.'

Copperspeak. Never changes, thought Danny. *And they're not even real coppers.* Although distracted by the notion of the alcohol that had been poured over and into him, it was clear that Danny was going to get nowhere telling what he knew to the PCSOs. He pulled himself up straight, trying to shake off the effects of being choked into unconsciousness. 'Okay,' he said. 'I'll keep it down. Am I under arrest?'

'Well, we could detain you while one of the local officers get here, but let's hope it doesn't come to…'

'Good!' Danny turned around and sprinted unsteadily back towards Beth's house, half fell up the steps and banged on the door with his fist. The PCSOs were right behind him. He alternated between banging on the door with his first and jabbing at the intercom button. 'Out!' he shouted. 'Come the fuck out, right now!'

Unsurprisingly, there was no reply. 'Please, sir,' said of the PSCOs. 'We're happy to listen to your side of the story, but you're not doing yourself any favours here.'

Danny stopped banging and jabbing. Several people were now watching proceedings from a safe distance. Danny heard some of their chatter.

It's him off the telly.

The alkie?

Yeah, that's him.

Danny felt the fury drain away. He looked at the PCSOs.

Both were in their mid-to-late twenties. Both seemed slightly frightened. They reminded him of the policemen out on Black Moss all those years ago. 'Really?' Danny said, the anger almost gone from his voice. 'My side of the story? You want to hear my side of the story? Somehow, I don't think you'd believe me.'

He held up both of his hands to the officers, palms facing them, in a peaceful gesture: defeat rather than surrender. 'It's probably best if I just get myself home. Sleep it off.'

'A grand idea, sir.'

Danny walked backwards from the scene, his hands still in the air. When he turned the corner, he started to walk quickly in the direction of the tram stop, pulling out his mobile phone as he went. A note was wrapped around the phone, secured with a thick elastic band. It was written in bland block capitals with a marker pen. It said:

BE ON THE TRAIN BACK TO LONDON BY SIX TONIGHT OR PEOPLE YOU KNOW WILL DIE

First, he rang Gary. Then he rang Kate. He asked both the same question. *How quickly can you meet me at my hotel?*

Then he started to run.

FIFTY-SEVEN

6.35 pm Thursday 23 June 2016

'Right,' said Danny, raising his voice over the chatter that filled his hotel room. 'Can I get a fucking word in edgeways here, please?'

'Sorry, Danny,' said Kate, pointing at Gary. 'But I haven't talked to this bastard for twenty-odd years, we've got some catching up to do.'

'That's because you turned your back on a proper job in radio to become a zillionaire, you capitalist cow,' Gary replied, rifling through Danny's replenished mini-bar.

'Dead right. That was stupid of me, wasn't it?' she said.

'Shut the fuck up and listen.' Danny had spent the last half hour in the shower, trying to wash away the smell of alcohol from his skin and hair – and the sense of fear and lack of control that the small amount he'd swallowed had given him. He'd only stopped showering when Gary and Kate had arrived. His teeth and gums tingled from the scrubbing he'd given them with his toothbrush. He'd used half a tube but could still taste vodka.

Gary and Kate sat side by side on Danny's double bed and looked at him. 'Okay. Here's what I know. Beth and Jan Cave are tied into this together somehow. I don't know how, but they are. It was Beth that sent me out to the Moss that morning in 1990 when the kid's body was discovered, and it was Beth that conned me into going to her house today. I'm pretty sure it was Jan that choked me into next week back at the house and it was probably her that played basketball with my head against a couple of brick walls back in the day. Plus… she collects kids' teeth. Which is a bad thing, as far as I'm concerned.'

'Agreed,' said Gary.

'Plus,' Danny added, 'they doused me in vodka to make me look like a drunken headcase. Who's going to believe me? No fucker, that's who. I couldn't even convince a couple of volunteer community cops that I was worth listening to. So, as a great man once said – fuck the police.'

'It's getting really weird this,' Gary whispered to Kate. 'Really, really weird. I've known Beth most of my life. Okay, she was a cow in the old days but, covering up child killings? Jesus Christ. She's got M.S.'

'They also gave me this,' Danny said, throwing the note onto the bed.

Gary and Kate read it. 'I assume you aren't going?' Kate said.

'You assume correctly,' Danny confirmed.

Gary pushed his glasses up his nose. 'So, what's the plan? Whatever it is, I'm bang up for it. I'm serious. Heads need breaking here.'

FIFTY-EIGHT

1.25 am Friday 24 June 2016

'There you go,' said Gary. 'I got the most expensive ones they had. I think you get what you pay for when it comes to baseball bats, I really do.'

Danny looked at the bat Gary had handed him.

'That's sixty quid's-worth of Louisville Slugger, that is,' Gary said, giving his bat a slow-motion swing through the air. 'Whammy,' he whispered. 'Fucking *whammy…*'

'Sure. Whammy,' Danny said in reply. *This is mad.*

'Here's the genius bit,' Gary added. 'I bought a ball and a glove too, so if we get stopped we can legitimately say we're just out for baseball practice.'

'At midnight?' queried Danny.

'We're very keen,' Gary countered.

'Of course we are. Kate, come on, what are you doing?'

'Just texting Dad with a few reminders about Jonathan for the morning. The pair of them are like two kids having a sleepover.'

She looked at the two men, testing out their baseball bats. 'Don't I get one?' she asked, stepping down from the front seat of Gary's van. 'Or are women not allowed to smash heads in, you sexist bastards?'

Gary handed Kate a bat. 'Of course I got you one,' he confirmed, speaking in a slow, patronising voice. He handed Kate a rounders bat that was half the size of the other two weapons. 'Not quite a Slugger, but you don't mind, do you?'

Kate looked at the bat. 'Wow. Had they run out of My

Little Pony ones? I would have preferred something with a bit of glitter on it, but it'll have to do, I suppose.'

She briefly gave the bat a swing back and forward, then, slightly embarrassed, tucked it into the pocket of her overcoat. 'Okay,' said Danny, getting out his iPhone and switching it to video mode. 'I'm on camera. Kate, you're on lighting, but wait until we're at the door. We want every scrap of evidence we can gather. Gary, you're in charge of twatting anything that moves.'

'I can do that,' the engineer confirmed.

'Thought so,' said Danny. 'Let's go.' The three walked quietly to the front door of Beth's house. Danny, Kate then Gary. There was a warm breeze and the moon was bright, lighting their way along with the orangey glow of the street lights. Kate was tapping the bat against her leg and whispering something under her breath. Danny walked a little slower, holding back so he could hear: 'Shit. Shit. Shit. Shit. Shit,' she said.

'Okay, Kate?' he asked.

'Definitely,' she replied. Then the whispered chant started again.

They got to the door and the three of them huddled in the small porch of the house. They looked around. The road was empty. 'Give me a little space here, will you?' Gary said, gently shooing them off the steps. 'Kate, step back and give me a little light from your phone. Danny, you'd better start recording.'

Danny and Kate looked down and began changing the settings on their phones. There was a clunk and Beth's door opened with a quiet beep. 'How the fuck did he do that?' Kate asked. Danny shrugged.

Danny and Kate peered around Gary into the house. It was silent. It was dark. 'What if there's someone here?' Kate asked in the quietest voice she could manage.

Gary tapped the end of his bat. 'Whammy,' he replied.

'Jesus Christ,' she sighed, 'I would really like my old life back, if that can be arranged, please?' She turned on her phone light, shining it thorough the gap in the doorway. The cold, white LED beam made the hallway appear frozen like a museum exhibit. There were tasteful art prints on the wall and several framed awards, including at least two for "Beth Hall – Independent Radio Newsreader of the Year." There was a stairlift too, with the chair ready to take someone upstairs. The light cut through the dark, well into the rear of the house.

Danny turned on the video function on his iPhone. He held it out in front of him. 'Let's go.'

They searched the downstairs front room first. More prints, furniture with expensive-looking throws and cushions and more framed awards. Gary picked up a photo from the fireplace surround. It showed a group of people at a Christmas party, looking the worse for drink. He was one of them. 'I have no memory of that photo being taken,' he said, mainly to himself.

The kitchen next. Kate nearly slipped on the small ramp that smoothed out the step, allowing access for Beth's wheelchair. 'It's not here,' said Danny.

'What isn't?' asked Kate.

'Beth's wheelchair,' Danny said, allowing his voice now a little louder than before. 'It's not here. Unless she drags it upstairs every night, that must mean that she's not here either.'

'Unless it's in here,' Gary said, tapping on the cellar door that featured an electronic lock similar to one at the front door.

Danny and Kate both spoke at the same time: 'Let's find out, shall we?'

Gary's bulk covered their view of the cellar door. In a matter of seconds, the double click signalled that the door had been opened. 'Gary,' Kate said. 'If we manage to not get put in prison for this, please promise me you'll show me how you do that.'

'Don't waste your time,' Danny said. 'It's ancient magic passed down through generations of hairy-arsed radio engineers. They're sworn to secrecy.'

Gary pushed open the cellar door and the three of them looked down into the darkness – it seemed to absorb the iPhone light rather than be illuminated by it. It was unusually robust for an internal door and banged hard against the wall leading down into the cellar. The three winced at the noise it made and stood in silence for at least a minute afterwards. Nothing. They walked down the harsh, stone steps then banked right as the room opened up. The cellar was the size of a large living room with a small window at the far end providing a little weak light from the street outside. It was filled with tools, boxes, old paint tins and spare furniture. All were neatly stacked on metal shelving units. There was also a large first aid kit attached to the left wall. It looked out of place, more like it belonged in a factory or large office rather than a house. Underneath it was a tent-like shape – several sheets pulled over something low and oblong. Danny lifted one of the sheets. There was a single, metal-framed bed underneath it. The mattress on it was dusty and soiled. Danny stared at it, scrunching the section of sheet that was in his hand into a tight ball. Gary's voice dragged his eyes away, but his mind was still captured by the bed. 'Nothing here,' said the engineer. 'Upstairs?'

'Wait,' said Kate. 'There.'

She shone a light onto a dilapidated Welsh dresser that stood against the far right-hand wall. It was partially covered with another sheet and had been painted a sickly light green colour. Behind it was a door with another keypad lock. Kate and Danny gestured towards the door to Gary. They moved the dresser as quietly as they could as the engineer hunched over the lock. True to form, it popped open in seconds. 'Move the dresser a bit more, so I can open the door wider. I'm not as slim as you two,' he said.

Kate and Danny did as they were asked. Kate's light revealed a larger room, five feet wide and fifteen feet long. On one side of the room ran a shelf. On it were boxes of gear that reflected twenty-five years of technical advances in camera equipment. There were Polaroid cameras, camcorders, digital cameras, Hi-8 units and DV cams. There were several developments in mobile phone technology represented too: many of the boxes boasted of the mega pixel quality offered by the phone's camera capability. The boxes were creased and yellowed but in remarkably good condition, given how old some of them were. Each camera or phone had clearly been used, then neatly returned to its original packaging and then stored as the next new gadget had come along and superseded it.

On the opposing wall of the narrow space were framed newspaper front pages, their headlines going back more than a quarter of a century. The stories told of IRA bombings in Manchester and Warrington, the murder of a Manchester aid worker at the hands of ISIS, child sex abuse rings in Rochdale – story after story, about a dozen in all, demonstrated moments in time over the last twenty-five years or more when Manchester and its surrounding areas had been the centre of national and international attention. Each front page had been carefully mounted and framed. In the bottom left-hand corner of each frame was a photograph. The earlier pictures were Polaroids, the newer ones were digital pictures that had been printed off and cut to the same size. Each photo was dated with extremely neat handwriting. Each was of a child, looking directly at the camera, like police mug shots. They were mainly boys, but some were girls. Some looked smiling and hopeful. Others appeared scared. Very, very scared.

Danny looked at the children's faces. One frame in particular caught his eye. At the far end of the room was a headline from the *Manchester Evening News'* coverage of the Strangeways' riot – it said: "20 DEAD". Danny remembered it well, remembered it being passed around the newsroom. He walked towards the framed front page. Unlike the other pictures, there were two photos inside this one. He stared at the pictures, both were of young boys. The picture in the right of the frame was dated 5 April 1990. The boy looked dirty and distraught. His eyes were half closed; he appeared to be crying.

The second photo was also dated: 25 April 1990 – the last day of the Strangeways' riot.

Danny looked at this photo – a boy with brutally short hair stared defiantly at the lens. Danny touched the glass of the framed page. His eyes began to burn with tears. 'Little Paul,' he whispered. 'Oh, Little Paul, you poor bastard.'

'What the fuck am I looking at here?' demanded Gary, no longer bothering to keep his voice quiet.

'The dream team's trophy room, Gary,' Danny said. 'The fucking *dream* team. They figured out that the best way to steal something and not get caught is to steal something nobody wants... Care home kids that no one gives a shit about. And just to make sure you can do as you fucking well please, you take control of the way it's seen by the outside world too. So, a cop to manipulate the cases and a journalist to manipulate the coverage. Oh, they fucked it up the first time, out at the Moss. Dropped that kid before they could sling him in the water. Probably panicked or got disturbed. But they got better, lessons were learned, they *refined* it, for fuck's sake. Somebody gets in your way like Peter Jeffries? Send them off the road and twist the coverage to suit your purpose. Make it look like he had a guilty conscience. Need a scapegoat when things start getting a little too close for comfort? Get a local grass, fill him with drink and guide his hand to cut his own throat up on the moors – make it look like he killed a kid at the same spot. Need a diversion? Do it all during the biggest stories of the last twenty-five years while the media is looking elsewhere.'

'Christ All-fucking-mighty,' Kate whispered. 'I can't take this in. I really can't take this all in.'

Danny looked at Gary. The engineer pulled a dirty hankie from his pocket and wiped his eyes. 'Jesus wept, Danny. Jesus fucking wept. Those vile, murdering fucking cunts.'

Danny rubbed his eyes. He spoke more quietly this time: 'Oh yes. One more thing. And this one's a belter. Need to be seen to be covering a murder while the really big story is unfolding elsewhere? Send the shittiest reporter you've got out there – he's *bound* to fuck it up.'

'Danny…' Kate began.

He was smiling now. 'A cop and a journalist,' he said. 'What better team could you ask for? It's perfect. The fucking *dream team.*'

Danny continued to stare in wonder at the framed front pages as Gary reached for one of the camera boxes and took it down from the shelf. He opened it and pulled out a clunky camcorder. He tried the power switch, but the battery was unsurprisingly dead. He moved on to a newer model and flipped open the DV cam playback screen – the camera came alive, but the power level was very low. Danny and Kate heard the slight whirring noise the unit made as the power kicked in. They looked at each other. Then at Gary. Then at the screen. They gathered around it.

They saw a bed – it appeared to be the same one as the room behind them – and there was a sheet over it. Nothing happened. Just a bed with a sheet. Gary put the camera into rewind and the picture went into reverse, showing them what was on the footage in reverse. They saw the sheet appear to be pulled back to show a child with a pillow on their face. They saw a desperate struggle – skinny arms and legs shaking and waving uselessly against the attack. They saw the pillow come away from the child's face. And they saw a boy, aged about ten, his face bruised and bloody, cry and plead and shake his head. All in reverse. Then the battery died and the screen went blank.

All three were still – unable to move – for at least a minute. Finally, Danny looked at Kate. She was weeping, head down, shoulders moving almost imperceptibly. Danny looked at Gary. The engineer was staring at the ceiling, breathing heavily.

Danny broke the silence. 'Grab a camera box and a picture frame each and let's go,' he said.

Silently, they did as Danny asked. They didn't bother to

tidy up after themselves; Gary knocked several boxes from the shelf. He didn't pick them up and put them back, he left them there. They didn't even bother to put the dresser back in its place. There seemed to be no point in pretending that they hadn't been here. Gary went upstairs and half-heartedly checked the bedrooms – he wielded his bat as if hoping, praying, that he would bump into someone, but all three seemed to know that the house was empty.

As they headed towards the front door, Danny noticed an iPhone taped to the side of the door frame. He pressed the home button and it came out of energy saving mode. It was eavesdropping on what had been happening via Facetime video. Danny looked at the screen. The person at the other end appeared to be driving a car, but he couldn't make out any faces. Then the connection was ended. 'We need to go,' Danny instructed, pulling the phone from the wall and jamming it into his pocket.

'Go where?' asked Kate.

'To Oldham Police station. Right now. There'll probably only be a duty sergeant and a few drunks there, but we need to go now. Looks like we're going to be in the twenty-four-hour club before the night's done. Just like the old days.'

'Sure,' Gary replied. 'Just like the old days, mate.'

'Can we go via my dad's? Just to make sure everything's okay.'

'Absolutely,' Danny said, putting a hand on Kate's shoulder. She pulled him close and hugged him.

'Those poor kids,' she said.

All three got into Gary's van. Danny took the frames and cameras and placed them carefully behind the seats. He took care not to look at the faces in the photos, especially the one he had grabbed, dated 5 April 1990 that showed the boy from Black Moss.

Gary pulled away from the kerb and the van headed down Princess Parkway, the main connecting dual carriageway from south Manchester to the city centre. All three sat in silence. After a few minutes, the engineer spoke: 'I didn't even vote,' he said.

'What?' asked Kate, still in a daze.

'Fucking Brexit. Completely forgot to vote.'

FIFTY-NINE

3.25 am Friday 24 June 2016

'The lights are on,' cried Kate as Gary's van pulled into the driveway of her father's house. 'Shit, shit, shit. No, no, no. It's half past fucking three in the morning and all the lights are on.'

As Gary came to a stop, Kate pushed Danny out of the way and climbed out of the van. She hit the gravel drive running and dashed straight to the front door, which was already open. 'Dad!' she shouted. 'Jonathan!'

Danny and Gary were right behind her. Both had their baseball bats. 'I'm going to use this thing tonight if it fucking kills me,' Gary shouted as they barrelled their way through the front door. Kate was still shouting for her father and her young son as she ran upstairs. Danny headed for the living room. John Smithdown was lying face down on the carpet, with the shattered remains of a glass coffee table surrounding him. Chips and shards of glass were stuck to his bloodied face and he was perfectly still. Danny stared at him, unable to make a decision about what to do next. He heard Kate shouting in a state of pure fury from upstairs, followed by the sound of her stomping down the stairs. 'Johnny's not here, Danny,' she shouted, taking the stairs two at a time. 'Those fucking bitches. He's gone.'

The sight of her father turned Kate's shouts into roars. Gary was moving John Smithdown's body into the recovery position, shifting the old man's arms and legs with surprising gentleness. 'Ambulance,' the engineer said. 'Now.'

As Kate dialled 999, Danny's mobile pinged. He didn't recognise the number but there was no doubt in his mind as to who it was. The message read: *Bring the pictures and equipment you stole – plus all mobile phones – to postcode OL3 6LF. Do not copy or send any footage, the phones will be checked. We will know if you call the police. It's the time for this to end. Everyone can walk away if you do exactly as you are told.*

As soon as he'd finished reading it, a second message arrived. A video file this time. Danny looked at Kate and tried to give her a reassuring smile. He walked out of the room and turned down the volume before opening the video. It was Jonathan Smithdown. Danny didn't need the sound to know that the boy was hysterical. The video was a close-up of his face – an arm was wrapped firmly around his throat, he was hitting the arm ineffectually, clawing at the pure white material of his abductor's shirt. The video lasted just a few seconds before freezing on the final frame of the boy's face.

'Danny!' shouted Gary. 'Where are you? Get the fuck in here, now.'

Danny returned to the front room. 'Was that them?' Kate asked. 'On the phone, was it them?' She seemed calmer now; the shouts and screams had been replaced with a quiet rage.

'Yes. They've got Jonathan. They want the evidence – the pictures, the camera gear and our phones – and they say they'll let Jonathan go. We've got to meet them – fuck knows where it is – but they've given me a postcode.'

'Punch it into Google Maps,' said Gary, still on his knees tending to John Smithdown.

Danny did as he was asked and showed it to Kate and Gary. 'It's a lane out towards the Yorkshire border,' Kate said. 'It goes for miles past some old shooting lodges then just fades out into the moors. Danny, we can't leave my dad here. He's in a bad way. But I've got to go to Jonathan.'

Gary unclipped the keys that seemed to have been welded to his belt since at least 1990 and tossed them to Danny. He followed it with his phone. 'Take the van, take the gear and go where they ask. Do whatever they say and get your lad back, Kate. We'll figure something out when he's safe. I'll wait here with your dad until the ambulance arrives.'

'That's a better plan than anything I've come up with,' admitted Danny. 'We'd better go.'

As they got to the van, Danny handed the keys to Kate, remembering he wasn't allowed to drive. She looked at him as if he were mad. 'You're right. Fuck it.'

SIXTY

4.45 am Friday 24 June 2016

Coming off the main Huddersfield to Manchester road, Danny turned the van into a series of lanes and tracks, each narrower and bumpier than the last. Street lighting had ended a good ten minutes earlier. There was the slightest sense that sunrise was on its way from across the edge of moors, but the retreating darkness was being backfilled by a heavy mist that the van's fog lights were struggling to cut through.

Danny and Kate had barely spoken since leaving her father's house. At one point she'd asked him why Gary hadn't text her about John Smithdown's condition. Then she had answered her own question, remembering that they had Gary's phone, along with the rest of the items they'd been told to bring. Danny idly flicked on the radio. The local all-night radio host was fielding calls about Brexit. 'Fucking hell,' said Danny. 'We're out. That's all anyone will be talking about today. And the next day.'

'Perfect, isn't it?' Kate said, staring at the ever-diminishing lane in front of them. 'Who will be interested in a missing kid on a day like today?'

Danny looked at her: 'They've got this diversion thing down to a fine art, you've got to give them that.'

'Danny? What are we going to do when we get there? It doesn't seem right to just let them disappear. Not after what they've done.'

He thought for a moment. 'Gary's right. Get Jonathan

then worry about it later.'

'It's not right,' she repeated, glancing to the back of the van at the picture frames they'd taken from Beth's house.

'No,' agreed Danny. 'It's not right at all.'

The lane passed through a series of wooden buildings that they assumed were part of the shooting range; then it went down to almost nothing. A strip of grass ran down the middle of the track; it led the way and demonstrated how little traffic came through the route. The track continued to shrink until the hedgerows running alongside it touched the van on both sides, scratching the exterior as if the branches were trying to get inside the vehicle.

In the distance they saw a figure. Jan Cave stood at the end of the track, one hand in the air telling them to stop. She was wearing a dark overcoat, but the fog lights caught the white of her shirt and illuminated her. The look on her face chilled them both; totally calm and business-like without a trace of emotion.

Danny brought the van to a halt but kept the motor going. Jan made a cutting motion across her neck with her thumb and he killed the engine. 'Yes, that's a good idea, you bitch,' whispered Kate. 'Let's see if we can get that throat cut before all this is done.'

The ex-policewoman walked away from the van and motioned for them to follow her. She walked slowly towards a disused concrete bunker-like building at the very end of the track. Danny gathered up the frames, held them flat and asked Kate to pile the camera boxes on top of them. She took the phones and they walked towards the bunker. Danny was starting to panic. *Look at us. Like we're taking presents to a party. It just gets weirder and weirder. I'd do anything to be back in London now. Anything. I'd even do that skiing reality show my agent talked about. Please let me be anywhere. Anywhere but here.*

He looked across at Kate. He envied her calm. She was staring at Jan Cave's back as she slipped into the darkness of the abandoned building. As she stared, she moved her lower jaw slowly left to right in a series of tiny movements. Danny could hear the click-click noise she was making as she ground her teeth together.

Jesus Christ, we're fucked. Really, really fucked. No one is coming out of this tonight. Not one of us.

He was about to tell Kate to turn back but she'd quickened her pace and was now ahead of him. The blackness of the bunker took her too. For a second Danny was all alone. He looked around – the moors gave nothing back. He went inside.

Dressed all in black and using a single forearm crutch to support herself, Beth Hall stood inside the building. All of the windows had long since been smashed and Danny could see the stars thought the roof – a third of the tiles were missing. Bird droppings, discarded bottles and the burnt remains of a small bonfire were the dominant features, along with some old car seats arrange in a semi-circle. Jonathan Smithdown was sitting on one of them. He was conscious but was struggling to stay awake, as if he'd been drugged. Both of his hands had been bound together at the wrist with shiny grey tape. Jan Cave stood next to him. In her hand was a huge kitchen knife. She stroked Jonathan's black, curly hair, gently at first. Then she took a handful of it and pulled his head to one side. She put the knife to his throat. Danny heard Kate whisper her son's name. The pain in her voice pushed away the panic Danny had been feeling and replaced it with guilt and shame. *We wouldn't be here if it wasn't for me and my great big fucking ego trip. Kate was right. Go back and sort out the one thing that's been eating me up for years? Then everything will be all right. What a walking, talking cliché.*

'Let's crack on, shall we?' said Beth. 'Danny, it's very important that you do as you're told, understand?' She spoke with calm and clear authority. It was her newsreader's voice.

'Yes,' he confirmed.

Beth glanced over at Jonathan. 'And it's very important that you answer my questions concisely and honestly. Do you understand that too?'

'Yes, I do.'

'Grand. Danny, have you brought everything that you took from my house with you?'

'Yes.'

'Have you got all three phones with you?'

'Yes.'

'Have you sent any messages or footage from them?'

'No.'

'Have you been in touch with the police, Danny?'

'No.'

'Does anyone know you're here?'

'Just Gary,' Danny replied. 'He wanted to come, and he sends his best, but he's busy tidying up the mess you left at John Smithdown's house.'

'Maybe we'll pop down to the hospital later, just to say hello. We'll see. Danny, put the frames and cameras on the floor please.'

He did as he was told. 'Good. Now then. Kate. Hi. Long time no see and all that.' Beth took a roll of tape from the pocket of her long, dark coat and threw it to Kate, who caught it, instinctively. 'You need to tape Danny's hands together please.'

Kate didn't move. 'Fuck this,' she said under her breath. Jan grabbed Jonathan's hair tighter and shook his head backwards and forwards. She was smiling.

'Now!' screamed Beth. Kate jumped with shock. 'Now! Now! Fucking now! Or she'll cut his fucking head off. Now!'

Kate moved forward. She seemed unable to look at Beth. She certainly couldn't look at Jan and Jonathan. She was staring at the compacted soil that served as a floor in the lodge. Her eyes looked up for the briefest of moments, then she crossed the room, pulling out a length of tape as she went. It made a *skrawking* noise. She bit it and tore off a two-foot-long piece. Danny put out his hands and gave her the merest nod, to let her now that it was okay. She wrapped the tape around his wrists as Beth looked on.

'You know what I'm going to ask you Beth, don't you?' asked Danny. He kept his eyes locked on Kate's trying to work out what she was thinking. Trying to read her thoughts. *I haven't got a clue,* he thought.

'Oh, fuck off, Danny,' shouted Beth. 'Oooh... Why did you do it?' Her tone was whingey and sarcastic. It was the 'cry baby' voice that she used to use in the Manchester Radio newsroom. 'Why, why, why oh fucking why?'

Kate finished strapping Danny's hands and put the tape into her coat pocket.

Beth looked at him. She was breathing heavily. 'Because we could. That's why. Because we fucking *could*. And because we fucking wanted to. That's it. Nothing more. Just that. Happy now? All nice and neat and resolved for you, Danny? Lots of lovely closure? What a dickhead you are. We don't all need some convoluted backstory to justify what we do – not like you. You fucking cry baby. Oooh, I'm all messed up and drunk all the time because of what happened to me and my sister in the past. But I can make it all better. No, you can't, Danny. You *can't* make it better, not for you, not for Kate here and not for your sister out in Wythenshawe either. We don't all need the past to justify what we do, Danny. Some of us just fucking *are*.'

Danny looked through the roof at the sky. The stars were fading. Dawn was coming. Jan spoke now. 'And some of us are actually close to our sisters, Danny. Not like you.'

Danny looked from Beth to Jan. And back again. *They have the same eyes. Jesus Christ. Sisters?*

Beth nodded at him. And winked. 'Kate. Come here please and bring the tape that you put in your pocket with you, please. Your turn now. Then it'll be time – and it'll *all* be over.'

Kate hesitated, then did as she was told and approached Beth, putting her hand into her pocket as she walked. She stopped and stood in front of Beth, who was still smiling. Then, for the first time since they'd arrived, Kate looked directly at Beth. There was silence for a moment. Then Kate took her hand from her pocket, pulled out the rounders bat and smashed it across Beth's jaw with a single backhanded stroke. She brought it back and hit Beth's face again from the opposite side; the woman's jaw wobbled slackly, free of its broken hinges on both sides. Kate hit her a third time, higher now, across the side of the head. Beth's crutch fell away and she dropped to the floor as blood splashed from her mouth and head.

A heartbeat after Kate's first strike, Danny ran directly at Jan who was shouting her sister's name. She'd loosened her grip on Jonathan's hair, but only slightly. Danny put his shoulder forward and tucked his head down, preparing to put his full weight behind knocking her off her feet and away from Jonathan. Just as Danny's shoulder was about to connect, she spun him round with shocking ease, slammed him against the wall and jabbed the knife twice into his shoulder and upper torso. Kate ran towards them both, swinging the bat wildly. Jan met it with the point of the huge knife, which stuck into the bat. She yanked the bat from Kate's hands, sending it across the room, then lifted her foot and kicked Kate square in the chest, sending her backwards. Jan picked Jonathan up by the tape that bound his wrists, put him over her shoulder in a fireman's lift and ran out the lodge through the rotten remains of the back door. As she went she turned and looked at Danny; she motioned with her head as if to say: *come on. Come and get me.*

Kate was still gasping for breath but managed to get to her feet. She staggered towards Danny and began unwrapping the tape from his hands. He pulled his wrists inwards and shook the remainder of the tape free. Although he was fully aware that he was bleeding heavily, he wasn't in as much pain as he'd expected. Kate bent double, her hands on her knees, fighting for breath. She pointed at the doorway. Danny headed off onto the moors. Kate followed as best she could.

The light was slowly spreading across the eastern edge of the moor. Through the mist, Danny could see Jan Cave in the distance. She was half walking, half running through the clough that stretched north of the shooting lodge. Jonathan was on her shoulder. The boy's head lolled from side to side. He was starting to move. Then he began screaming.

Danny followed them as quickly as he could. Kate was moving more slowly behind him, shouting her son's name. The moorland peat was soft and wet with dew under their feet. The depth of the terrain varied wildly; sometimes Danny's foot would drop into a wet and muddy hole. Next, he'd be jumping over mounds covered in sharp moorland grass. He was tiring quickly, but he was gaining ground. He looked ahead. Jan passed by a small reservoir. *Little Black Moss,* thought Danny. *She's heading for the Pennine Way and then the main road.*

As she passed the small reservoir, Danny saw her let the boy slide from her shoulder. He landed unsteadily on his feet. His knees buckled slightly but he stayed upright. Jan then dragged him onwards towards Black Moss itself. He screamed and screamed.

When she got to the path she stopped and turned. She slipped an arm around the boy's neck and held up the knife; its point was tucked behind his ear. 'FUCKING STOP!' she screamed. 'Do not take another fucking step. Come an inch closer and I'll slit his throat.'

Danny stopped. Kate came up behind him and they grabbed onto each other. 'Please,' Kate said. 'Please.'

Jan walked backwards up the Pennine Way path, the knife still threatening the boy's throat. Danny and Kate stayed where they were, afraid to make even the slightest movement, fearful it would be interpreted as a step forwards.

Jan edged away from them. As she got close to the brow of the hill, with the Manchester Road behind her, Gary Keenan ran at her from behind. Jonathan was knocked to one side of the path, Jan to the other. Gary landed on top of the woman, his weight pinning one arm behind her back. She yelled in pain as her arm snapped above the elbow. Her free hand moved with astonishing speed as she stabbed at Gary with her knife. Four times, five times the knife went into his side and neck before Danny and Kate got to them.

Danny kicked the knife from her hand. Shouting and swearing, Gary rolled to one side and Jan twisted around on to her front and crawled free. Gasping to replace the air that Gary had knocked out of her, she pushed herself upwards, but her hands sank into the wet sand around the edge of Black Moss. Kate jumped on her back and put her knees across Jan's upper arms. The ex-policewoman screamed in pain. Kate then put both hands to the back of Jan's head and began pushing her face into the sand at the water's edge of Black Moss.

Danny watched them, transfixed. The fight was draining from Jan Cave as Kate suffocated her. Her face had disappeared into the sand up to her hairline. The sun broke over the edge of the moors and the three of them were flooded with light.

I suppose I could do the right thing and stop her, Danny thought. *But fuck me I want that woman to die right now. I've never wanted anything more in my whole life. Die. Die. Fucking die.*

EPILOGUE

10.30 am, six weeks later

Danny was quite enjoying his Community Payback work. He didn't especially care for the orange vest he had to wear, or the toots he and the rest of the six-strong clear-up team would occasionally get from passing motorists. But there were worse ways to spend a summer's day. The sun was shining, he was out in the fresh air and clearing rubbish from the roadside seemed like a reasonably worthwhile task. He wasn't about to kid himself that the exercise was going to wipe out decades of heavy drinking, but it certainly wasn't doing him any harm. He felt healthy and strong. Picking up the roadside litter with a grab-stick was good exercise for his shoulder too. The sheer weight of the knife that he'd been stabbed with had caused more damage than the sharpness of the blade, but the fracture on his collarbone was healing reasonably well.

Another driver bibbed his horn and waved. 'They never get tired of doing that, do they?' Danny said to one of his fellow workers, a teacher in her thirties who'd punched a sixth-former who had been beating up another pupil.

'No,' she said, smiling at Danny as she grabbed at some takeaway cartons before popping them in her bag. 'They seem to get endless pleasure from it.'

The court had initially wanted Danny to do his community service near the site of his car crash in London, but Danny's lawyer had successfully argued that he would be more use here on the outskirts of Oldham, where he could continue to help the police build their case against Bethany and Janet Cave.

Though he'd been commended by the judge for his actions, Danny was still a convicted drink driver and as such had another 130 hours of litter picking and graffiti scrubbing to do.

The initial charges that came about as result of what happened in the early hours of the 24th of June – one count of murder, two counts of attempted murder and one of child abduction – didn't receive as much attention as they normally would have done. Everyone was initially too busy looking at the Brexit result to care too much. But as the weeks went by – and more children were identified – the media's interest began to grow. The tabloids had even given the case its very own nickname. Danny winced every time he heard a mention of the 'Twisted Sisters'. *That's a terrible, terrible name for a case. Awful.*

He was also slightly annoyed that he hadn't thought of it himself, particularly as his publishers were adamant that his book about the case should have that very same name.

Beth and Jan still weren't cooperating with the police. After her face was put back together, Beth had been placed at Bronzefield prison in Surrey; Jan was at Foston Hall in Derbyshire. Little Paul had been identified by the teeth found at Jan's office, but there was still no word as to who the boy was that Danny had seen on the 'beach' at Black Moss in 1990.

Danny thought about the boy a lot. He was thinking of him as he cleared away rubbish when a voice from a passing car that had slowed down next to him snapped Danny out of it. 'Put your back into it, you lazy fucking bastard,' said John Smithdown, leaning out of the window.

'Dad!' Kate cried from the driver's seat. 'Language in front of Jonathan, please.'

The boy gave Danny a thumbs up from the passenger seat. Danny returned it.

Kate pulled the car to a stop. 'Shall I pick you up at five?'

'Yes please,' said Danny. 'Gary's wife is expecting us. I know we've been to see her already this week, but she was in a bad way at the funeral. Of course she would be. Stupid thing to say. So yes, five would be perfect.'

As the car pulled away, John Smithdown dropped an apple core onto the verge in front of Danny. 'You missed a bit,' he shouted as the car headed off.

Danny gave John Smithdown the middle finger and watched them go. It was a hot and hazy day and the moors seemed to shimmer. He saw some children head down the Pennine Way path. They were probably going to take a paddle in the cool waters of one of the reservoirs. One kid pulled his t-shirt off and waved it around his head, shouting at his friends as he ran bare-chested towards the water. Danny knew that going into reservoirs wasn't allowed, but there were more dangerous things in the world.

He took a swig from the water bottle attached to his belt and caught up with the rest of the community payback team as they made their way steadily up the Manchester Road and away from Black Moss reservoir.

An official report has found fundamental deficiencies in the way the police deal with child abuse and the sexual exploitation of children. The Inspectorate of Constabulary found unacceptable delays in obtaining evidence, a failure to take certain cases of missing children seriously and a lack of awareness among local officers about registered sex offenders in their area.

BBC Radio 4 News Friday 25 November 2016

THE END

About the author

David Nolan is an a multi award-winning author, television producer and former crime reporter.

He has written a dozen books including *Tell the Truth and Shame the Devil,* the true story of the largest historic abuse case ever mounted by Greater Manchester Police. He presented a BBC Radio 4 documentary based on the book called *The Abuse Trial* . It won both the Rose D'Or and the New York International radio awards in 2016. He was also given a Royal Television Society award for his documentary *Riot! - Strangeways Ten Years On.*

He lives in the hills overlooking Manchester.

Acknowledgements

Many thanks to former Detective Constable Nicola Graham and to Paul Lockitt for their expert advice in the fields of child protection and radio.

Chris McVeigh and Christopher Rhatigan - thank you too.

Although many of the locations in *Black Moss* are real, all the characters are fictitious, except for the Strangways rioters.

More books from Fahrenheit Press

Rubicon by Ian Patrick

Two cops, both on different sides of the law – both with the same gangland boss in their sights. Sam Batford is an undercover officer with the Metropolitan Police who will stop at nothing to get his hands on fearsome crime-lord Vincenzo Guardino's drug supply. DCI Klara Winter runs a team on the National Crime Agency, she's also chasing down Guardino, but unlike Sam Batford she's determined to bring the gangster to justice and get his drugs off the streets.Set in a time of austerity and police cuts where opportunities for corruption are rife, Rubicon is a tense, dark thriller that is definitely not for the faint hearted.

Rubicon has recently been optioned by the BBC.

Burning Secrets by Ruth Sutton

It's the spring of 2001 and Foot & Mouth disease is raging across Cumbria. Twelve-year-old Helen Heslop is forced to leave her family farm and move in with relatives in a nearby town because the strict quarantine means she can't travel back and forth to school in case she inadvertently helps spread the disease. As the authorities and the local farming communities try desperately to contain the outbreak, tensions run high and everyone's emotions are close to the surface. And then Helen disappears. The police search expands all over the northwest coast where farms are barricaded and farming families have been plunged into chaos - not least the Hislop family, where potentially explosive fault lines are exposed. Under the strain tensions build inside the police team too, where local DC Maureen Pritchard is caught between old school DI Bell and new broom DS Anna Penrose. Will Helen survive? And can life for the Heslop family ever be the same, once burning secrets are discovered and old scores settled?

Vinyl Junkie by Tony R. Cox

England, 1974. Reporter Simon Jardine and DJ and part-time private investigator Tom Freeman, attend a homecoming gig for a megastar band. After the show, Jardine and Freeman see a record company manager roughed up and threatened, later that night they hear a man was murdered yards from the gig. These events mark the beginning of a thrilling chain of events that leaves even the hard-bitten Jardine breathless and in fear for his life. As the stakes rise Jardine and Freeman are bounced between dishonest record companies, corrupt cops in the pocket of violent criminal gangs, and IRA terrorists who control the drug trade. The plot pushes relentlessly forward and climaxes when a shipment of drugs sails into a remote Scottish loch, where the forces of good and evil face each other down in a violent, fatal and bloody finale.

When The Music's Over by Aidan Thorn

When Benny Gower murders his business partner few people doubt his good reasons for doing so. Unlike Benny, it's not as if Harry Weir was popular. But he was the heir to Birmingham's most violent and dangerous criminal organisation. For Wynn McDonald, dragged out of retirement for the sake of his old gangland accomplices, motive doesn't matter. All he cares about is tracking down the nightclub manager turned killer. But before Wynn can extract necessary vengeance he'll need to turn over every stone on his way to finding answers. And not everybody's going to be happy with the truths that come crawling out.

30888854R00171

Printed in Poland
by Amazon Fulfillment
Poland Sp. z o.o., Wrocław